Ruff Cut

A Riverview Mystery

By Kasey Riley

DEDICATION

I would like to dedicate this book to several people without whose help, it wouldn't have been finished. First to my husband, Jeff. Thanks to you the story is more complete and the formatting and publishing are done – I love you and appreciate your help more than you can know. Secondly to Leslie Helm and the Write Away group in Crossville. Your help in editing and thoughts have made this book stronger and better. Thank you all. This book has been in the works for about a year due to our move in 2016 and the other book that demanded me to finish it before I could work on Ruff Cut. Thanks to everyone whose ears I've bent and who I've bored with my jabbering as I worked out the details. Thanks everyone.

Ruff Cut

A Riverview Mystery

Chapter One

A blinding flash, a deafening roar, a blast of air pushing her under the desk as she reached for her fallen pen; pain, burning pain, just before darkness overcame her. Voices, guttural voices, Afghanis close by. Coming to her senses long enough to stifle the pain-induced groan caused by her broken and bleeding shoulder, Megan opened her eyes. Darkness surrounded her as memory rushed in of the deafening blast which threw her under this desk. Megan realized the squad must have tripped a booby trap as they cleared the building. But, what were the Afghanis doing here? How long had she been unconscious? Where was her squad? Lack of light under the desk gave the time as night. The explosion had happened shortly after lunch.

Cautiously, Megan fished around in the dark until she found her com unit. Listening to the Afghanis, she translated what the enemy forces were discussing. She heard them pumping each other up with stories of driving the American troops away. Using her workable hand, she managed to send out short bursts of text, praying someone was receiving them. The Afghanis were making plans to attack a nearby village, they planned to kill everyone for helping the Americans. Creaking, debris falling, hitting her injured shoulder, nauseous pain and then blessed unconsciousness. Awakening with the darkness still surrounding her, the aridity in her throat brought on convulsive swallowing, but even that didn't ease the dryness. Her stomach cramping, Megan wondered how much time had passed since the explosion. Touching her wounded shoulder, the blood felt thick and sticky; obviously hours or perhaps even days had passed. Silence reigned around her, the building felt empty and abandoned. Her awareness fading, Megan dozed—then gunfire, grenades, screams...shouting in English, and the sound of a distant chopper.

****

"Oh, my God, noooo!" Her own scream roused Megan to tears, trembling, and gut-wrenching pain in her long-healed shoulder. Looking down at her cold-sweat-saturated tank top, panting, she sat and looked around the dimly-lit bedroom; her eyes still bleary and her ears still hearing the long-ago battle. The nightlight she could never sleep without gave the room depth, proving she wasn't trapped again in the rubble. Hanging her head and rubbing her face with shaking hands, the sweat on her palms mingled with the tears on her cheeks. Her shoulder ached with the movement, the scar pulling as her muscles flexed. Moving increased the blood flow, easing the burning pain, but the twinge reminded her of the episode, which changed the course of her life forever.

Years of training as a Forensic Computer Specialist and Cryptologist were useless if she couldn't sit at a computer and work with both hands. Her Middle Eastern language skills were unneeded if she couldn't carry a weapon and follow her squad-mates to the villages where they needed her to interrogate the locals. It wasn't only the loss of her military career which changed her life; but would these nightmares never end?

After she got back from Afghanistan, while her shoulder healed, she spent time with others in group therapy sessions trying to talk through the emotions and trauma. For the most part, she was better by far than she had been in the beginning...but, every so often, her subconscious would bring back the incident in horrifying detail. Megan understood some of her fellow soldiers relived the war every night and she was thankful to be beyond that situation.

2

However, she felt it wasn't right that her brain couldn't let the incident go and let her move forward without looking back.

This had to stop! It had been months since the last episode but, even so, every night she tossed and turned before sleep claimed her; worried the dream would visit again. That might be part of the problem. If she could simply fall asleep thinking only of positive things, perhaps she would cease having the dream. For a moment, she debated about taking some of the medication the shrink had given her to help her fall into a dreamless sleep. Determined not to become dependent on the medication, Megan decided against taking the pills. Too many of her friends and fellow soldiers had earned drug habits because of combat; she vowed not be one of them.

A Purple Heart and a Silver Star would never replace the Army life she had planned. The citations looked great in her records, but they couldn't help her sleep without nightmares or move without pain. As a sheriff, her medals helped her win the election, she knew that. The Army skills and discipline she had gained helped her to ace all the classes she had taken since her election but, given a choice, she would trade them in a second to keep from having the nightmare.

Still shaking, she wondered whether Aaron was awake. She wanted—almost needed—to hear his voice. He would understand her need for comfort or simple communication with another soldier, another veteran. She hated leaning on him as much as she did. It wasn't fair to use his shoulder and accept his comfort without being able to offer him anything emotional in return. He said he didn't care. He wanted her to feel she could call anytime but she couldn't help knowing how much he wanted her, and how much he cared about her. Compared to the man who couldn't even bother to visit her in the hospital, the one who told her to "keep the ring," Aaron was a prince who deserved so much more than she was brave enough, at this time, to give him.

The difference between her service and Aaron's was that he had planned on leaving the Army Rangers by the time he was thirty. The wound in his leg didn't do much more to change his life's plan than force him to adjust back to civilian life at twenty-five. Roger Meadows had already offered him a job at the R-M so, as soon as Aaron was able to walk or, more accurately limp away from the Army, he moved into a job he loved. Aaron's limp didn't interfere with managing the R-M. That was five years ago. Now days, his limp only appeared after an especially physical day of riding or working on his feet. Aaron coached the little girls' soccer team in his spare time and Riverview had accepted him as one of their own.

Megan felt a part of the community from her summers spent with her Aunt Marge. Aunt Marge was head of the Methodist Ladies Auxiliary and had helped Megan win the office of Sheriff of Riverview with as much energy as she put into the yearly Bazaar. As a teen, Megan spent several weeks each summer helping her aunt ready the town for the annual fund-raiser. She fell in love with the area. When her life fell apart, Riverview was the *only* place where she felt at home. The moment she left the hospital and returned home to Texas, she knew she had to move away from her over-protective family. Marge set her up with a job working for Roger Meadows taking care of his uncle's ranch while the man was in prison. The arrangement suited Megan to a "T". A house, a barn, pasture for her horse and a job she could do at her own speed. Lots of quiet time to lick her wounds and come to grips with the forced changes in her life.

Soon, her shoulder healed and she gained strength and mobility. Living by herself in the old house helped her find peace of mind, and become secure in her own talents. Six months she held that job before the position of sheriff opened. With Roger Meadow's support, she applied to the Riverview Town Council to let her fill the position until the next election. A year later, she was officially Sheriff of Riverview and she'd taken every course available to help her learn what she needed to know to protect her friends and the community. Now, six months into her four-year term, she felt confident in all aspects of the position.

Everyone in town knew how Aaron felt about Megan; he didn't try to hide it. Megan knew that many wondered why she and Aaron seemed to be only friends, when it was obvious how much he cared. Few people could understand how she battled daily for her sanity, or the embarrassment she felt about the scarring of her shoulder. Some who had seen active duty could; those were the ones who understood how far she had come in the past year. They even sympathized with how much further she needed to go before she could lead a reasonably normal life and be able to give Aaron the love he so richly deserved. Perhaps she did love him, maybe she was ready to admit it, but the thought frightened her. She simply wasn't prepared to commit yet.

"Damn it," Megan muttered, reaching for her phone to text Aaron. It seemed to jump into her hand as she touched it, both ringing and vibrating under her palm. Hitting the button, she said, "Sheriff Megan Holloway here. This better be important; it's way too early on my day off."

"Sorry, Boss. We've got a missing child. One of the campers at the R-B has a six-year-old boy and he wandered off during the night," Deputy Joseph Kaleo explained. Calmly he continued. "We're mounting search parties and I thought you might want to either be part of one, or at least know what's happening."

"Thanks, Joe. Sorry I snapped at you. I need my coffee. I'll meet you at the R-B in half an hour, but don't hold any group for me. Send them out as quick as they come in to volunteer, groups of at least two. Section the area, let locals choose ground they know. Make certain the entire camp's been thoroughly scoured. Search inside every trailer, outhouse, pavilion storage, anything with a door needs to be opened—got it?" Her brain whirling, Megan pictured the area and all the different spots that might draw a child.

"Check the hay barn—look for any bales that aren't level, in case he got up in there and the hay shifted." She began moving toward her bathroom, barking directions and taking charge of the search.

"Did you call Marcia and Matt at the Gunnison Valley Ranch? They've been raising two dogs for that rescue group. I don't know if the dogs are trained yet, but it might be good for the animals to be part of this. Also, both Marcia and Matt are backcountry certified. I'm hanging up. I'll be there as soon as I can find my clothes and gear."

Even knowing Joe could handle things until she got there, Megan had a bad feeling about this. The R-B had been open less than a year. The surrounding woods still had deadfalls, treacherous not only because of possible shifting, but because of the snakes and other hazardous creatures they might hide. If something drew the child into one of those piles, he could get bitten; lost was the least of the risky situations a child might encounter in this region.

Walking out of her bathroom five minutes later, she began pulling what she considered her "backcountry" clothing out of her closet. She dressed in layers, lightweight fabrics next to her skin, and durable, tightly-woven nylon and cotton for the top layer. Wool socks, tall western hiking boots, a multi-pocket vest and her badge completed the outfit.

Heading to the kitchen, she quickly put her favorite flavored coffee on to brew. While the coffee brewed, filling the room with a rich caramel and caffeine scent, she grabbed a fanny pack and began stuffing it with apples, canned oranges, granola bars, a bottle of electrolytes on one side and a bottle of plain water on the other. If she were going to be out in the woods, she needed to be ready to keep herself— and possibly the child—fed and hydrated until she could get back. Satisfied with her pack, she poured coffee into a lidded mug and snagged two additional granola bars for her to eat on the way.

Driving the Dodge Durango assigned to her as Sheriff of Riverview over to the R-B, she reviewed what she knew about the campground. The facility belonged to Bethany and Roger Meadows who also owned the R-M cattle and horse ranch. The facility was Bethany's brainchild. Roger had created the equestrian campground and pack station to her exacting specifications. With twenty full-service pull-through sites for campers with horses, or for horseless campers in RVs; it was state-of-the-art. Each site had two covered pens in the shed row and there was space behind the rigs for those who wanted to set up portable corrals. The outer ring surrounding the full-service sites was open ground for rough camping or portable pens, as needed. Six family cabins ringed the lodge at the north end of the facility, amid the trees.

In the center of the camp, there was an open field, flattened and cultivated to provide excellent footing for horse and rider. Bethany insisted this ground be maintained and kept open for horses to be hand-grazed, and also for group events. Riding groups could gather there to head out on trail together. It was also a perfect space to set up vet checks or trail obstacles for competitions. A couple of shaded picnic tables and a two-sided covered pavilion sat at one end, giving an open view of the whole field and campground.

The north end of the property housed the lodge, showers, public restrooms, and restaurant. The large barn at the south end housed the pack-string and dude horses as well as featuring a large hay storage section and another section for shaving storage. Behind the lodge the cook had a private cabin, while the pack-station wrangler's cabin sat behind the barn, to be closer to the horses. Each position was a "live-in" and included free rent, horse stall, and meals along with their monthly salary. It was great work during the summer, but the R-B could prove lonely in the winter. The wrangler worked year around, caring for and training the horses. The current plan for the cook was to move her over to the R-M to help at the main house in the winter. With this being the first year of operation, both jobs were floating until need was known. If the job didn't prove to be required in the off season, next year the jobs would change to seasonal positions.

Megan figured it was close to a quarter mile from one end of the R-B to the other, might actually be over. A small child could find lots of hiding spots, or get into any number of situations in the dark. Nearing the property, she slowed and began searching for any signs of movement along the last mile of dirt road back into the camp. Even knowing she had little to no chance of seeing anything from her Durango, she still found her eyes straining at the brush along the road.

Pulling up close to the pavilion at the head of the open field, she observed the scene for a moment. In the center of the field, six volunteers with horses were preparing to mount up. Two had dogs, one a hound of some type and the other a shepherd, from the looks of it. The dogs sat obediently next to the horses, waiting for the signal to head out on the trail.

Standing in the middle of the semi-circle of horses, riders and dogs, Deputy Joseph Kaleo looked out of place but clearly in charge of the situation. His size dwarfed most of the riders and at least one of the horses. Megan watched him hesitantly pass the map he held to Matt Ward of the Gunnison Valley Guest Ranch, while Matt's dog bared a tooth at him. Casually, Matt reached over and lightly swatted the dog's nose. At 6'4", Joe should've been unconcerned about the dog, but big dogs worried him. His fear was more that he would hurt the animal than the other way around; at least that's the way he explained it, but Megan had her doubts.

With a heavy sigh, Megan took a final sip of her cooling coffee and climbed out of her Dodge, shaking her head as she walked toward the group.

"Hi, Joe." She called to him and the riders behind him. "What area is this group covering?"

"Hi, Sheriff. This group will follow the Skeleton Loop with the dogs searching above and below the trail." Joe seemed happy to see her. Megan understood why when a distraught woman in a thick fleece robe with tied sash and fleece slippers came up and grabbed her arm.

"Wait a minute, Ma'am. Let me get these volunteers going and I'll be right with you. Why don't you sit at the pavilion where I can find you?" Megan shook the hand off her arm, turned the woman toward the tables, and gave her a nudge in that direction.

"You have your rifle, Matt?" Megan asked.

Matt patted the butt of the rifle snugged in its scabbard on the off side of his stout gelding. "Yep. If we find anything, I'll fire one shot. If we hear one shot, we can return to camp."

"Right. Good hunting, and ride safe. Be back well before dark, whether you find anything or not. I don't want searchers lost in the mountains, too," Megan warned the group.

She stepped back to stand beside Joe while the riders mounted and filed out of the field toward the trailhead. Megan wondered what could draw a small child out of camp in the wee hours; but kids were curious, and some would always have less sense than others.

Turning to her deputy, she smiled at his worried expression. "Come on, it's early yet. Weather's looking fine and more volunteers are arriving. We'll round up this child before noon—I hope. He's got to be getting hungry by now and he'll start making noise. The dogs will find him."

The pep talk was designed to lessen the big man's concern, it seemed effective when he smiled at her. The talk did little to lessen her own fears. A child lost in the wilderness was in danger from wildlife, plants, cliffs, and rivers in the wet season. Luckily, at the end of October, there was little water in the creeks and ravines. The longer he stayed lost, the higher the risk. Everyone was aware of that and a sense of urgency hung over the field as riders saddled up and horses whinnied and stomped away flies.

Turning, Megan eyed the woman sitting at the table in the pavilion with her head resting on the table, sobbing into her arms. She could only be the mother.

"That's the boy's mother. I think her name is Rebecca Stroud." Joe offered, following her gaze and confirming Megan's unspoken thought.

Patting Joe on the shoulder, Megan turned to her next task. Climbing the mild incline to the weather-protected enclosure, Megan noted the coffee urns set up by the Ladies' Auxiliary, who were bustling around in the background. One, her Aunt Marge, had come forward to offer comfort to the distraught young mother. She was rubbing the woman's shoulders and talking to her as Megan arrived.

"Now, Sweetie. It's going to be okay. Your boy'll be found safe and sound. All these volunteers know this country so well, there won't be any spot a youngster can get into without them finding him. Mostly because they ran in this forest when *they* were young." Marge assured, still rubbing Rebecca's back. "Let me find you something to drink. Coffee, tea, chocolate?"

"No, I don't want anything except my Jamie back!" snarled the woman. She raised her head and looked around, sniffling, but no longer sobbing. "I'm sorry, I didn't mean to be rude. I'm so worried about my baby." She touched the hand still rubbing her shoulder.

"Sweetie, I understand. I'd likely be snippy myself. I'll bring you a cup of hot chocolate; it'll help you focus." Marge moved away, heading for the urn of hot water.

"Ma'am. I'm Megan Holloway, Sheriff of Riverview. Joe called me in to help." Megan moved to sit across from the woman and take her hands. "I know this is a trying time but I need to know as much as you can remember or can figure out about why Jamie might go off and what he's wearing. How old is your boy?"

"Hello, Sheriff. I'm Rebecca Stroud, Jamie's mother. I would say nice to meet you, but this moment has nothing nice about it." She sighed and gazed vacantly around the pavilion and field. "Jamie's six. Well, six-and-a-half by the calendar. He went to bed in his Spider-Man pajamas, as far as I can tell he didn't change out of them. But, his cowboy boots and a jacket are missing from by the door. He's very good about not going out without shoes and jacket," she boasted.

"Does he wander out at night often? Would he go out to look at the stars? Most kids are scared of the dark. Do you know why would he leave the cabin? Did he see something yesterday, which might lure him out?" Megan watched Rebecca take a deep breath and rub her hands together, possibly to relieve their shaking.

"We went to the zoo last week and took a tour. The guide led us into the darkened area where nocturnal animals and birds shelter during the day and explained about how the sun hurts their eyes so they only come out at night. Jamie was fascinated because he's timid about the dark and the thought that some creatures only come out at night amazed him." Her face softened at the memory.

"What color are the pajamas and the jacket he's wearing? Are his boots simple flat-soled cowboy boots?" Megan prompted the mother for a more detailed description of the child.

"His jammies are blue, with red from the knee down. The top is red with blue arms. The jacket that's missing is his favorite. Bright orange body with black arms. It has a tiger on the back. He got it from Santa last Christmas." Her eyes misted, thinking of her child. "The boots are almost worn out; he seldom wears anything else. Black, with pointed toes and stitching up the calf. I yell at him for wearing them when it gets icy because they have flat soles."

"Do you recall anything yesterday that caught his fancy or that he wanted to explore and you held him back? Sometimes kids will return to something they didn't finish examining." Megan looked into the face of the woman, pressing and prompting her to remember.

"We got here after lunch and I made him take a nap before we went exploring the camp." Her gaze wandered around the camp as if trying to place her location in relation to her cabin. "We left the cabin and walked through the lodge. I showed him the showers and pointed out the kitchen and told him he could only go there with me. We came out the front door and walked toward the stables. It's quite amazing, with the stalls and barns in amongst all the trees. We live in the city in an old brownstone so this is incredibly different from home." Rebecca sniffed, wiping a gathering tear from her eye before she continued. "We kept to the right and circled the entire camp. He got to pet a couple of horses down at the stables and the wrangler showed him the pony he could ride today. Then we worked our way back up to the lodge, had a snack and returned for his afternoon nap. Rain moved in and we spent the evening playing checkers in the lodge. He doesn't actually know how, but he enjoys stacking the pieces."

"Thanks. That was very descriptive. Was he excited about riding? Did you see the trails heading into the woods?" Megan asked. Her mind seemed to be zipping from spot to spot, trying to come up with something that would pull a child from his bed in the dark.

"Oh my, yes. He petted the pony for almost twenty minutes, giving it hay and picking grass for it before he would move on with our hike. I remember the trails into the woods but I don't think they excited him much. He did see a few squirrels on a log pile and a deer took off up the hill as we approached. Jamie loves all animals and has no fear of anything--wild or tame."

"I'm going to suggest you go back up to your cabin and dress for the day. I'm going to mount a small search party close to camp. Once you're dressed, why don't you retrace your steps from yesterday, looking for anything we might miss. But, *do not leave camp*. We don't want to search for you, too. If you see anything, come find me and I'll check it out with you," Megan ordered.

Mrs. Stroud glanced down at her robe, finally noticing she had yet to dress for the day. "Oh, oh my. I didn't realize I was still in my nightgown." Her hand went to her throat, pinching closed the overlapping fleece fabric. "What must everyone think of me?" Her eyes filled with tears as she looked up at Megan.

"Everyone realizes you've been too busy helping us find your boy to change. That long robe looks comfy. I wish I had one like it to sit and watch TV. I'll bet those slippers are warm, too. My feet are always getting cold." Megan helped the smaller woman to her feet, turning her toward the cabins. She watched the woman head toward her cabin and nodded to her aunt, Marge, to follow and assist the distraught mother.

"Boss, I'm so glad you came in time to do that interview. I really lose it when a woman cries in front of me. My brain just freezes." Joe shrugged at Megan, admitting a typical male attitude.

"I feel for her, but I wish I knew what could have drawn the child out into the dark or early dawn. I don't suppose she mentioned if his bed was still warm when she realized he was gone?" Megan glanced at her deputy in question.

"No, and I didn't think to ask. Sorry."

"I didn't ask either; should have. It wouldn't have told us much but it might have made me feel better to know he only had a half hour's start on us." Megan gave the man a wry smile. "You had the compound checked and all doors opened. What about the lodge? Especially the kitchen?"

"We checked all the closets and the shower stalls in the bath facility. I even had Sheena, the cook, check all the downstairs rooms. No luck there."

"Did she search the kitchen? The boy could have gone looking for food. I need to talk to Sheena, so I'll check the cupboards." Megan turned and headed for the lodge, keeping a fair distance behind Marge and Mrs. Stroud. At this point the mother was better off in her own cabin, not out here hindering the search with questions and tears.

She found the cook, black-haired and curvaceous Sheena McDonald, cleaning up the kitchen after offering coffee and breakfast to any waiting volunteers. Sheena had made simple sausage biscuits, something the volunteers could handle as they tacked up their horses. As early as it was, she knew many of those volunteering had awakened to a telephone call and gone straight out to load horses and head over here to search. Food would help keep them going on the trail.

"Hi Sheena, how are things going? Thanks for feeding the volunteers. You might want to make up a bunch of sandwiches too—bill the office for them. Volunteers need energy and if we treat them well, they'll be back for the next lost hiker." Megan smiled at the short, cute woman in front of her. Megan envied her fair skin and deep-blue eyes. Only the Scots seemed to be able to carry that genetic trait for black hair and deep blue eyes. Her own dirty-blonde hair matched her sun-bronzed skin, but her eyes were light sky-blue compared to the periwinkle color of the eyes regarding her.

"Not a problem, Sheriff. Boss Lady said to see that anybody who showed up was treated better than family." Her voice had a lilt instead of a pronounced Scottish burr. Her phrasing and syntax plainly showed her heritage and time spent with her Scottish kin. "I'd rather stay busy than sit about worrying over the poor lad."

"I remember you have a walk-in cooler and a walk-in pantry. You searched them for him, didn't you?" Megan asked, watching Sheena's economical movements as she moved from sink to cutting boards to range. Sheena must be about her age; she didn't appear any older. Megan couldn't help but wonder what brought her to this area.

"Yes, when I found out the boy had been running around before daybreak, I sent his mother to search the rooms upstairs and I opened each and every cupboard as well as walking into the pantry and the cooler. I even opened the freezer, in case he tried to get himself ice cream. Boys are always hungry. Nothing is safe from them." Sheena nodded toward the stainless-steel upright freezer.

"Good job. Are you certain his mother checked everything upstairs?"

"The way the woman was screeching and wailing, the boy would've had to be either deaf or unconscious not to hear. But, you know, if the scamp was feeling guilty, he might have hidden. Let's take a look around in the guest rooms." Sheena suggested. "They're all unlocked since there're no guests and we need to freshen them before the weekend. Who knows, if we're quiet we might be lucky and find the boy. I truly hope so."

"Okay. I'll start on the second floor and you on the third. Open every door and look under the beds. Don't call him, just look. That way, if he's scared, he won't run or hide from us," Megan suggested with a grim smile at the cook.

"I'm on my way." Sheena turned on her heel and headed for the stairs with Megan not far behind.

Megan turned to the right at the second floor landing and looked out over the reception area, eyeballing the front desk. If she found nothing upstairs, she would check under it when she returned to the first floor. Walking to the first room past the balcony overlook, her boots rapped hollowly on the wooden floor. Megan paused at the door to listen. Other than the sounds of Sheena moving on the floor above her, the lodge was quiet. Everyone was outside searching for Jamie.

Opening the door, she softly walked into the room, crossed to the bathroom, opened the door, the cupboard under the sink, and pulled back the shower curtain. Then she turned back to the room and checked the closet before dropping to her knees to search under the bed. Using the bed, she pushed herself back to her feet and left the room. She searched the four rooms on this side of the hall in the same fashion. Silently, she listened for any sounds outside of each door before she opened it. At the end of hall, she crossed to the other side and began working her way back toward the balcony.

Megan heard Sheena still searching the rooms above. She sighed. She hoped the boy wasn't out in the woods somewhere and this was a futile effort, but it had to be done. With her hand on the knob of the final room on the second floor, she paused for a second to listen. Was that a quiet sob from inside the room?

Chapter Two

Soundlessly, Megan turned the knob and pushed the door open a crack, leaning her head against it to hear better. Again, she heard the soft noise. Releasing a deep breath of relief, she pushed the door open a little more, saw nothing and knew he had to be hiding. Stepping into the room, she folded one of her long legs under her as she sat down on the bed, her pant leg catching on the top of her tall cowboy boots.

"Wow, am I tired! I think I'll sit here and rest. I hope poor Jamie isn't getting cold and hungry, lost out there in the woods. I'll bet he is. He doesn't know how much he's missing. We're having peanut-butter and jelly sandwiches for lunch, with a huge pile of chips. Then after lunch, I know the wrangler was planning to take Jamie for a ride on that cute pony. What was her name?" She hesitated to see if her question would lure him out.

"H'—her name is Twinkles," a small voice stammered from under the bed.

"Are you sure? I thought her name was Sophie or something like that." Megan replied, knowing this line of conversation was working.

"The man at the stables intro'--introduced me to her. I 'member her name is Twinkles because her eyes look twinkly in the sun." Even stuttering over the harder words, the voice gained confidence.

"Well, that's good to know. My name is Megan. What's yours?" Megan wanted him to come out from under the bed at his own speed, and at the same time she wanted to tell all the searchers he was okay. Containing her impatience was crucial; if she was to bring him out without fear and panic.

"My name is Jamie. My mommy is mad at me, so I'm hiding." His voice wavered and a small sob escaped.

"Are you scared your momma will spank you?" Megan hoped this wasn't an issue of the child running away due to abuse, but she could protect him if it were.

"Mommy don't spank me. She gives me a time-out until she gets over being mad. Sometimes I sit in the corner, *forever.* " Sniffling, he continued. "I heard Mommy screaming for me. I'm in so much trouble," he wailed, no longer able to contain his grief and fear.

A few muffled thuds told Megan the child was moving out from under the bed. Soon a small head appeared on the far side of the bed.

"Why do you think your momma is mad?" She asked.

"I wanted to see Twinkles sleeping, so I went outside. I went to her stall. She was eating and it made me hungry so I went into the kitchen where I found apples and oranges in a bowl. I took two without asking. Is that stealing? I can pay for 'em; I have some money left from Grandpa George." His face mirrored his emotions. First excitement, then fear and finally hope at the thought of righting a wrong he had committed.

"So your momma didn't know you were going outside? Why didn't you wake her and ask?" Megan patted the bed next to her and Jamie climbed on it. He crawled into Megan's lap before answering.

"Momma was tired from our hike. She needs her sleep. I came upstairs with the food. A door was open so I found a sink to wash my apple. I sat down between the two beds and made believe I was in a fort. I ate my apple and climbed under the bed to hide from the bogeyman. I fell asleep." Jamie yawned and leaned into Megan's chest, looking up at her.

"Is that why you stayed gone so long that your momma was scared you were lost? Why didn't you come out when you heard her calling?" Megan rubbed Jamie's back and rested her chin on the top of his head.

"Momma waked me up with her yelling and I knew she was mad, so I stayed quiet under the bed. Then I fell asleep. When I waked up again, I knew I was in big trouble and I cried. Then you came. Do you think Momma will ever let me play and ride Twinkles? I'm sorry. I didn't mean to make Momma scared. Honest." He sniffled and rubbed his face, snot, tears and all, into Megan's unscarred shoulder.

"Oh, I bet if I ask her to let you out of the corner after just an hour, she will. I'm the sheriff so she should listen to me. She's more scared about you being lost than she is mad at you for going out by yourself. Come on, let's go let everyone know you're safe." Megan moved him away from her shoulder, pushing his hair back from his reddened eyes. She smiled down on his sad face and tweaked his nose. "You know; a lot of people are here looking for you. Some even brought dogs to smell you in the woods. You've caused quite a stir. Let's go find your momma."

A small smile played across the boy's face, lighting his brown eyes and deepening the dimple in his left cheek. Megan stood up and let him slide down her leg to the floor. Taking his small hand in hers; they left the room. "Can I have a sandwich? I love peanut butter and jelly. Grape is my favorite." His eyes pleaded.

"First we find your mom, and then we'll get you a sandwich. I promise. It's almost noon and you missed breakfast. But, you did have that fruit, didn't you?" She attempted to frown at him, but a smirk twisted her lips.

"Do you think fifty cents will be enough to pay for it? It's in my jeans pocket." Jamie seriously offered, frown lines wrinkling his brow.

"I'll bet that the cook, Sheena, is going to be so happy you're okay that she won't even charge you for the fruit." Megan stopped at the top of the stairs. "I hear her coming now. There she is." She turned her head to watch Sheena come down the final two steps from the third floor.

"Well, I see you have a new friend. Is this Jamie?" Sheena's blue eyes twinkled at the sight of the small child clinging to the sheriff's hand.

"Yep, it sure is. Jamie, this is Miss Sheena. She's going to tell everyone you've been found while I take you to find your momma. Then, Miss Sheena will make you that peanut-butter and grape-jelly sandwich we spoke of, okay?" Megan looked from the boy to the cook, using her head to direct the woman out to the group pacing the pavilion.

"T'ank you, Miss Sheena. I didn't mean to steal the fruit. I was hungry." Jamie shyly smiled up at Sheena.

"Honey, if it is sitting out on a table or counter, then I mean for it to be eaten by anyone who wants it. You didn't steal, you just helped yourself." Sheena ruffled the boy's hair as she passed him and jogged down the final flight of steps. She continued out the front door, breaking into a trot until she reached the pavilion.

Megan watched her speak with Joe, then step over to Aaron to repeat the news. Aaron lowered his head to hear her and Megan noted the slight blush on Sheena's cheeks and the sparkle in her eyes while she conversed with the handsome cowboy.

Megan's heart dropped to her feet. Could Aaron possibly be interested in the cook? The cook's interest in the tall cowboy was obvious by the blush on her cheeks and the slight movement of her body closer to his. While Megan couldn't blame Sheena, she wanted to strangle her. No, that wasn't exactly right. She wanted to scream and stomp both of them. Watching Aaron, he seemed to be overly polite and attentive to the pretty, curvaceous, petite young woman. A woman who was as different from Megan as light to dark. Tall, slender, scarred Megan versus petite beauty. Tears burned her throat, but Megan refused to give in to her emotions. No way would she let anyone, especially Aaron, see how his attention to Sheena made her feel.

Quickly, she turned from the scene unfolding across the drive and picked up the boy. Heading out the back door of the lodge, she asked him, "Which cabin is the one you're staying in?"

"I can read numbers. There's a big three on our door," he boasted.

Carrying him toward the cabin, Megan forced herself to reason out the scene she had witnessed. Aaron was a free agent, while he professed an attraction to her, and a sincere friendship, they had not established a romantic relationship; physical or otherwise. They enjoyed each other's company and Aaron had kissed her, more than once, but he hadn't pushed to get closer because of the barriers she kept erecting. She should be happy if another woman flirted and he smiled in response; he deserved more than she could offer. Unable to convince herself of this, she arrived at the door to cabin three.

At the sound of her footsteps on the porch, the door flew open and Rebecca Stroud rushed out to grab her son from Megan's arms. Megan wrapped the other woman up with her free arm, creating a group hug, while trying to calm her.

"Look what I found. Jamie is very sorry he scared you. We've talked about it and agreed an hour in the corner will help him to remember not to leave without permission again." Megan let Rebecca have her child and drew away from the group hug. Megan watched Rebecca's face, waiting to see how she responded to the suggested punishment.

"My baby! Thank God, you're safe! You had momma so worried. Where were you?" Rebecca hugged Jamie tightly with tears streaming down her face. Kneeling to set him down, she pushed him away to look at his red face. "Why did you go out in the dark?"

"I's sorry momma; I wanted to see horses sleep. Then I was hungry, so I found some fruit in the k'chen. I went upstairs, to find me a sink and potty. After I washed t'fruit, then made me a fort 'tween the beds to eat. I got to playing the boogeyman was looking for me, so I hid under a bed. I was so sleepy. I'm sorry you was scared, honest. Please don't cry, Momma." Jamie patted his momma's arm while telling his story and tears began to trace down his cheek. "I'll sit in the corner forever if you won't cry no more." He seemed more affected by his mother's tears than the thought of her anger.

"Baby, don't you *EVER* do this again! You hear me?" Rebecca gently shook the boy, then pulled her hands away.

"You know I was terrified and now I'm getting very angry with you. I think you should go sit in the corner while I speak with the sheriff and when I'm done, we can discuss just how long you will need to sit there. Now go." She glared at him and pointed, arm extended in the age-old fashion of mothers everywhere.

Both women watched the boy walk, head down, into the cabin. Megan heard the scrape of a chair being dragged across the room.

"Sheriff, I'm so thankful. Where was he? Has he eaten today? Do I need to take him to see a doctor? He's awful clean for a lost child." The questions poured from the trembling woman.

Megan put a soft but firm hand on Rebecca's shoulder. "Slow down, take a few deep breaths. Everything's okay." She watched the distressed mother collecting her emotions and felt the shaking lessen under her hand.

"There, that's better. I found him on the second floor of the lodge. He heard you but was scared to come out because he knew he was in trouble. He told me you would never hit him but that you would make him sit in the corner—forever." She smiled at the stricken look on Rebecca's face. "I know better, but he didn't. I told him I would negotiate his punishment down to an hour and you would listen to me because I'm the sheriff. I know I don't have any say, but I think you need to show mercy in this case."

"I've never kept him in the corner more than thirty minutes. Don't you think an hour is a bit long for a six-year-old?" Rebecca glanced over her shoulder, through the open door, to see her baby boy sitting in the corner.

"Yes ma'am, I do. However, until he learns to tell time, you can let him out of the corner whenever you want and tell him it's been an hour. He's hungry. Sheena will bring over the sandwich and chips I promised him. I also told him the wrangler was expecting him to ride this afternoon—but I expect he knows he hasn't earned the treat today. Your call, of course. He's such a sweet boy; he told me he didn't want to wake you because you had a long day yesterday. That's why he left without telling you." Megan grinned as she relayed Jamie's excuse.

"That's my Jamie, always thinking of me, or at least so he says." An exasperated sigh left the mother. A shot rang out in the distance causing her to flinch. "I guess that was the signal to the searchers..."

"Yes, calling them in or at least telling them the child has been found. Some will continue to ride a while, but most will return to camp to find out what happened. I'd better go to the pavilion to hold the post-search meeting." Megan touched the woman's arm and then stepped down off the porch.

"Sheriff?"

"Yes, Ma'am?"

"Thanks. For everything. Simply having your shoulder to lean on and knowing your people were willing to spend the time searching has made this ordeal less painful and frightening for me." Rebecca swiped her eyes with the back of her hand, giving Megan a small watery smile before reentering the cabin.

When she reached the open field, Megan's eyes scoured the assembled volunteers for Aaron. She found him in the group below the pavilion, still talking to Sheena. While she watched, he dipped his head lower seemingly in deep conversation with the cute cook. Sheena batted her dark lashes and smiled, clearly savoring his attention. Sighing, Megan tried hard to keep from frowning at the couple. She told herself there was no need to become emotional. Aaron was a free man; he could show interest in the sexy cook. *Damn it all to Hell.*

Pasting on a smile, she walked over to Sheena, not looking at Aaron. "Excuse me, Sheena, I told Mrs. Stroud you would bring over a plate with a peanut-butter and grape-jelly sandwich, along with a pile of chips for Jamie. I think it would be best if we let mother and child bond over this without a crowd of well-wishers hanging around them. Give them about ten minutes before you head over to cabin three, okay?"

Sheena turned from her conversation with the good-looking cowboy. "That sounds like a great idea. Is she going to paddle his little bottom for all the commotion he caused?" Her soft voice thickened with irritation, her Scottish heritage showing.

"No, he's sitting in the corner and may stay there most of the day. He was terrified he would be in the corner until he grew up when I found him." Megan laughed, forcing herself to be cordial. While she wanted to strangle Sheena for flirting with Aaron, she knew the cook had as much right to flirt with him as any woman. Aaron was a dear friend, nothing more—yet. They spent a lot of time together and Aaron was her most staunch supporter, but neither had committed to any personal relationship beyond friendship.

"I'll head to the kitchen then and get the food." Turning to go, Sheena turned back to Aaron and said, "We'll continue our discussion later. Come by the lodge whenever you find the time." A twinkle in her eye and a gamin smile expressed her interest.

Megan turned away from the departing cook. Looking up at Aaron, she smiled. "Hi Aaron, how are you? Did you go out in a search group?"

"Nope, I just got here to offer when Sheena came out and gave the word the boy was safe. You found him hiding under a bed? Damn, kids are strange creatures." Aaron's eyes studied Megan's face, seeming to see through her smile to the pain within.

"Yes they are. Well, I need to go help Joe for a while in debriefing the searchers." She turned to head up the rise to the pavilion, then paused and turned back. "I almost texted you this morning. The dream came back, with a vengeance. I've forgotten the details, but I woke myself screaming. That hasn't happened in a while," she confided.

"Sorry to hear it. Want me to come by this evening? We could talk it out. It helps sometimes to figure out what triggered it. You might've remembered more details by then. I could bring pizza." Aaron looked longingly at her, his expression serious.

"If you don't have anything else going on, I would really appreciate the company. I don't want to be alone with my thoughts right now," Megan admitted.

"About seven?"

"Perfect, I'll supply the beer." She turned from him and started up the small hill where her deputy, Joseph Kaleo, stood talking to the ranch owners, Roger and Bethany Meadows in the pavilion.

"Hi Bethany, Roger. Good to see you, but I could wish for better circumstances," Megan greeted the couple, smiling at Bethany's rounded belly.

"Yeah, this is a first, and I hope a *last* for the R-B." Bethany hugged her friend. "I hear you completed the final courses and are now certified in several fields. Great! If we need a negotiator or a marksman, Riverview will be prepared."

"Thanks. The courses really weren't needed, but they look great on my résumé." Megan found herself laughing.

Stepping away from the couple, Megan faced the others waiting in front of the pavilion. "*Okay people, gather round.* " Megan called. Some led their horses; some simply gathered in groups discussing the events of the morning. Once they had moved forward and formed a semicircle in front of the pavilion, she addressed them.

"First and foremost, I want to thank all you for your quick response to the call for volunteers. We were very lucky the child was found so fast. If he hadn't been hiding, we could have found him sooner and saved ya'll the effort of hauling over here to search." Megan let her exasperation show in her tone of voice along with her stance in front of them. "I want you to know your efforts have not been in vain. Ya'll now know where this place is and you're invited back for a barbecue potluck this Sunday afternoon in appreciation of your efforts today. I'll supply the hotdogs, hamburgers, buns and condiments; the rest is pot luck, whatever you want to bring. Bring your horses. Come explore the new trails and enjoy the benefits of having this facility so close to home." Megan waited while applause politely sounded through the crowd.

"I want to tell you where and how the child was found. Jamie woke up in the dark and decided to go "watch the horses sleep". Only a six-year-old would want to do that." She snickered. "From there he wandered to the lodge where he found a spot to build a fort in one of the rooms. Honest, folks, I could not make up this scenario if I tried. He created a make-believe fort between the beds and ate fruit filched from the kitchen. He hid there from imaginary monsters and fell asleep. When he awoke to hear his mother frantically calling, screaming his name, he knew he was in deep trouble. Jamie decided to continue to hide under the bed because of her anger. Soon, he fell asleep the second time certain he would be spending his entire life in a "time out" for his misbehavior. I found him because he was crying. He wanted to come out, but was scared about the punishment. I used my recently-acquired negotiation skills and the child psychology from college to talk him out from under the bed and give him the courage to face the consequences of his actions." She paused again, waiting until the applause died.

"Jamie and his mother are both grateful for your help and he will be making up "thank-you" notes as part of his punishment. You may collect yours at the dinner on Sunday." Megan made a mental note to speak with Rebecca and have the child work on this chore. "At the barbecue there'll be a sign-up sheet for anyone who'd like to join a mounted search-and-rescue team for situations like this. I think with two guest ranches in the area and many trails in the National Forest, it's time Riverview had a trained group for emergencies. I'll research the training information. I'll remind you on Sunday to sign up. That is about all I can think of. Anyone have any questions?"

No hands raised or voices called out. Megan searched all the upturned faces and smiled again. "Thanks folks, I'll look for you on Sunday." She turned to her deputy.

"Joe, I'm heading home after I speak with Rebecca to enjoy the remainder of my day off. Think you can handle the reports?"

"Yes, Boss, not a problem. You go have a quiet rest of the day off." Joe automatically touched his hat in farewell as Megan turned to leave.

Minutes later, she was knocking on cabin three. "Mrs. Stroud, may I have a word with you?"

The door opened. Behind his mother, Megan saw Jamie sitting in the corner, a plate in his lap, eating a sandwich. "I see the food made it. Good. I think I have an idea for a punishment, which might reach him better than sitting in a corner. Do you think he could hand print about thirty thank-you notes for the searchers who spent time and effort looking for him? You know, a simple 'Thanks for your time' or 'Thank you for searching' phrase on paper will work." Megan watched the light come on behind the woman's eyes.

"Oooh, that's a wonderful idea. It would teach him courtesy as well as remorse for his actions. Where can I find some construction paper? I didn't bring much with his toys."

"I'll send you some paper and markers this afternoon."

"Thank you again for the great idea. We'll be back for future stays, and I'm going to tell everyone just how helpful and friendly this area is to strangers."

"Have a great day, Ma'am. Jamie, you be a good boy and do what your mom tells you, okay?" Megan heard his small voice follow her down the steps.

"Yes, Sheriff."

Hiking back around the lodge to where she parked her Durango, Megan felt the pressure of the search and the stress of the lost child lift from her shoulders. Even exhausted, she couldn't keep the smile from her lips. This could have ended so badly and yet, by the Grace of God, it had a wonderful ending. Silently, she offered a prayer of thanks.

Unlocking her Dodge, she noticed the slightly slimy spot on her shoulder where the boy had rubbed his face against her and smiled. As she headed home, she wondered if the remainder of her day off would hold any other surprises.

On her way back to her small ranch, Megan's mind replayed the events of the morning. The search proved one thing to her. Riverview needed an organized Search-and-Rescue group. It was time to move the local volunteers into the modern age with GPS units and up-to-date handheld communication systems. These mountains were too rugged for effective searches, without training and proper gear. Some extensive first-aid training would be a smart idea too.

First, the picnic and volunteer sheet for sign up. Once she had a number, she could hold First-Aid and Grid-Search classes for them, or find classes being offered by educational or emergency-response groups. Those with horses could learn how to "see" from horseback, while others could travel the many jeep and logging tracks by ATV while searching.

If she worked this right, she could have help any time it was needed. Properly trained and outfitted help. A well-trained group could save lives. Mentally, she made a note to search the internet for training information and suggested gear for mounted Search-and-Rescue teams. Raising the money to fund the group might be challenging but, between grants, fundraising events, and perhaps local donations, she could visualize the group forming.

Chapter 3

Megan's mind rehashed the plan as she drove from the R-B toward her small ranch. She wasn't distracted but she wasn't completely focused on her driving. Movement caught her attention a split second before an animal stumbled over the guardrail onto the shoulder of the road, then limped into her lane of travel. Fast reflexes, no oncoming traffic, and luck kept Megan from hitting it. She pulled to the side of the road and stopped; her heart racing in reaction to the near collision. Looking in her rearview mirror, she saw the animal hobbling down the middle of her lane toward her. From what she could see, it was either a miniature horse or a large shaggy dog, either way, it appeared to be in sad condition.

Putting on her flashers, she hopped from her Durango and quietly moved around to kneel behind it on the passenger side. The animal slowed at the sight of her and then the tail began to wag. Yep; it was a very big, shaggy, matted, hurt dog.

"Hey buddy, what are you doing out here? There are no houses for miles." Megan crooned softly as the dog cautiously approached. The tail, wagging a slow beat, the head drooping, it wobbled, leaving bloody tracks on the pavement. This dog had done some hard and painful traveling over rough ground. Long white hair lay matted and tangled around stickers, while the golden brown eyes pleaded for mercy above a pink mark at the top of a dry black nose.

"Easy, baby. Sit," Megan soothed, her hand extended. The huge dog sat then lay down within a foot of where she knelt. "That's it. I'm not going to hurt you. Just relax. Good dog." She leaned forward and smoothed the stickered mass away from under its eyes and tugging at a couple of foxtails to remove them. "There, is that better? Ahhh..." Megan ran her fingers into the belly hair to discern the gender. "Girl."

The dog released a deep sigh as Megan's fingers forked through the double thick rough coat to scratch her belly. Her fingers encountered what felt to be stitches, but the dog's coat was so thick and matted, she didn't investigate for fear of causing the animal more pain.

"Oh, you like tummy rubs, do you?" Megan smiled at the mostly white shaggy dog, trying to recall the breed name. She knew it was some sort of stock guard dog, but this dog, while large, was painfully thin.

"What did you do; follow a predator and then lose its trail? Where are your owners, I wonder?" She continued to run her fingers through the rough body coat, over the deep chest and stout neck. The long hair, well rounded rib cage and thick neck mane gave the dog the appearance of mass, but Megan could feel every rib and the pink tongue lolling out of the poor dog's mouth seemed dry. She realized the dog might have gone without water and food for a day or more out here in the high desert. This dog wasn't a hunting dog, but it might have brought down a rabbit or two. Finding water could be difficult for a city-bred animal without the instincts that a wild animal develops.

Megan ran her hand down the muscular right forearm to the right paw. "Let me see, baby. How badly have you worn your feet down? I need to see if I can get a sense of how far you've come." Talking to the dog, for some reason feeling the need to explain herself, Megan gently turned the paw under to have a better look at the pads and claws. Ouch.

The poor dog had almost no claws left and each section of pad showed blood where the surface had worn through.

"Okay, baby. I need to get you into my Durango. You can have the back; I think you'll fit if I put the rear seats down."

Megan stood and taking hold of the thick mane on the dog's neck, she tugged and said, "Come on, girl. Only a little more and you'll be at Doc Rayburn's clinic. I know it hurts, but you can do it. Good girl." She cooed to the dog as the animal slowly stood and hobbled with her to the SUV. "Such a brave girl you are." She scratched the dog's ears before opening the rear door. Folding the rear seats flat, Megan scowled at the height of the compartment from the surface of the road, praying the dog weighed less than she should for her breed.

Turning back to the dog, Megan sighed and began to bend down to help the tired animal into the back. "Whoa. Easy girl. Wow, you made it." She breathed a sigh of relief and grinned at the back end of the animal now filling the rear third of her Durango. Megan closed the door before the dog could back out, just in case she had second thoughts. Jumping into the driver's seat, Megan started the motor and headed out.

She passed the turn to her ranch and continued on until she reached the driveway belonging to the local large-animal veterinarian. Riverview had no small-animal vet, so Dr. Rayburn treated anything that showed up on his property. Rolling to a stop in front of the metal building that housed his office, Megan honked and grinned at the stout, swarthy man just coming out.

"Doc. I'm glad I caught you. I have a patient for you." Megan opened the rear door. "She's dehydrated and malnourished. I can handle those, but her feet need to be treated, and there's a spot on her belly...she might have some old stitches. She's worn her pads down so far that the meat is exposed." Megan turned in time to catch the dog when she launched herself out of the Dodge. *"Oomph."* Megan stepped backwards under the sudden weight, trying to keep from falling. "Easy girl. It won't help either of us if you break my leg!"

"Did you carry a foal in the backseat? No wait, it's not a horse. It's one of those Pyrenean Mountain Dogs, you know, Great Pyrenees dogs." Paul Rayburn looked at the dog struggling to jump down from Megan's arms. "Set her down. She won't go anywhere, Sheriff," he advised.

"If you don't set her down, I'll be treating both of you," he warned.

Megan let the dog slide down her body until its hind feet touched the ground. She winced when the dog yipped at the sudden contact with the rough surface. The dog immediately rolled over on her back, taking all weight off her painful feet.

"I told you to take it easy. Poor baby." Megan chided the dog as she knelt next to her as the vet approached. "This is Doc Rayburn, Baby." Megan caught herself making introductions and laughed before she continued. "Doc, this is Baby. At least that's what I'm calling her at the moment. She was limping down the highway. I almost hit her. Poor thing. I don't think she could have gone another mile. I can't remember any lost animal reports for a dog of this size. Have you had any?"

"No, there's been no report of a lost Pyrenees. She could've escaped in a different county. These dogs can cover a lot of miles without much trouble. We've had a lot of east-coast trail riders in the past couple of weeks. I know, I had to treat one horse for colic and another for a bowed tendon. I think most of the horses were arena animals they brought out here and expected to go mountain climbing on them. I wonder if the dog got away from one of them...a lot of those people never train their dogs to stay close—they expect the dog to follow tamely through the wild lands. Riders should understand that a herding dog or guardian dog are going to follow their instincts—it's what they do." Paul reached down and easily picked up the dog, carrying her like a huge baby, with all four feet in the air.

"Open my office door, if you would, Sheriff. Then go straight back and open the door on the right." He followed Megan into his clinic and only passed her to lay the dog on the exam table. "Easy big girl. Megan, grab me a syringe and the first vial in the medicine chest next to where my clipboard is sitting. Yeah, the one on the shoulder-height shelf." He gave directions without taking his hands off the dog.

Megan found the vial and lifted a syringe from the jar sitting just beyond the clipboard. "Do you need an alcohol swab or anything, Doc?"

"There are some in the jar next to the one with the syringes."

Grabbing two, Megan passed them to the vet. "Here you are. What are you giving her?"

"Well, I don't want to give her anything, but I can't have her struggling to get up when I start cleaning those feet. So I'm giving her about a quarter of the dose of ACE that I'd give a healthy dog her size." He peeled back the dog's thick double layer coat, swabbed the skin on her neck. Sliding the needle into the dog easily, he pushed the serum before the animal could move or otherwise object. "There you go sweetie. Just relax. You're going to be fine." His soft voice soothed the nervous dog. He quickly examined her gums, teeth and tongue. Moving to look in her hears, he paused and then lowered his head to get a better look. "Sheriff, this dog's got a tattoo inside her ear. Left one," he moved to examine her right. "Yep, right one too. It looks like Arabic script. Come look." He stepped back to let Megan get closer.

"Wow, Doc. You're right. It is Arabic script and numerals. Grab a pencil and write this down. B A N D I 07839. Megan read the letters and numbers tattooed onto the inner cheek of the big dog. She had automatically separated them as she read them to the vet. "I doubt it means anything, but 'bandi' means prisoner in Pashto. Well, bandi kind of fits, she's our prisoner now." Megan scratched the dog's ears.

"I'm going to set up an IV for fluids. She's very dehydrated." Watching the dog closely, Doc. Rayburn noted how quickly she relaxed, showing the effectiveness of the sedative. "There, I told you it would be okay," he petted the dog's head, pausing to scratch behind her ears.

"Megan, would you keep her head down while I put a soft muzzle on her? She won't be able to bite, and she shouldn't panic at the restraint." The vet moved over to a cabinet where he pulled out what appeared to be a short sleeve with a strap from one side to the other on the wide end. Confidently, he slipped the wide end over the dog's black nose, sliding it up to below her worried golden eyes before securing the strap behind her head with the hook and loop closure fabric.

"There, now keep her distracted while I work my hands over her to see if there are any injuries under all this hair."

"No problem, Doc. I felt something odd on her belly, but with all that hair I didn't examine her other than lightly brushing her tummy." Megan kept her hands on the dog, petting and scratching while the vet skimmed his hands over the large body.

"Humph...this looks like a recent spay incision; but it feels wrong and her hair hadn't been shaved back around it." His hands began prodding the stitched wound that ran up from where her leg joined her body toward the rib cage for several inches. "Kind of long, even if she is a big dog. Feels lumpy. That *is not* what I want to see." Shaking his head, he walked over to a locked cabinet where he pulled out a vial and another syringe. "I'm going to knock her out because I need to open that incision to find out why it's lumpy. She might be bleeding into her belly," he explained to Megan as he picked up a scalpel and some pro-size clippers before turning back to the exam table. "Strange though, if she's bleeding into her belly, I would expect her to be either in shock or feverish but she shows no symptoms of either."

"Is it scar tissue forming?" Megan asked. She was only guessing, she had not a clue what would cause lumps in that area but thought scar tissue was as likely as any other suggestion she could make.

"Too soon, the stitches seem to be less than four days old. The edge of the incision hasn't fused yet. In fact, there isn't even much scab or healing evident." He slid the needle into a vein, pulled back some blood and pushed the drug, watching the dog's eyes close and her breathing become even. "There, now I can work without worrying about her jumping off the table." Grabbing the clippers, he began shaving the thickly matted fur from the edges of the wound.

"This gets stranger and stranger. I thought it was a new incision because there was no scabbing or fusing. But, now I see that the opening has been here for some time. The edges of the skin are healed, just not fused. This is like something you would see around a drainage tube, only larger." He snipped the sutures allowing the wound to open. "I'll be *damned*. Look at this." Paul stepped back and pointed to a baggie protruding from the wound. Grabbing his cell phone, he clicked several shots of the odd incision with the baggie protruding. He tugged on the plastic, trying not to cause damage, but needing to retrieve it from the belly of the dog.

Megan began using her cell phone to snap photos while the vet worked. He kept his hands away from in front of the bag he was removing so the photos would show dog, incision, and the bag spilling out of her belly.

"What the hell? Doc, is that a baggie? What could a dog need that would be sewn into its gut?" Megan stepped closer to the side of the dog for a better view, snapping three more photos of the baggie and the wound.

"This dog didn't need what's in this bag; someone else does." He pulled the plastic bag open and watched in awe as a velvet inner bag slid out. "You want to open that, Sheriff? My guess would be drugs or gems." He stepped back to give Megan room.

Megan shot a couple more frames and then eased the velvet bag open allowing the contents to slide out on the metal exam table. "*Holy Christmas!* Would you look at that? Diamonds, not small ones either. Wonder what the value is for this batch?" She picked up a particularly bright stone and held it to the light. "Someone is using this dog as a 'mule'. Guess I'd better get the Feds involved." Megan shot some photos of the sleeping dog, the velvet bag and the fifteen stones scattered beside it. She put the gems into a small, lidded container, which she stuck into her pocket with the now empty velvet bag.

"I'll clean out the cavity. Do you want me to put some cotton and pebbles into a baggie and place it in the dog?" Paul began cleaning out the cavity where the bag had rested. "I would expect the Feds are going to want to 'play dumb' over this and see if the dog gets claimed."

"No, this dog deserves better. Do what you need to do to get the wound to heal well and sew her back up. We'll find a way to protect her and draw out the smugglers. If they claim the dog, they risk the stones have been found. They could cut their losses and leave the dog to those who found it but I think they'll be greedier than that." She laughed as she thought about the problem facing the thieves.

"Of course, we could advertise finding the dog and its current location, keeping it under tight surveillance while we wait for the smugglers to steal it. But, they might just kill the dog and rip the bag out, saving the trouble of loading such a huge animal. I would hate to see you put the dog at risk like that." The doctor paused in his work, looking seriously at Megan. "You know they don't value the dog and for that I think they should suffer as they made this poor girl suffer."

"I'll go into town and call the FBI. I'm not certain this is their jurisdiction, but it isn't drugs or people so that might rule out Homeland or DEA." Megan frowned and walked toward the door. "Keep her safe. Don't give her up to anyone or let anyone know she's here, especially your twins."

"Don't worry, Sheriff. I'll put her somewhere the twins never go...both of them are allergic to cats and they steer clear of the feline patient's holding room. I'll make a bed up for her in there. Let me make a copy of the letters and numbers in her cheek. I'll check tomorrow to see if I can figure out what it means. I heard a while back that a humanitarian group was removing working dogs from war-torn countries in the Middle East. Maybe she's one of those and the tattoo is a registration. I've got a few friends I can call" Dr. Rayburn waved as Megan smiled and walked out.

Back in her SUV, Megan sighed. Sometimes her job simply sucked. Putting a helpless animal in harm's way was pretty sucky to her. *Damn, damn, damn! Why do people use animals, children and harmless citizens to carry drugs and goods, not to mention bombs, across borders and into secure places?* She remembered Afghanistan; how the enemy had used anything and everything to attack the American troops. Heartless bastards. Now this! She wanted to find those slime balls using animals to do their dirty work and put them away. Frustrated, she gunned the motor, her Dodge pitching gravel as it fishtailed back to the highway.

At her ranch, she showered and dressed in a clean uniform. So much for a day off, she'd wanted a peaceful ride on Radar today. Just take off into the hills and enjoy the scenery. Oh well, maybe next week. "This is why I earn the big bucks. Assigned days off belong to non-elected officials," she muttered as she climbed back into her Durango and headed to town, her mood easing only slightly with the beauty of the drive.

Driving down Main, as she neared the Sheriff's Department, she scowled. The building was a multi-purpose community building, housing EMS and fire dispatch, the city jail, her office and the court room/town council chamber. Deputy Kaleo's personal car sat in the parking spot assigned to the Sheriff. Taking a deep breath and exhaling Megan let go of her irritation, her lips turned up at the edges. Of course, he had her spot. He was in charge today and that space belonged to whomever was in charge. She knew she couldn't fault him for parking close to the door when she wasn't on duty.

Finding a spot under a shade tree, just down the street from the office, Megan headed for the office front door. The shaded spot was better anyway. Her Durango would be cool when she left work, instead of sweltering. Megan's mood lifted and she hummed a bright country tune as she walked up the steps.

"Good morning, Sheriff. I didn't expect to see you here today. Guess Joe called you out for the lost child?" Shirley glanced up from her desk at the customer counter. The phones were quiet and it appeared she was working a crossword puzzle.

"Yes, that started my day. Could you see that some construction paper and colored pencils or crayons are delivered to Cabin 3 at the R-B? Take the cost from petty cash. The lost child is going to make Thank You cards for those who searched. In addition, could you find David Harrison's personal telephone number or his personal office number in Denver? I need the FBI and it's fun to have a name to call. I hate that switchboard." Megan frowned at Shirley, picked up her messages from the IN basket on her way to her office. "Thanks Shirley." she called over her shoulder before closing her office door.

Megan's smile faded when she glanced at her clear desk and knew she would be cluttering it up over the next six or so hours as she filed reports, spoke with the FBI and did work that should have waited until tomorrow. At least it was clean to start. She'd stayed until seven last night, getting it that way. Looking at the stack of notes and messages she had collected from her IN basket, Megan sighed and sat down at the neat, clean desk. No time like the present to get started.

First of the messages was one from old Henry at the Library. "Sheriff, have you seen that funny-looking truck that's been cruising around town since last Monday? It's lime green and so low to the ground I'm surprised it doesn't scrape when they enter the parking lot." It was the kind of rhetorical message Henry often left. Ever since he helped identify the arsonist stalking Stephanie and Doyle last year, the man thought he was an ace investigator. He spent most of his time looking out the library windows and noting unusual people or cars and trucks. She had a list going of those he'd told her to "look out for".

He was a sweet old man, but sometimes she wished he'd pay more attention to overdue books and less attention to strangers in town. This was prime tourist country. Lots of strangers came and went, most staying at the R-B or the Gunnison Valley Ranch. None of them terrorists, arsonists, or kidnappers. She set the note aside to add the truck to what she thought of as "Henry's List" in case she needed it for future information. She noticed he even included the Nevada license plate number. At least he was thorough.

Next was a message from John at the Truck Stop, complaining about a few bikers who'd spent more time at his gas pumps than needed. Megan didn't know what John expected her to do about it so she began a pile for "what the heck" messages. A note from Ida Mae Bailey asked her to come by later to speak with a new boarder who seemed to be frightened about something. Another for the "what the heck" pile. She laughed aloud as she read the next, seems her Aunt Marge was giving her notice that if she didn't come to dinner on Monday, she could expect one of her own deputies to collect her. Marge would do it too. Megan noted on her calendar "Dinner with Marge" in large letters over Monday's date.

The final message was from Betty at Betty's Diner. She wanted Megan to stop by because "something fishy is going on". That was the total message. "I need to talk to you if you can come by. Something fishy is going on." Betty truly loved mystery.

Betty was one of the town's gossips, but the woman had a nose for trouble. Megan stared at her watch. A little early for lunch, but the diner might be quiet and Betty could spend a few minutes explaining the "something fishy". Megan stood, grabbed her hat from the rack, thought about removing her gun belt, then thought better of it and headed for the door.

"Shirley, I'm going to Betty's for lunch. I'll be back in about an hour. Joe is technically still in charge today, so page him for any calls." She waved as she headed out the door. Pausing on the steps, her gaze slid toward the diner before she walked a half block in the opposite direction to Christopher's Gems, Stones and Precious Metals. Christopher had gone to college in California and returned to Riverview to set up his small business because his mother needed his help after the death of his father a year ago. The bell over the door jingled a happy sound as she entered the quiet store. Sighing, Megan hoped his mother had enough to support them since the store seemed too quiet.

A clean-cut man in a moderately well-fitting suit came out from the back. "Hi, Sheriff. What can I do for you today?"

"Hi, Christopher. When you opened, I remember seeing the story about your gemology skills and how you expected to help people with all their precious and semi-precious stone needs."

"Yep. I earned the degree and bought all the most modern equipment to handle just about any kind of stone." Christopher seemed to stand taller and his smile broadened when listing his credentials.

Reaching her hand into her pocket, Megan brought out the container holding the diamonds from within the dog. "I need some way of identifying or marking these stones. They are evidence in a case I'm working and it's critical to keep a valid chain of evidence. What can you suggest?" Megan sat the container on his counter, watching his reactions. It was unlikely that he was any part of the smuggling ring, but no one was exempt from suspicion at this point.

"Got a machine in the back that will 'capture a diamond's unique optical fingerprint.' I'm even qualified to be an expert witness. The machine will photomicrograph each stone and its internal characteristics. As good as a fingerprint of a person since no two stones are exactly the same. I bought it because it's also great for identifying real or fake stones too. Let me get my gloves." He walked to the end of the counter and reached into a desk drawer, retrieving clear latex gloves. "Sheriff, please bring the stones and follow me to the back room. I know you can't lose sight of them or it could jeopardize your chain of evidence."

Picking up the container, Megan followed Christopher through the curtained door into his workshop area. Looking around, she recognized a rock tumbler from her childhood days when she had a much smaller version of it. The sunlight played through a skylight, giving the room a bright and cheery ambiance. "Nice shop."

"Thanks, I'm proud of it. Over here is the machine, Sheriff. Have a seat where you have a clear view and hand me the container. You can photograph the process if you think it will help." He stretched out his hand and took the container, setting it on a small clean surface to the left of the machine. "Let me get a cloth to put these on." Returning with a large black velvet cloth, he covered the workbench on the right of the machine. "There. I'll empty the container on the velvet and as we scan each stone, I'll put it back into the container. Sound okay?"

"I'll take photos of the process. Spread the stones out so it's obvious how many are there. This photo can be compared to the photo taken when they were confiscated." Megan pulled out her phone and took a photo of the fifteen stones. She shot frames of him inserting each stone into the machine and pulling it out again until all stones had been scanned. "Okay, now what? May I have a copy of the scans?"

"I'll give you a disc. If I upload this to the mainframe, they can be compared to find out if they are stolen. Do you want me to do that?" Christopher was keying in data, but paused to question Megan.

"No, not yet. We don't know who is smuggling the stones or what kind of equipment they have or where they plan to distribute them. Let's just keep these stones anonymous for the moment. Once we have the smuggler, we can see if the stones are stolen or just being used to launder money." Pausing for effect, Megan glared at the man. "I expect you to keep your mouth shut on this one. You can't even tell your mother until we've solved the case. You understand? It could be hazardous to let the criminals know you've handled the stones and could testify against them."

A worried frown creased Christopher's brow. "Wow, I never thought I could be in danger for this kind of work. No problem, Sheriff. I won't tell a soul, I swear."

"Good. I'll take the container. Thanks. Send the bill to Shirley, I'll let you know when I'll need your expert testimony. Take care, and tell your mom that Megan says hi." Waving over her shoulder, Megan walked out of the shop, putting the disc and the container in separate pockets, and smiling, she headed for the diner.

The brightly-colored mesas and surrounding hills contrasted with the bright blue of the Colorado sky. Megan's heart lifted and her smile grew bigger as she strolled along Main. Riverview never ceased to make her smile. The friendly people waving, the never-ending changes of weather which she'd loved as a child visiting her aunt and that she loved even more now as an adult.

She loved her folks, her brothers and the ranch where she'd been born and raised but Riverview seemed more like home. The people here accepted her as an adult, not just one of the Holloway kids or as her brothers "little Sis". She didn't have to live up to expectations or live down things done by her siblings. She was part of the community, accepted first because she was Marge's niece, but mostly because she fit in with the town of Riverview. This was rough country where people stuck together and often knew more than needed about their neighbors but, most times, didn't judge.

Chapter Four

Megan noticed the parking lot at the diner held only a few old ranch trucks. Not the crowd of trucks and cars it would hold in an hour or so. She smiled as she entered. "Hi Betty, George, Billy, Michael," she called to the owner and the customers seated at the counter, before taking over a vacant stool.

"Sheriff. I'm happy to see you. I heard you found the lost kid at the R-B. Good job. It could have been really bad if he'd gone out in the woods someplace. Most city folks just don't understand this rough country." Betty brought Megan a glass of water. "Why don't we take the back booth so I can keep an ear on the kitchen?" She pointed toward the back with the hand holding the water and carried it that direction, not giving Megan a chance to agree or disagree. "I need a BLT, bacon crisp, tater tots and a small salad for the sheriff," Betty called to the kitchen as she passed the door.

"What makes you think I'll order that today?" Megan grinned, knowing exactly Betty's response to the question.

"Cause it's what you order every time you come in here for lunch."

"One of these days, I'm going to change the order just to surprise you," Megan threatened lightly.

"When you do, I'll eat the BLT," she laughed, seating herself to face the door. Lowering her voice and looking around to make certain none of the customers followed them, she continued, "There's something fishy going on. There's been five very strange vehicles driving slowly around town this past week. I mean, we've all seen them over and over, going a lot slower than most visitors. It's like they're lost... or casing the area. Any of your deputies noticed them?"

"What kind of vehicles? Henry reported the lime-green lowered pickup truck," Megan prompted, pulling her notebook and pen from her shirt pocket.

"That's one of 'em. They all have those tinted black windows so you can't see anything going on inside. Spooky and evil looking, if you ask me." She gave Megan a nod, looking for agreement.

"Well, tinted windows aren't against the law, so long as they meet our statutes on darkness and aren't mirrored. They're unusual around here, though. Besides that, what can you recall about the cars?"

"Well, one is a SUV. I think it's an Escalade—that Cadillac thing. It's that pearly white color, makes those dark windows really odd. Another is one of those gigantic things...I think it's a Humvee or Hummer, I can never get the names of those dang things right. Looks like it might be able to carry a whole squad of big men. You know the thing I'm talking about?" Betty seemed to be at a loss for words, so Megan nodded to show she understood the vehicle in question.

"What color is the Hummer?"

"That thing is black, but it has a metallic-looking shine to it. Then there's the really sleek-looking one. It's a silver that leans toward blue. I saw the numbers on the side and one of the customers called it a Mercedes S500L. It purred so quietly, I hardly heard it pull up next to the door. You should've seen what got out of it. I swear the woman had to be almost six feet tall and she had on heels that were about six inches high! You only see clothes and hair like that on TV. She strolled in, just like she knew what she was doing and ordered a grilled chicken salad with dressing on the side. Wanted a bottle of water with lemon. Real snooty, but she left a nice tip. She asked where you go to adopt a dog, a big dog. I told her to check with Anna over at the shelter off Second. That car's been driving around town just about every day this week but, she hasn't been back. Guess she didn't like our brand of water." Betty snorted at her summation of why her customer hadn't returned.

Betty continued with her tale. "The fifth car is an almost orange kind of gold sports car. John from the truck stop was here when it drove by and just about dropped his pie. I've never seen lust for a car before but, John had it bad. He breathed something about wanting to get under the hood or behind the wheel of it, swallowed hard and blushed. I think he got hard watching it and was embarrassed. I asked him what it was and he said it was a Lamborghini Hurricane. He said it was faster just standing still than any car in the county. Like I said, he was lusting after that orange-gold car something fierce." Betty looked around the diner, smiling and waving at the customers who were beginning to file in for lunch.

"Hey, ask your deputies to watch out for those black-windowed cars. No one needs windows that dark, unless they're hiding something illegal inside. Let me know if you want me to try getting tag numbers the next time I see'em. The sleek thing and the lime pickup were from Nevada and the one John wanted was from New Mexico but, the other two had Colorado plates." She stood, walked into the kitchen and returned with Megan's sandwich. "Here you go. Today's lunch is on me, kind of congratulations for finding that little boy."

"Why thanks, Betty. You're just too sweet." Megan smiled up at the older woman and watched her walk over with menus for her latest customers. Looking down at the sandwich, tots and salad, Megan realized just how hungry she was. It'd been a busy day and it wasn't yet noon. She finished making notes on the suspicious vehicles and tucked her notebook back into her pocket before she began making her way through the delicious meal.

She puzzled over the strangers but knew it could be anything from a house party at one of the celebrity ranches up near the ski slopes to a group at one of the dude ranches. Gunnison Valley and R-B often had groups rent out all or part of the spread for an event or gathering. Thinking about it, she knew it wasn't the R-B because of the lost child. She made a mental note to call Gunnison Valley Ranch after lunch. All this was probably for nothing. The visitors had likely headed back to wherever they came from by now.

She was biting off a corner of the sandwich when the Lamborghini cruised by the diner. Cruised, the only word to describe how it moved. Cars like that don't "drive" or "motor", they "cruise" or sometimes "speed". This one cruised and Megan swore she could feel the eyes of the driver looking in as he passed. The black windows gave no clue, but she got goose bumps and a tingle up her spine from the slow, almost evil cruise. " *Holy shit,* " she breathed around the mouthful of food.

Pulling out her notebook, she scribbled down the New Mexico license plate data while trying to swallow her suddenly very dry bite of sandwich. Betty was right, those dark windows were downright spooky. Next to the plate number, she noted, "check windows with meter, compare to NM tinting laws". She would remind her deputies in the morning to feel free to pull over suspicious vehicles to check darkness of tint and compare to regulations for the state of registry. If the driver had a local license, the car would need to conform to Colorado's 27% Visible Light Transmission regulation. She felt certain the sports car would prove to be darker but might meet whatever the New Mexico regulations happen to be.

Picking up her water, she washed down the food with a couple of gulps, wrapped the other half sandwich in her napkin, left a healthy tip for Betty and headed for the door. "See you later, Betty. I've got a few things to check and I'll let you know if I find anything useful. Bye." Megan found her legs moving quicker as she headed back to the office than they had as she strolled to lunch. Her mind whirled. Still might be nothing evil but, damn, that car felt wicked. If a car could make a person feel worried, that one worried her.

Shirley flagged her down as Megan entered the building. "Sheriff, I got a call through to David Harrison. His wife told me he was working today and gave me his direct line. His assistant answered and told me he was at lunch and will call you back as soon as he gets back into the office. Is that okay? She actually didn't offer any choices." Shirley handed Megan a note with a tentative smile when Megan paused at the reception counter.

"Thanks, good work. What's this?" She glanced at the message.

"From Henry, up at the library, just one if his messages. You know, he makes me read them back to him like he doesn't trust me to put down what he's saying. I'd be insulted if anyone else treated me like that but Henry used to give me a sucker for each book I read when I was a kid, so I can't be angry with him." She giggled at the memory. "In the city, if a man gave a little girl candy, he'd be under investigation. Here, it's just Henry encouraging kids to read. I think he still gives out candy with children's books to this day."

"Thanks. I missed the candy since I was only here a few weeks every summer and too busy to read. Love the thought of him doing that, though. I knew there was a reason why I liked him. If it makes you feel better, I think he calls with the messages just to 'help' me and keep me from missing clues. In his world, everything is a mystery or suspense—unless it's a romance." Megan laughed when Shirley agreed with a nod.

Taking the message and her sandwich into her office, she pulled up the national program covering vehicle registrations. Inputting the license plate, state, and car model, Megan hit enter and sat back to wait for whatever data was on file for that particular license plate. She reached into her small fridge and pulled out a bottled iced tea. Opening it, she used it to wash down the remainder of her sandwich while waiting for the results.

Beeping sounded from her computer. Nicodemo Poggi of Socorro, NM popped up, the result of her search. At least he had a Post Office box address in Socorro. Records gave him a physical address on Vista Drive. Furthermore, the records showed the local officers had tested the window darkness of the vehicle more than once. Doing a quick search on the owner's name popped up a short rap sheet. Cited once for "Failure to maintain a lane" which in her experience just meant the officer wanted to get a closer look at the driver and/or the vehicle. They also cited him once for "burning without a permit" which sound like the local police wanted a reason to invade his property without getting a warrant. Neither citation showed any fine or payment. Neither citation made it to court. Megan had no doubt the man had both citations dismissed.

Other than the fact the man had money, a foreign-sounding name and a liking for fast cars, Megan wondered why local police seemed to be finding reasons to question or harass him. Making notes of the citing officers and the station information, she closed the files. She dialed the Socorro police department.

"Hello? This is Sheriff Megan Holloway of Riverview, Colorado. Is Officer Minton in the office this morning?" Megan reached for the clean notepad sitting on the left side of her daily calendar. She was surprised the receptionist seemed able to connect her to the officer, she'd expected him to be off or working out of the office at this time of day.

"This is Captain Draggle, Sheriff. I understand you are looking for Officer Minton. I'm sorry to tell you, but he was run down on the highway last month. Hit and run, no evidence other than the tag number of the car he stopped and the tag was stolen." A deep sigh punctuated the statement. "Can I ask why you want to speak with him?"

"*Damn*, I'm so sorry to hear that, Captain. I wanted to ask him about Nicodemo Poggi. From the reports, it looks as if he was the only officer involved with citing Poggi on misdemeanor offences. Do you have any background on the situations?" Megan gripped the phone tighter and worked hard not to react to the death of a fellow officer.

"Poggi? Minton was trying to hang something well enough for it to stick on that slimy bastard. We've arrested his underlings for everything from drugs to human trafficking. I'm pretty damn certain hassling Poggi is what got Minton run down. It was a hit, plain and simple. Then Poggi left the area. We hoped he'd gone back to Chicago where he'd come from. We've been too busy to track him. How do you know the name, is he in your jurisdiction now? Watch your back, Sheriff." The Captain halted to allow Megan to answer.

"His Lamborghini has been cruising around town lately. When I ran the tags, I came up with the two citations on the owner. I don't know if he's moved into the area, or is staying at one of the many guest ranches around here. Are you working with any other agency? DEA, Homeland, FBI? Also, would using animals to bring in contraband sound like something Poggi would be involved with?"

"Look Sheriff, I don't know if the Feds are after this guy. I do know his underlings smuggle humans so it's not a big leap to other contraband. If he's moved up to your neck of the desert, I say good riddance to bad rubbish and warn you to tread very carefully. He's a snake with a pit full of associates who are almost as deadly. What's your email? I'll send you Minton's files on the man. Nothing concrete enough to catch him, but it may help you to have more background data."

Megan rattled off her email and fax number to the Captain. "Send the non-essential data by fax. Nothing is sacred around here, so I don't want sensitive data by fax. If you have photos of known associates, fax them too. We've had several vehicles with dark windows and one Mercedes with Nevada plates that might be part of this man's organization. Appreciate your help and, again, sorry about the officer you lost. I'll be careful." Hanging up the phone, she sat there staring at it, wondering if the officer had a family. Megan and her deputies acknowledged this job put them into harm's way. Any traffic-stop or family-disturbance call could turn deadly in a heartbeat. The risks were part of the territory. However, that didn't stop her from grieving every time she heard about an officer who paid with his or her life. Damn, it pissed her off too. She let go of the grief and held onto the anger. Anger would take her further than grief.

Pushing back from her desk, Megan went out into the office to see if Joe had returned from the R-B. Looking at his empty desk, she saw Dwayne just beyond, filling his insulated mug at the coffeepot. "Dwayne, I thought you had traffic detail?"

At the sound of her voice the man spun, sloshing coffee on his hand and swore. "Damn Sheriff, you startled me. I thought you had the day off."

"Is that why you're hanging around here rather than out on the highway?" Megan's voice was deceptively soft but her eyes were hard as she surveyed the young deputy.

"No Ma'am. Uh...I stopped in for a fresh citation book and thought to fill up my cup before I headed back out," he stammered.

"Well, while you're here, I'll fill you in on some data I just received. I want you to keep an eye out for vehicles with darkened windows. I need license data and see if you can follow one to see where it goes. Don't get close or let them know you're following. It's possible these people are dangerous, so don't stop them unless there's a damn good cause. I don't want you hurt, I just want to know where they're living." Megan punctuated her statement by shaking a finger at the man. "There's nothing on them except local gossip and you know how this town loves to gossip. I spoke to the sheriff's office where the Lamborghini is registered and the owner is a 'person of interest' in the death of one of their officers. No evidence, no concrete link but, the officer had stopped it twice in the days before he was run down on the highway. Watch your back and don't give them any reason to come after you." Megan tried to pound the warning into the young man's head. The last thing she needed as a gung-ho youngster following and harassing Poggi.

Watching the deputy leave, she hoped she'd not made a mistake in alerting him to the strange vehicles. She went over to speak with the dispatcher, asking her to call Joseph to ask for his estimated time of arrival back to the office, telling him she needed to speak with him in private.

Back in her own office, she looked at her watch. Two o'clock. David might have returned to his office by now. She picked up her phone, dialing his number.

"Hi, this is Sheriff Megan Holloway. Has Agent Harrison returned yet?"

"His line is busy. Would you care to hold? I'll see he knows you are waiting." The receptionist seemed helpful, not abrupt, as Shirley had reported.

"I'll hold; it's important I speak with him. Thank you for the effort. I appreciate it." Megan had found that politeness earned more effort than rudeness with government employees. She doodled on her notepad, thinking of the dog and the diamonds. Pulling the container of stones from her pants pocket, she opened the lid, admiring the sparkle inside. Yep, someone was missing these and likely would do just about anything to get them back. Poor dog.

"Megan, hi. Great to hear from you. What's happening in Riverview?" The friendly voice of her friend's husband boomed into her ear.

"Hey, David. Riverview might have a few new, unsavory residents. First, we have found a Great Pyrenees with diamonds sewn into its belly and a tattoo in her cheek written in Pashto. Appeared to be a spay incision, but the vet thought it felt wrong and opened it. We found a baggie with a pouch of gems. Poor dog is being used to smuggle." Megan paused to see what David would say.

"Sounds interesting. Kind of international for a small town in Colorado. Any idea who owns the dog?"

"Not a clue. No collar on her and her feet have seen a lot of rough ground recently. Dr. Rayburn is going to research the tattoo. He remembers hearing about a group rescuing working dogs from Afghanistan and Pakistan for new homes in the USA. Maybe this was one of those dogs. Question is, were the stones in her when she left the Middle East?" Megan wondered again about the possible connections.

"While I was trying to call you, I found out we may have some new residents. The kind that might just be involved with something like money laundering or smuggling. Betty informed me we've had vehicles with blacked-out windows cruising the town for the past four days. Might be linked with a lost dog. What do you think?" Megan had just associated the cruising with a dog search. Like a firefly buzzing over her head, the thought shed light on some of the things she'd been told.

"The new residents have records? Anyone I should know about?"

"The chief character is a Nicodemo Poggi. No specific record, but has employees with convictions on drug trafficking and charges of human trafficking. Following the money, the path leads to their employer, Poggi. A deputy down in New Mexico tried to get a better look at the man and ended up a speed bump on the highway within days of a search. Can you think of any specific agency or agent who would be investigating a person such as Poggi?" Megan waited while David seemed to be pondering her question.

"Let me make some inquiries and either I or an interested agent will get back with you. Mind if I give out your information?" David paused when Megan didn't respond. "Only to vetted and trusted agents." He assured her.

"No, give the work data out to anyone, but my private number to no one. Trusted or unknown. If they leave a message, I'll get back with them. Or better yet, you can give my email out to anyone and I'll respond to inquiries online. I think I'd prefer that to telephone calls. Cuts out the switchboard here."

"Will do. I've got your email, both private and work. Okay to give both?"

"No, just the work email. I check it from home. Thanks, David. Could you email me later with who you've passed this on to? Kind of a verification if I get email from a stranger."

"Will do. Keep your head down and your butt covered. If you've got high-level criminals working in your area, it could get risky. I'll tell Kam you called and will email her later. Okay? Take care." David warned her.

The line went dead before Megan could respond. Just like the man, always abrupt and in a rush. It was nice to have a contact to call, but sometimes he seriously irritated her. Getting up, she took the container of diamonds to the safe located behind the reception desk. She used her thumbprint then her personal pass code to open it. She had thought the elaborate entry excessive, but now, as she placed the diamonds and velvet bag inside with the completed evidence tag, she was happy no one else could access the safe. Next, she took the disc and put it into the locked filing cabinet in a file she labeled "Lost Dog".

"What're you doing, Boss?"

Megan jumped at the male voice behind her. "Dammit Joe. Quit sneaking up on me." She whipped around to face the big man. "None of your business. You're safer if you have no clue at this point."

"Okay. What did you want to see me about?" Joe followed Megan back into her office.

"Well, it's been an interesting day. Missing child, Henry seeing villains again, Betty being suspicious of vehicles with black out windows and I damn near hit a dog on the way back to town. Doc Rayburn has the dog. From the looks of it, the poor thing has been running loose a while. Have you had anyone ask you about a lost dog?"

"Busy day off, what do you do on a work day?" Joe snorted, remembering waking his boss up that morning. "No, as far as I know none of the local dogs have been reported missing. But, I'll tell anyone looking to check with the Doc."

"*No!*" Megan turned to glare at her deputy. "In this case, I want you to take the name and telephone number of any person searching and give it only to me. *Do not tell ANYONE where the dog is.* Do you understand?"

Joe put his hands up defensively. "Sure, Boss. I'll do that. Why don't you want me to direct them to the vet? It's what we would normally do."

"Sorry, didn't mean to snarl. The dog has been abused. We might need to protect it and Dr. Rayburn from the owner." She didn't exactly lie, the treatment of the dog by its owner was abuse in her book. "Also, watch for vehicles cruising through town and down the side roads. Might be the owners looking for her. Take down tag numbers if you see anything suspicious but do not confront them. This could be a dangerous situation. In the same manner that domestic abuse can get you killed, these people are not nice and not likely to react in a manner you would expect from law-abiding citizens. Pass this on to Deputy Jacobson when you see him. Do not approach."

"Got it. Is that all? There's still forms to fill out about this morning."

"That's it for now." Megan dismissed him with a wave and looked back at the notes on her desk. She should run the plate Henry had given her but she figured it could wait until tomorrow.

Chapter Five

Even though Megan needed to pick up beer, she still managed to swing by Stephanie's Closet for a new shirt first. If she hurried, she might even be able to get Alyssa to style her hair. Maybe get a different cut or something. A new style could bolster her courage to begin the next chapter in her relationship with Aaron.

Aaron had been smiling at the R-B cook. Megan no longer doubted that she felt jealous, although she had no right. She had no claim on him; they were only friends. Her memories of the night he had held her on his lap while she sobbed brought a wistful smile to her lips. Feeling his erection under her thigh had embarrassed him, especially when she giggled. Okay, so they could be more than friends if she wanted. Did that give her the right to keep him away from other women? Well, maybe it was time to make a decision about taking their friendship up a level. She couldn't expect him to wait forever. His patience would only last so long and she knew she needed him in her life. Therefore, it was off to shop and primp before buying the beer and heading home. She picked up the message from the Bailey's and headed out.

Later, sitting in her Dodge Durango, Megan turned the rearview mirror to get another look at her reflection. All she could think was "wow, what a change." She'd given Alyssa free rein and the stylist had made some major changes. Megan no longer had long, below her shoulder, naturally wavy, light-brown hair. The woman in the mirror had a Marilyn Monroe-style curly head of hair in mahogany brown with layers of shades and highlights from ash blonde to deep red. The curls were loose, wavy and felt soft to her touch. The color had just enough red to give the curls depth, catching highlights from the sun when she moved. The layers of shades and highlights made her think of a summer spent outdoors. One wave kept dropping across her forehead and Megan knew she would need to hold it back or it would drive her insane...but for now, it looked sexy as hell. Goose bumps played up her arms and butterflies did cartwheels in her stomach as she contemplated the completeness of the change from her normal appearance.

On the seat next to her was the bag holding not only a new embroidered shirt, but also a pair of formfitting jeans with sparkles on both back pockets. The shirt would tie and expose her midriff, the butterflies embroidered across the front outlined the cut-outs across the yoke. Eyes would gaze from the cut-outs of bare flesh down to her full breasts. Not an outfit she would wear locally unless she wanted the attention of all the cowboys. Uncertain if she had the courage to wear it for the one cowboy who mattered to her, she would keep it handy. At least, the outfit would be in her closet just in case.

Looking at her watch, she realized she barely had time to grab the beer and get home before Aaron arrived. Stopping at the Bailey's would have to wait until tomorrow. Running into the liquor store, she grabbed the beer and had the clerk toss in a couple of those little sample-size bottles of booze they kept in the case on the counter. One of those would settle her nerves. Unconsciously, she ran her fingers through her new style and tossed her head, not noticing when the clerk swallowed hard at the sexy movement. He stammered goodbye as she left the store. Strange, Bill didn't often stammer. Shaking her head, she threw the bag on the seat of the Durango and headed out of town.

She tried to keep her foot light on the gas pedal, but caught the SUV speeding up beyond the limit twice. She laughed each time, forcing herself to back off the speed. This was just another evening with her friend. Nothing special to be worried about. *Yeah, right.*

At the house, she put the beer in the fridge and downed the sample bottle of peppermint schnapps as she headed upstairs with the bag from Stephanie's. The liquid burned all the way down her throat. Throwing the bag of clothes on her bed, she stripped as she ran for a quick shower, needing to rinse off any hair ends before they began to itch.

Shaking her head over the tub, she freed up any loose ends from her curls. Next, she stepped into the tub. Pulling the shower head free, she turned the water on warm and hosed down her body from the neck down, rinsing off any ends that had made it down her shirt, in spite of the hair dresser's cape. Alyssa had assured her the curls would stay since they were natural but Megan didn't want any rude surprises this close to Aaron's arrival so she kept her hair dry.

Wiping the steam from the mirror, she shrieked at her reflection. The coils were there...but so was frizz. Her hair which had lain smoothly, now bounded out from her skull in a wild profusion of curls. She wrapped a towel around her still wet torso and moved out into the bedroom where she grabbed her long-handled round-headed brush. Sitting in front of her mirror, she began brushing her hair, hoping the pull of the brush would settle the frizz as the humidity decreased. Mechanically, she ran the soft brush over her skull, winding it tight where she wanted her hair to curl.

Pouring a drop of styling mousse into her hands, she rubbed them through the curls, and then opened her fingers to pick and fluff the hair next to her skull. The frizz disappeared while she worked, and soon the soft curls of the new style reasserted themselves. Megan reached for her makeup, but heard a truck pulling into her ranch yard. Holding the towel, she ran to her open window and called out from the shadows. "Hey, I'm just out of the shower. Beer is in the fridge; I'll be down in a moment. Help yourself."

"Sure thing, Babe." Aaron's deep voice called back.

Megan heard the door close and his steps within her house, heading for the kitchen. *Damn.* Panicked, she grabbed the first panties she felt in her drawer. She had them on before she realized it was the sexy lacy almost-nothing pair she'd bought because they were so daring. Again letting chance rule, she reached into the drawer and put on the first bra that came to hand. Looking at her image in the mirror, she blushed. OMG, she stood there in the raciest panties and bra she owned. Her ample breasts rested in the push-up cups, giving her more cleavage than she felt decent. Maybe the shirt wouldn't show off the display. She looked longingly at the bag on the bed, making the decision before she lost her nerve.

With slightly shaking hands, she buttoned the shirt and tied the ends into a loose knot. Next, she slipped on the tight jeans. Her damp legs grabbed at the denim, making the chore difficult. The zipper insisted on sticking when she tried to pull it closed until she buttoned the waist first, taking the stress off the mechanism. Looking in the mirror, Megan felt her jaw drop. The long-legged, softly-curved image in the mirror looked like sex on a stick. Shit, she couldn't go down there like this. Her face reddened and she reached to unfasten her jeans.

"Hey, what's keeping you? The pizza is getting cold." His voice coming closer, Aaron sounded a little irritated.

He reached her door before she could close it. He stood there staring. His beer can slid through his fingers. He managed to close his hand and hold it before losing it entirely, but he could hardly tear his attention away from the woman in front of him.

"Hey, I was just trying on this new outfit. What do you think?" Her voice sounded scared and uncertain.

"Uh... *Wow*. Simply wow." Aaron entered her room, took her by the hand and turned her around to get the full view of her outfit and her hair. His voice reverent, his breathing shaky, he asked; "Who are you and what have you done with Megan?"

"Does that mean you like it or not?" Her voice squeaked. Taking a deep breath, she continued. "I felt it was time for a change, so I had Alyssa cut my hair and Stephanie had the clothes. Like the rhinestones on the jeans pockets?" This time her voice sounded more normal.

"Babe, you've always been beautiful to me, but now..." He stepped closer to her, moving his hand to her waist. "Let's get downstairs before I help those clothes fall off you." He pushed her out the bedroom door and guided her to the stairs.

Megan tried to hide her satisfied smile and the heat she felt at his touch. "I guess I can assume the change is acceptable?"

"Yeah, I like the changes. What made you decide you wanted it?"

They walked into the kitchen and Megan grabbed plates while Aaron took another beer from the refrigerator. She kept her back to him as she tried to be honest with herself before she answered him. "I remembered what you said last year and thought maybe a visual change could be the signal you wanted. Like maybe I'm ready to make other changes as well."

"Okay, but I talk a lot. Can you give me a clue exactly what I said or when I said it?" Aaron's voice sounded husky and confused.

Turning, Megan noticed he was laughing through his confusion and she couldn't help but laugh with at him. Oh well, it was worth a try but if he didn't remember asking her to let him know when she had accepted herself and adjusted to her scars, obviously she would need to be more plain spoken. "Well, you said I needed to adjust to my scars and the changes in my life after I was wounded. I was to let you know when I reached that point. Well, I think I have." She felt her face flush and her voice failed, making it impossible to finish what she wanted to say. Taking a deep shaky breath, she continued, "I still have bad dreams on occasion, but I'm stronger and more confident about how I look. I think I'm ready to move forward with my life and possibly our relationship, if you're still interested."

She reached for the beer he had set on the table for her, giving it her full attention. Her face felt like it was on fire and she knew it was beet red. "Pass me a couple of slices, would you? I'm starved." Her voice filled the silence; she refused to look up, uncertain what his face would tell her and unwilling to find out.

"Now, I remember that conversation. It holds true today, the same as it did then. But, I have a question...does this sudden readiness to move forward have anything to do with that cute cook at the R-B inviting me to come by 'anytime'?" Instead of passing her some pizza, he reached over and lifted her chin with his index finger. "Just because I smiled at her, doesn't mean I would take her up on that invitation." He looked deep into her worried eyes. "Back to our conversation of last year. I think what I told you then was that I wouldn't notice your scars because I would be too busy worshipping your luscious body and making love to you to see anything ugly."

Megan looked up at him, unable to keep from it. His face told her everything she needed to know. He *did* remember and he *did* still want her. Her eyes watered. "This outfit and the change to my hair were as much for me as for you. My shoulder is still ugly, no matter what you think, but I'm ready to face it and not be ashamed of the scars. They are now and will forever be a part of me and they'll shape me into the person I'll become in the future. I earned them with honor and anyone who looks away from my shoulder has more serious emotional scars than I have physical ones." She felt her chin raise and her spine straighten with pride, in herself and her military service.

"Well said! Now, let's eat before the pizza is cold. Then you can tell me about the dream that woke you this morning. I'm not going to be distracted from the first reason I'm here this evening. Once we hash out the dream, we can maybe work on a dream or two of mine." His eyes heated and Megan felt the color rising in her cheeks again.

The sound of munching pizza punctuated with occasional moans of gastronomic pleasure filled the kitchen while they enjoyed the meal. After each finished two slices and emptied their beers, Megan sighed. "Thanks, I needed that. Want another beer?"

"Yeah, I could use another. If you're done, why don't we move to the couch where we can discuss your dream?" Aaron stood, smiling at the view of her rhinestone-decorated pockets when she bent over to take two more beers from the fridge. "Babe, those jeans are fine, but your butt makes them amazing." He laughed when she tucked her ass and spun around to face him. "Come on, you wouldn't have them on if you didn't want me to admire them, would you?"

"When I'm walking in front of you, yes...bending over, well...okay yes to that too," she admitted, blushing and passing him his beer. Turning, she led him into her cozy living room and took one end of the couch. "Okay, where do you want me to start?"

"What do you remember, and more importantly describe your emotions as much as you can. Is this a dream of fear, worry, or guilt?" Aaron sat himself down within touching distance, but not close enough to make casual contact.

"It was like the whole episode was happening again. I felt the power of the blast, saw the flames and felt the pain of my injury and then, woke to fear for my friends and the powerful need to warn them. I even faded in and out of awareness as I did during the time I spent under the desk. My fear was all for my fellow soldiers. My pain was so real but I knew I couldn't succumb to it until I had warned the others. Finally, I was fading when I heard sounds of battle overhead. The gunfire, grenades and my scream of pain and fear woke me. It took a minute for me to realize it had been only a nightmare of the initial incident. I'm so tired of this kind of thing. I haven't had a nightmare in months and hoped I was past them—but now I'm worried they'll never go away. When I woke the emotion I felt was fear for myself. Does that make me selfish?" Megan realized she had picked up a couch pillow from next to her and was hugging it for comfort.

"No, that makes you human. You did your duty, got the word out about the coming attack and saved many lives. You weren't selfish then and you're not selfish now. Has anything happened in the last few days to stress you enough to bring the dream back?" Aaron had watched the anguish play across Megan's expressive face while she recounted the dream; now he watched her face clear as she concentrated on finding the possible trigger.

"Mrs. Miller's boy, Raymond, was just wounded over there. I went with Dr. Samuelson when her daughter, Isabel, called because her mom was hysterical. I held Mrs. Miller and told her he'd be home soon. It was difficult because I had no idea how seriously wounded he was and if he'd be home at the hospital or home in a casket. That was two days ago. I learned yesterday he'd lost his leg to an IED and was lucky it didn't kill him. One of his squad wasn't so lucky. His mom's doing better but is scared she won't be able to be strong for him when he gets home." Megan wiped the tears from her cheek brought on by the memory of consoling Mrs. Miller and trying to help her come to terms with her grief and anger about the pain and suffering her son was and would be enduring. Megan's other hand unconsciously massaged her damaged shoulder.

"That could do it. At least you can understand the trigger and maybe that alone will keep the dream from recurring. Facing your own pain and suffering in sympathy for the pain of others is something you need to learn how to handle." Aaron found a tissue to hand her. "You can sympathize with others, but you need to get control over how deeply you empathize with them. Life will always have victims and you can't shut them out—just know it's their pain; not yours, and try to distance yourself from it. That sounds simple, but we both know you're overly compassionate and putting space between yourself and the pain of others will never be easy."

Aaron scooted closer and put his arm around Megan's shoulders, letting her face rest against his shoulder. "The day you stop feeling and caring will never come, but you will learn to either cry out the pain or work through it before you sleep. When you sleep too soon, your mind plays back the time you spent under that desk. You relive your own pain and suffering. That's not a good thing. You've suffered enough." He took the pillow away from her and held her tighter, feeling her shoulders shaking as a storm of tears overtook her.

"That's it, Honey, cry it out. Cry for yourself, Raymond, me and all the other soldiers who have paid for politics with body parts or lives." He tucked his chin down to nuzzle her hair as he comforted her in the only way he could. "Maybe, someday, mankind will be able to live in peace, I doubt it, but I pray for that day. Until then, soldiers will march to the tunes of politics, greed and religious beliefs. If they are lucky, they'll understand what they are fighting and dying for, but most will never understand the why; all they know is the orders of those above them. God help us all."

Time passed and Megan's tears soaked his shirt. Taking another tissue to blow her nose, she rested her head against the drenched fabric. As the storm of emotion passed, Megan felt his body reacting to her nearness. His hands massaged her spine, from shoulders to waist. Turning her face up, her lips grabbed his in desperation, much like a drowning person grabs for floating wood. Her lips opened to the swipe of his tongue. The kiss deepened, her arms encircled his neck, pulling him closer while her tongue danced and warred with his. Aaron pulled her onto his lap and his hands wandered up her chest to palm the fullness of her breast where it strained against her shirt.

Sensations washed through and around Megan at Aaron's touch. His mouth caught her moan when his thumb rubbed against her tight nipple before he lightly pinched it. The kiss broke and she nibbled across his cheek and down his neck, turning just enough to give him better access to her flaming body. While his one hand teased her breast while his other hand wandered down her belly, stopping to unbutton the waist of her jeans and tug at the zipper.

Her free hand fumbled at the buttons of his shirt, aching to feel the power of his chest under her palm. Blindly, she turned her face up to his, again finding his mouth with hers. Under her butt, she felt him growing and pulsing. She ripped at his shirt buttons, finally getting to touch the heat of his lightly-furred skin at the same moment his hand found the moistness of her mound. Her body bucked against his hand when one finger slid around the lace of her panties to enter her hot folds.

His kiss swallowing her gasp, Aaron felt her dampness and his tongue invaded her mouth, mimicking what he wanted to do to the hot, moist folds under his fingers. Megan moved against his hand, pressing and presenting herself for his invasion. "Woman, you're killing me," he moaned against her clinging lips. He pushed her back so he could see her eyes; half closed and dazed gazing back at him. "Are you certain? Babe, we go any further and I won't be able to stop."

"I can't stop now." Her voice shook at the admission and her hand wandered from his chest to the hard bulge in his jeans. She smiled at his groan, quickly followed by a huge exhale when her fingers massaged him. "I need you, Aaron, I want you so much, it hurts."

A pounding at the door brought both back from the rage of passion.

"*What the Hell?*" Megan looked incredulously toward the front door when the pounding sounded again. Sitting up, struggling to zip her jeans closed, she realized her visitor had a perfect view of the couch through the glass panes on her front door. *Damn. Damn. Damn.* She felt her face redden and she glared at the person discreetly looking away from the door. Well, Dewayne definitely got an eyeful. *Shit.* Now the entire town would be talking. Up until now, hers and Aaron's relationship posed many questions—but few answers. Oh well, it could have been worse. Getting caught necking like teenagers on the couch was bad—but five minutes longer, and who knows what he would have seen?

"*Sonofabitch!* Do you often get visitors at this time of night?" Aaron helped Megan to stand with a well-placed hand on her amazing ass, then spent the time it took her to walk to the door trying to arrange his erection within his jeans to ease his discomfort. No way could he stand up. Megan laughed over her shoulder at his condition.

"At least you didn't flash anything. Poor Dewayne will need therapy after getting the view he probably got before knocking. Wonder what the hell brings him out here at this time of night?" She faced the door, trying to appear calm and collected, unashamed of the situation.

"Sheriff, Sheriff, you've got to come. Joe's bad off. I couldn't wake him and his head's bleeding." Deputy Dewayne Jacobson looked away from the unbuttoned condition of his boss's shirt and jeans. The darkness covering the red in his cheeks, he struggled to keep his eyes on her face. Damn, he should have called but once the paramedics had Joe, all he could think of was to get to the sheriff.

"What? Slow down, Dewayne. What happened to Joe? Did you get the paramedics? Start from the beginning and tell me what happened." She didn't pull him into the house, but rather let him stand in the doorway while Aaron was collecting himself behind her. She maintained eye contact with her deputy while her fingers finished buttoning her blouse and checked the button at her waist. When Dewayne's eyes dipped from hers, she scowled. "Well?"

Dewayne's eyes darted back to her face. "Dispatch got a call from an anonymous motorist that there was a body over a guardrail just east of town on Highway 50. Dispatch called Highway Patrol but I was sent too because I was closer. They also dispatched the paramedics. Sheriff, it was Joe. Someone stripped him naked, and handcuffed him to the guardrail with his own handcuffs. I opened them and laid him out. Scared me to death, his face, it was so pale. He was out cold and I couldn't wake him. Sheriff, he had a note in his mouth. It read: 'Mind your own business or next time he won't be naked; he'll be dead'."

Dewayne swallowed hard, his prominent Adam's apple bouncing, his face reflecting his fear for his coworker and friend. "The paramedics managed to rouse him, but he wasn't making much sense. They took him to Montrose and the Highway Patrol took pictures of him and the scene. They also took his handcuffs and the note with them to Gunnison. The last time Joe checked in, he was following one of those cars you told us about on the west side of town. His cruiser wasn't where we found him, the locator put it west, barely inside the town limits. In fact, I passed it on the way here. I thought you would want to check it out with me." He took a deep breath, looked down at the hat he held in both hands and continued; "I'm sorry, Sheriff. I should have called. I didn't know you had company." He intently studied his boots.

Megan felt Aaron at her shoulder. "It's okay, Dewayne," she said. "You couldn't have known, but you're right, you should have called. I could have met you at the car. Let me grab my hat and gun." Turning, she hid a smile at Aaron's frown. "Looks like we're gonna have to take a rain check. I'll call you once I've spoken to Joe and seen his car." She lowered her voice before continuing, "This isn't over, but maybe we'll have better luck another evening. I'm not certain just how much I'll be able to concentrate on work...but I'll try. Good luck getting home without pain, those roads are bumpy." She snickered and managed to accidently rub the bulge in his jeans when she attempted to pass him on the way to collect her gear.

Aaron grabbed her and kissed her, taking his time to enjoy the depth of her mouth. "Yeah, another time. Maybe at my place, less chance of interruption." He noticed her blush, but patted her on the butt and let her go. He turned back to the kitchen, picked up his hat and headed out the back door, never saying good-bye either to Megan or the deputy. Hopping into his truck, he headed home, still uncomfortable where his jeans rubbed painfully against his enlarged and sensitive groin.

Cussing under his breath, Aaron realized he'd missed his turn to the ranch. In his six years of working for Roger, he'd never missed the turn, even in a blizzard. Damn. She really had his head spinning. Too wired to think of sleeping, he took Big Blue Ditch road to the right, following it in the bright moonlight until just before the creek. There he turned left to the dirt track, continuing up to the land he'd purchased several years ago. Parking next to the cleared building site, Aaron got out of his truck and stood admiring the view in the full moonlight. Awkwardly, he walked the floor plan he'd staked out with string on the bare earth. Someday soon, he would bring Megan up here to show her his dream. He hadn't done so, because he'd been waiting for her to be ready to accept him and their relationship. He knew she hadn't been ready to share the dream with him— until now.

He'd almost lost hope, Megan had been very slow to accept herself and know that she was a strong and able woman. However, tonight...ahhh tonight, she shown him that maybe, just maybe she was moving beyond her wounds and seeing a possible future for them. His heart just about burst with the happiness he felt. Megan didn't realize she had been his world for the past year and a half while he waited for her wounds to heal. Her physical wounds had healed long ago, but the damage to her confidence and self-esteem had seemed insurmountable. He laughed aloud and fist pumped the air, wanting to dance with the joy he felt.

Tonight, he'd seen the girl she must have been before the military, before the battles, and death. Before the final ordeal in Afghanistan taught her physical pain and mental anguish. She would never again be the carefree girl she'd been before the Army, but she would be a confident woman who could laugh and enjoy life with him. He'd told her a year ago that when she was able to accept herself, he would be waiting and tonight she'd shown her readiness to accept her wounds and move on with her life. She wanted him as much as he wanted her, and she no longer displayed any fear of his rejection over some ugly scars. Damn, it was about time. His body still hard and throbbing from their interrupted foreplay, he paced again around the string-formatted floor plan. Maybe he should go back to her place and wait. No, with his luck, either she'd be out all night, or so preoccupied when she got back that she wouldn't be able to disconnect from work. *Shit, talk about bad timing...*

Chapter Six

Off balance from Aaron's last kiss, Megan continued up the stairs to collect her gear. As she entered, she caught a glimpse of herself in the mirror and giggled. She didn't look much like the Sheriff of Riverview in this outfit.

"Have a seat, Dewayne; I need to change, it won't take a minute," she called down the stairs. In her closet, she grabbed the closest uniform slacks and shirt, while she tried to wiggle out of the tight jeans. Her shirt came off over her head without unbuttoning once she had the waist untied, and she was buttoning up her uniform shirt when she took the stairs two at a time. "See, all I have to do is pull on my boots and holster."

She slid one foot into a boot and hopped over to the gun safe where she kept her weapons. Keying in the code with one hand, she pulled the boot firmly, skidding the sole on the carpet to push her foot all the way into it. She buckled her holster around her waist and slid her second gun into her boot holster before turning back to the deputy, smiling at his mildly dazed expression. "There, one more boot and we are outta here." Pulling on her second boot, she grabbed her hat from the rack and led him out the door.

"Damn, Sheriff, I never knowed a woman who could change clothes that fast. My sisters take hours, just to change from jeans to shorts." His voice held awe and respect.

"Thanks for the compliment; at least I think it was a compliment. Did you call the car in to the Highway Patrol?"

"No ma'am, I should've, but all I could think was 'there it is' and 'I need to get to the Sheriff'; I don't know where my common sense was. Anyway, it's within the town limits. Do we need to call them?"

"Well, I think we should. The case is pretty much theirs because Joe was found on the highway. I do want to see it before the Highway Patrol gets there so perhaps we can wait until we have the vehicle in sight before we call it in. Were Joe's clothes anywhere around where you found him?" She shook her head at the wonder of a huge Hawaiian, naked on the side of the road—handcuffed to a guardrail. Someone had a very wicked sense of humor or macabre wit to do that to the man.

"Well, let's go. You're driving." Megan jumped into the deputy's cruiser.

On the short drive to where Joe's patrol car sat, Megan spoke with Dewayne, trying to settle him down. His hands shook from the adrenaline rush of finding his coworker along the highway.

"You say Joe was unconscious when you arrived? He didn't wake up until after the paramedics got there?" Megan watched the man relax as he concentrated on the drive and his answer.

"When I got there, he was spread over the guardrail like it was a horse. His hands were cuffed around the damn thing. He was pale in my headlights, and you know how tan he is, against the silver rail and his head was bloody. Scared me shitless. 'Scuse the language, Ma'am. I thought he was dead."

Megan caught sight of the patrol car in Dewayne's headlights. "Hold that thought. I'll call the CHP to tell them where we found the car. They can meet us here." Megan used the patrol car radio to call Colorado Highway Patrol dispatch and give them the location of the wounded officer's cruiser. "Okay, Dewayne, continue. What was the first thing you did?" She prompted him as the deputy rolled up behind the other patrol car, parking a fair distance behind it. "Where's your undercarriage viewing tool?" Megan smiling at his blank look. "The mirror on a stick that should be in your trunk with the shovel and bucket."

"Is that what that thing is for? I haven't touched it because I couldn't figure out why or how it would be used." Dewayne hopped out, ran around to his trunk and returned with a collapsible pole with a lighted mirror on one end.

"Thanks. Now, I can see under the car without getting too close." Megan finished putting on crime-scene gloves before taking the stick from Dewayne. She began at the rear of the car, holding the extended mirror at an angle to see the undercarriage. Normal dirt, dried mud and tar greeted her inspection. She walked to the far side and once again pushed the mirror under the car between the front and rear doors. Megan breathed a sigh of relief...nothing but dirt. She hadn't expected anything else but when a criminal is willing to assault a deputy—they could be dumb enough to booby-trap his car.

Walking around the cruiser, Megan surveyed how it was parked—according to regulations, off the surface of the road, giving the officer room to work with traffic violators without endangering himself on the roadway. Something light almost glowed in the grass and brush along the roadway. "Dewayne, I need you to shine your spotlight over here so I can check out the crime scene." She waited for her deputy to play his light into the brush before she stepped carefully toward it.

Underwear littered the grass and Joe's shirt was caught on a bush. His boots were neatly placed side by side, but the remainder of his clothing seemed to be scattered around haphazardly. Joe must have been terrified. His gun belt, the holster empty, sat next to his boots. Stepping over to the passenger's door, she used her gloved hand to open it. No sign of his pistol, and the rifle normally locked across the back screen was gone. The scattered clothing led her to believe this was the scene of the attack. Joe must have been hauled across town and dumped where he had been found along the highway. The perpetrators must have been strong men or several men. Joe's weight wouldn't be easy to move if he was knocked out here. They must have woken him before moving him. Looking around, she couldn't tell if there was paint overspray due to the darkness. If not, did they paint him at the dump site on the side of Hwy 50? Or, did they haul him somewhere private to paint him and *then* haul him to the final spot to leave him handcuffed to the guardrail?

"Dewayne, get photos of the car, its position in relation to the road, and the interior of the cruiser. I want several shots of the clothing scattered in the grass. Don't move anything."

"Sure thing, Boss."

Megan circled the car, searching for any tracks or signs that it had been moved to this spot by someone other than the driver. They staked Joe out on the other side of town but why go to that bother if the car was going to be left on this side of town? Joe might know the reason. Maybe they ran out of time and didn't get a chance to take the car closer to where they left him. Maybe they felt by having the car in one place and the officer on the other side of town; there would be no way of knowing which direction the criminals actually were going. Standing by the hood, Megan pondered the situation; things just weren't making sense.

Over the buzzing of night insects, she heard the sound of an approaching vehicle. She turned toward the west and watched headlights cutting the darkness before the car rounded the curve. Watching the Colorado Highway Patrol cruiser pull between Dewayne's cruiser and Joe's, she waved.

"Hi. Sheriff Megan Holloway, nice to see you." She extended her hand in greeting to a petite young woman in CHP uniform.

"Officer Cherrie Morgan. I heard Riverview had a new sheriff. Nice to meet you, wish the circumstances were different." The handshake was firm, dry and brief.

"Were you one of the responders when my deputy was found on the east highway this evening?"

"No ma'am. That was the sergeant and his trainee. I only saw the photos and evidence when I came on duty. Sarge is still doing the paperwork and cussing about the trainee getting to go home, as I understand." The woman's smile was genuine, giving Megan the impression there was little love lost between Cherrie and her boss.

"Tell him that's why he gets the big bucks." Megan smiled with the trooper. "Dewayne, I think we're done here. I need you to drive me back to my place. I'm heading into Montrose to see how Joe is doing. If he's awake, I'll find out if he can fill in some of the details about what happened." Waving at the highway patrol vehicle, she ordered, "Stay safe Trooper; remember whoever did this is still out running around." Then she slid into her deputy's cruiser.

The drive back to her ranch was silent and uneventful. Megan hopped out when Dewayne stopped next to her Dodge. Without asking, he waited for her to start her SUV before he led her out the driveway. At the highway, he turned back toward town and Megan went west, heading for Montrose.

At the hospital, Megan made several inquiries before she found Joe. With his concussion, they put him in ICU for the night to monitor his condition. Megan found his bed, listened to the rhythmic humming and beeping of the monitors, found a chair in an out-of-the-way corner and sat down to wait for him to awaken.

Gazing sightlessly at the wall in front of her, her mind wandered over what had almost happened with Aaron. Damn, it didn't seem fair. About the time she felt confident enough to take their relationship to the next level; fate stepped in to block the action. Maybe she was wrong and it wasn't time to get closer with him. She ached with the memory of his kisses and the feel of his calloused hands caressing her sensitive body. No, it was past time to accept herself and have faith he wouldn't reject her because of her physical scars. Knowing only her fears and lack of self-confidence had held back the natural progression of their relationship, she sighed.

Of all the people in the world, Aaron would be the first to accept her in spite of her wounds and the last to mock or object to what she had sacrificed for her country. In her heart, Megan had known this for almost two years, *two years*. She only needed to face the facts and have the faith in herself, which Aaron already had in her. Wondering if the sight of Sheena flirting with Aaron *had* caused the sudden need she felt to move the longstanding friendship into something more, she snorted contemptuously. Of course it did! If there were no Sheena, Megan wouldn't have found the courage to move forward. She probably would continue putting off her decision as she had for the past year. Knowing he was there, waiting patiently, she had felt no need to progress into accepting all the changes her time in the Army had brought to her physically and emotionally. It's easy to stay blind to the changes when you know someone will be there if you need them.

Now, knowing Sheena was interested and worrying that Aaron might decide it was time he found a woman without so many self-doubts, Megan had no choice but to move forward. Aaron deserved a real relationship, not a distant or close friendship with her. As scary as it was, she needed to move ahead with her life. Ashamed that she was so shallow, she admitted to herself a more giving and self-confident woman would have let Aaron into her heart and bed a long time ago. Only the thought of losing him caused her to face reality and change her outlook now. Tears of self-disgust formed behind her eyes, but she refused to let them drop. By acknowledging the problem, she realized she was close to resolving it. She could not change how she had treated Aaron in the past, but she could damn well change how she behaved from here onward. The thought lightened her heart and she vowed to let him know how much she cared and relished the relationship they shared.

A rustling of bedding brought her back to the here and now. "Hey Joe, how are you feeling? Know where you are?" Megan stood and stepped closer to get a better look. His head had been shaved around the lump on his skull. Sutures held the skin together as it stretched across the bump.

"If one more person asks that, I'm going to claim I'm in the White House." Frustration reflected in his eyes and his lips formed a tight, straight line. "I'm in the Montrose

Hospital. I've got the mother of all headaches, my skin still itches from the scrubbing they gave me, and my wrists are swollen from where those jackasses put my own cuffs on too tight. They scrubbed me down because the medics reported some poison oak near the guardrail. Damn stuff grows where nothing else will."

"Well, it appears you're recovering. Your attitude could be better, but I don't blame you for being pissed. However, I'm more pissed that you didn't follow my orders than you should be at having to answer questions." Megan glared at the large lump of deputy hidden under the blanket. "When I tell you not to approach a vehicle, I *mean* for you not to approach it unless absolutely necessary."

"But, Boss, he had a tail light out. I thought that would be sufficient reason to stop him."

"And how did that work out for you? Want to tell me what you remember about the incident?" Megan moderated her voice, knowing the man was feeling rough.

"It was just after dark; I got behind the lime-green truck and followed it west out of town. Well short of the edge of town, I turned on my flashers to signal it over to the side of the road. The fool didn't slow for over a mile, until after I turned on the siren. I called in the stop to Dispatch and approached the pickup on the driver's side. I only saw one occupant; I have no idea where the person who hit me came from. Maybe he was riding in the back of the truck, I honestly don't know. I never got a good look at the driver. I was down before I made it to the driver's door." Joe rubbed his swollen wrists before he continued.

"When I came to, two beefy guys were pulling off my boots. My shirt and tee-shirt were already off and my hands were bound in my cuffs. I tried kicking, but one guy pulled a knife and told me he'd cut my cock off if I tried that again so I figured I might as well hold still. Once my boots were off, they helped me stand and made me shuck my pants and shorts. Right about then, I began to think that making a run for it might be in my best interest, but one guy pushed me from behind. I hit my head as I fell. I came to as they cuffed me to the guard rail. I tried to get my hands loose, and the guy to the left hit me over the head with something. That's all I remember until the paramedics woke me up. I saw them a couple of times, but my eyes were so crossed from being knocked out all I can tell is that there were two of them and both were good-sized, beefy, muscle-bound, morons. Sorry, Sheriff."

"Well, I'd say both you and the assailants were lucky. You, because you lived through the experience and the assailants, because they hurt you but didn't kill you. I thought from the way your clothes were scattered on the side of the road that you might have struggled. I'll put money on us never seeing that truck in Riverview again." Megan patted Joe's leg and walked over to look out the window. "Your car was found on the west side of Riverview, you were found east, on Highway 50. A note was stuck in your mouth, warning us to back off or worse would happen. All in all, these people are going out of their way to draw the attention of the law rather than flying under the radar. I wonder what they're up to and why they would move you to the other side of town. Confusion factor? I wonder where they're hiding out. Any thoughts?"

"I'd check with Zeke at the real estate office. He'd know if he sold one of the ranches to a buyer whose employee has a truck matching the lime-green one I stopped." Joe suggested.

"Good idea. Maybe I'll be able to locate their hideout. I also need to find out who lost the dog I almost hit today. You get better. Do you need me to send Deputy Jacobsen to collect you tomorrow?"

"No Ma'am. Molly will be here early and she'll take me home as soon as the doctors cut me loose. Thanks, anyway."

"Okay, you tell Molly not to do any damage, I expect you to get a thorough tongue lashing from her. I know that little dynamo. I'll see you when the doctor gives you a signed release for duty." Megan waved and left him looking large, uncomfortable and more yellow than tan against the cream-colored blanket...that paint had left some pigment behind. She chuckled, relieved his injuries weren't worse.

Megan enjoyed the twenty-five-mile drive home from Montrose. The beauty of the starry night with the outline of black mesas and mountains against the horizon soothed her nerves, giving her time to think. Traffic was light on the highway at this hour so, while her subconscious focused on driving, her mind wandered over the events of her day off.

Pulling over, she grabbed her cell phone and hit the app to record her thoughts before pulling back out on the road. "Tomorrow, have Shirley look into grants and possible funding for Mounted Search and Rescue group. Check with real estate agents in both Gunnison and Montrose counties for recent sales of larger properties—deputies can handle that. Have Cheryl work on setting up barbecue for this weekend. Oh yeah, work with the Feds to find out who is smuggling and how to catch them without wreaking havoc in town. That should fill the day." She tapped the screen to end the recording.

Absently, she rubbed her shoulder to ease the ache from a long day of use. The reconstructed muscles had adapted well to her trauma but after a fourteen-or-so-hour day of physical usage; they protested. She switched hands on the steering wheel, allowing her left arm to hang free for several miles, grateful when she saw the turn to her ranch. Radar and Sonny would be out in the high pasture, no feed needed there.

Megan knew she was lucky this place had good pasture to support her horses when she wasn't needing to add grain as she conditioned them for competition. Her only wish would be that she could find the time to condition and compete again. Maybe once Bethany had her baby they could team up again and haul to a few rides after spending some time working the horses back into shape. Yeah, right. Bethany would want to ride, but Megan doubted they would be hauling to rides anytime soon.

The house appeared a clean white skeleton in the moonlight, the dark windows upstairs looking down on her as she parked. Even with the porch light on, it was too lonely and quiet. Megan wondered if it was time for a dog or a cat. Something to be happy she returned home each night. A cat would be easier, but a dog would be more company. Remembering the Siamese cat, Sam, she had looked after while watching Phil's ranch, she felt a twinge of remorse. He'd been a hellion, but great company when she was there.

Thinking of the Great Pyrenees at the vet's office, Megan chuckled. She wondered if she could take the dog into protective custody until the case worked out. Yeah, that would work. The animal would be company and Megan could make certain those who mistreated it couldn't take her back. Maybe. Her heart lightened with the thought of having a pet again. Radar and Sonny were great, but you can't really cuddle with a horse and they could destroy a house if you tried to make them house pets.

Megan's hall clock chimed midnight as she climbed the stairs to her bedroom, but she felt relaxed and happy in spite of the events of her day. Maybe tonight she would sleep without dreams. Gazing at her reflection, she thought of Aaron. Okay, all she wanted was only hot dreams of a handsome cowboy tonight; she would have to call him in the morning and tell him about tonight's events. Of course, by morning, he'd know most of it, since nothing stayed secret or quiet in a small town. Slipping out of her uniform, she eased into her short sleep tank before turning off the light and sliding between the cool sheets. Her body tingled as she fell asleep, thinking of Aaron's tender touch.

****

Monday dawned warmer and bright. The azure blue of the Colorado sky stretched between the mountains and the high fluffy white clouds which shadowed them. Early November in the high country could turn fast, but they often enjoyed many days in the sixties and seventies, sometimes even reaching eighty. Praying for the good weather to last through the next weekend, Megan mentally planned her cook-out at the R-B. Driving into work, she swung in at Dr. Rayburn's place.

"Hi, Doc," she waved, exiting her Dodge. "How's the patient?"

"Eating like a horse and wanting more. I want to keep her one more day to make certain there's no infection." Dr. Rayburn warned.

"Fine with me. I decided I need a dog, so I'm keeping her; she is so sweet." Megan assured him. "Until this is settled, can you keep her hidden? I don't want her owner or the Feds knowing she's still alive."

"Sure. She's in the back room with the cats. I thought that would be the least likely place for anyone to search and she seems to love the cats, especially the one brought in on Saturday. He lost his eye and his owners wanted me to destroy him, but I talked them into giving the animal to me to place in a forever home." He led Megan into his clinic as he spoke, leading her down a long hall to a door marked "Cats".

"Hmmm, maybe I should take them both. I was thinking about getting a cat too. You know I spent some time with Phil's cat while housesitting for Roger before I became sheriff. I kind of miss Sam. I heard Phil had him put down last month and it made me want to cry. How strange the dog should bond to a cat also needing a home. What does the cat seem to think about the huge dog?" Megan put her hand out to stop the Great Pyrenees from rushing past and out the door.

"Spider is taking the dog's friendship in stride. He's Siamese crossed with something, neutered, big for the breed, and while he's adjusting to having only one eye, he seems confident in the world. You know Siamese; they think humans are here to serve them." Dr. Rayburn stopped at the open door to a cage at waist level. "There you are, let me look at your eye, Fella" He reached in and pulled out a cat that must have weighed over fifteen pounds.

"Wow, what's he crossed with, Maine Coon? I thought Sam was the biggest cat I've ever seen...this one looks larger than Sam." Megan reached out to stroke the cat. "Last time I saw a cat this large was at a show and the variety was Maine Coon."

"I would guess Maine Coon as part of his breeding, but I think he's at least three fourths Siamese because of the shape of his head, blue eye and the refinement of his coat." The vet turned the cat to inspect the sutures over its eye socket. "Whatever got his eye managed to tear some of the surrounding tissue. I sewed it up and there doesn't seem to be any infection. If you want him, I'll give him to you with the dog. Let me know the when you're set up and ready for them. If I have a house call your direction, I'll even deliver." The vet eyed her, waiting for her reaction to his suggestion.

"I need to buy some things, from a carrier for the cat to a new collar for the dog. Any food suggestions?" Megan softly stroked the cat before dropping her hand to scratch the dog's ears.

"Any higher-quality food will do; neither has diet issues but I suggest not free feeding. If you'd like, we can start them out on the prescription food I have out front. With these two, you might need to take out a loan for that diet!" He laughed at her expression.

"Quality counts but if I'm not eating steaks, neither are my animals. I'll do some research and stock up. I'll call you. So the cat is Spider? Perhaps I should name the dog Sparkle. Sparkle and Spider...hmmm, has a happy ring to it. Don't forget to keep it quiet that you have the dog; I still don't want it to be common knowledge." Megan fondled each of the animals again before turning to leave the room.

"Hey, Sheriff; you didn't ask me what I found out from my friends about that tattoo."

"Oh yeah, you were going to check into it. What news?" Megan turned back to the doctor.

"She's one special dog. It seems a contractor turned her over to the rescue group which has been collecting dogs left behind when residents were forced to flee the war. The man told them he'd already arranged a forever home for this particular dog with a ranch in Colorado because he had it on good authority she'd been trained to guard and herd cattle and goats. He gave the volunteers exact directions on how to get the dog to Colorado and who to call when she was on the final leg of the journey. Guess how long ago all this happened? A full week. The dog skipped quarantine because it was part of a group the volunteers had been holding separate before shipping; a pre-shipping quarantine, if you will. I don't know how much the man paid for the dog to get into that particular group of dogs, but however much it was, he got his money's worth in speedy delivery. A two-day flight, a nine-hour layover at the shelter and back on a flight to Colorado. All prepaid by this contractor who wanted the dog to find a good home with his friends. Hmmm, sounds suspicious to me; but the dog is proof and the diamonds in the dog were likely the reason for the rush."

Out in the parking lot, Megan made notes on the Dr. Rayburn's research and then wrote down a short list of items she'd need to get for the two animals. Good thing payday was last Friday; this could get expensive. Sighing, she started her Durango and headed for town, hoping the case would close quickly so she could bring her new roommates home.

Remembering the message from the day before, she drove directly to the Bailey's boarding house. She knocked on the door as she looked around to see if she could spot the new tenant's vehicle. A small gray-haired woman opened the door to her knock.

"Sherriff, so good of you to drop by. The new boarder is terrified of someone or something. She hides up in her room and doesn't seem to have a car. I don't have a clue how she got to town. She doesn't seem beat up, but acts like a whipped puppy. You have to talk to her. She needs protection from whoever is after her." As Ida Mae spoke, she pulled Megan into the house and pushed her toward the staircase. Behind Ida Mae, Lilabel held the shotgun, ready to protect her sister. Ida Mae continued paying no attention to Lilabel, "She's in the rooms on the top floor. Up the stairs, straight back and the door on the right goes up the last flight to the top."

Megan shook her head and started up the stairs. "I'll see what I can do, but you know she doesn't have to speak with me just because you're worried. Lilabel, I'd feel much better if you weren't pointing that shotgun at the door anytime Ida Mae answers it."

"Sheriff, so long as we don't know who is after that poor thing...the shotgun will be drawn when someone comes to the door. I keep it here in the storage closet under the stairs for easy access." Lilabel huffed, putting the shotgun away.

Following Ida Mae's instructions, Megan climbed the stairs and walked quietly down the hall, turning to face the final door. Surprisingly, that door was locked so she knocked gently on it. "Hello? Miss..." Megan realized Ida Mae had not given her the woman's name. Knocking a harder second time, she continued more loudly, "Hi in there, this is Megan Holloway. Ida Mae called me; she's worried about you. Could you please open the door?"

Megan heard shuffling then a light step on the stairs behind the door.

"What do you want? Go away. I'm fine!" The voice sounded tremulous, weak and teary.

"Well, we can talk through the door if you're more comfortable that way or you can let me in; but I'm not leaving until we talk." Megan worked to seem concerned and determined without sounding aggressive. She heard a deep sigh and then the click of the lock turning. "Okay, I'll let you in, but only because Ida Mae is downstairs. I'm holding my cell phone and 911 is on speed dial." The door opened, the young woman stepped back, her eyes rounded at the sight of Megan's uniform. "Why didn't you tell me you were the cops?"

"Would you open the door if I did? Some people are more worried about law enforcement than they are about other issues in their lives." Megan stepped forward, following the woman up a short flight of stairs. "Ida Mae didn't give me your name and I feel stupid calling you Miss... would you give me your first name?"

Looking wary, the woman pointed toward a couch, "My name is Nadia, Officer. What can I do for you?"

The woman's voice was rounded and deep with a hint of an accent which Megan couldn't place. She was taller in her bare feet than Megan by several inches. Megan's work boots added two-inches to her already impressive five-feet nine-inch height. Quickly doing the math, Megan knew Nadia had to be right at six-feet tall, barefoot. Nadia was willowy looking to the point of painfully thin, possibly due to stress and a lack of food from the hollows under her eyes.

"I'm Sheriff Megan Holloway. Ida Mae and Lilabel are worried about you. They called me because I'm the only one they could think of who could offer assistance. You're not in any trouble here and if you need help, the people of this town are good at helping each other. The real question might be 'how can we help you?'" Megan extended her hand to the woman with a friendly smile. She watched expressions play across Nadia's face as she considered Megan's offer.

A moment of silence passed between the two women before the stranger collapsed on the couch, covering her face with her hands. She began to cry. Her shoulders shook with the force of her raging emotional storm. Megan stepped forward and rubbed the closest shoulder, found a box of tissues on the table, and passed several to her.

"Whatever's wrong, we'll do our best to help. You're not alone any longer." She spoke soothing words and continued to offer the physical comfort of a back rub while Nadia cried. When her weeping slowed, Megan passed Nadia more tissues and sat down beside her.

"Now, can you tell me what's going on? How did you get here? Is someone trying to hurt you?" Gently, Megan asked the questions foremost in her mind.

"You must think me such a drama queen. I never cry like this. It's been so crazy and I've been so worried. Does everyone in town know I'm here? I should keep going and put more miles between me and that ranch. It was so dark and I hadn't eaten since breakfast. I rested in a hole between two boulders and only walked after dark. I think I walked in circles the first night. Then I found the road the second night and followed it, hiding when I heard cars. And then, I simply couldn't walk anymore. There are wild things out there in the dark; I heard them." She hiccupped on a sob as her story wound down. Wiping her eyes and blowing her nose, she continued. "He's bound to be looking for me. I never realized when Jimmy took me to the compound that his boss would object so violently."

"Nadia, who's looking for you? Why is anyone chasing you? Why are you running? Did someone threaten you?"

Megan clasped Nadia's hand, watching the fear come and go in her eyes.

"Jimmy worked for Nico Poggi for the last month he was located in New Mexico. He was Nico's driver. We fell in love when he filled his tank at the truck stop where I cashiered. When his boss moved up here, Jimmy moved with him. We tried to keep up a long-distance romance, but I missed him so much. He must have missed me too because he asked me to join him; he even sent me the plane ticket. I didn't know he hadn't asked his boss; it never occurred to me that my presence would get Jimmy *k'...killed*."

She burst into tears and began to rock back and forth on the couch. "We'd just gotten to the compound and Jimmy went back out for my suitcase after unloading the cage with the big dog into the garage. I heard arguing, first the boss was yelling at this guy with him. He shouted, 'I know why you had to leave Afghanistan; keep your fucking hands off my woman!' Then the voices got closer and I looked out the window. I heard Mr. Poggi yell at Jimmy, then he pointed at him, turned to one of his guards and said, 'Shoot him, then go take care of the woman'. I saw the man turn his gun on Jimmy and shoot. *He killed my Jimmy!*"

Nadia broke down, sobbing again. Megan patted her shoulder, uncertain what to do.

Taking a deep breath, Nadia continued, "I ran out the back of the building, through the garage to avoid the man with the gun. I turned the big, fuzzy, white dog loose as I ran, hoping they would chase it instead of me. Jimmy had been sent to collect her at the airport at the same time I arrived. I ran into the desert in the dark. I heard Mr. Poggi yelling 'Get the bitch! A grand to whoever brings her back! Dead or alive!' All I could think of was poor Jimmy. God kept me safe from falling and wild animals as I ran. During the day I hid out under a big bushy thing one day and between some boulders the second. Finally, when I knew I was going to die of thirst I found the highway and followed it until I saw a light. I realized I had reached a town, I fell in the dirt beside the highway and cried and then knelt and thanked God for bringing me safe through the wilds."

Instinctively, Megan put an arm around the woman, rubbing her back and trying to soothe away the images of the murder. "Who shot Jimmy? Do you know a name, or can you identify the man with the gun?"

"Armando, Nico's bodyguard, did the shooting, but Nico told him to do it. I heard the order, the other man with Nico did nothing to stop Jimmy from being killed. Now they want to kill me. I know they do. I have no family and nowhere to run. What am I going to do?" Nadia straightened her shoulders and sat up, drying her eyes. "I want them to suffer for what they did to poor Jimmy. He never deserved to be murdered. Those *Szemetek,* fatherless dogs..." Her accent thickened as she cursed the killers.

"Nadia, I am so sorry for your loss. I want you to know I'll do everything I can to protect you. I like your accent. Where did your family come from?" Megan asked, hoping she wouldn't learn Nadia was in the country without papers.

"My family emigrated from Hungary when I was five. I grew up speaking both languages but, since I am citizen, I try not to use my mother tongue. When I get angry, I find certain words in Hungarian work more than English," she explained.

"I understand. My cousins in Wales taught me some cool words when I visited them in my teens but, fortunately,

I've forgotten most of them." Megan smiled and stood. "Now, I need to go to work. I'll contact the Marshal Service about the Witness Protection Program. If you're willing to testify, I think they'll help you find a new life. If you don't want to testify, then I'll see what I can do to help you build a new life somewhere Nico won't find you. I don't believe in terrorizing witnesses; you've been through enough. For now, sit tight. I'll get Ida Mae to bring you whatever you need. Things are going to work out. Nothing will replace Jimmy, or wipe out what you saw but decide if you want to put Nicodemo Poggi behind bars for his crimes." She left Nadia sitting on the couch with a tissue in her hands. At the foot of the stairs, she called back. "Lock this door. Ida Mae will knock twice, pause then repeat, pause, and end with a single knock. Don't open the door for anyone else."

Downstairs, she spoke with Ida Mae. "Have you or your sister mentioned your new boarder to anyone? Think. I need to know. Anyone at all?"

"No, Sheriff. When we realized she was scared—and that was the moment we opened the door—we decided to keep her a secret until we found what the problem is. Did she tell you what's wrong?"

"She's witness to the murder of her lover. I'm going to get her into Witness Protection, if I can. Until then, we need to keep her a secret for her sake and for your own protection. The people involved wouldn't hesitate to take out everyone in the house, if needed. So, absolutely no gossip. Not to anyone, no matter how much you trust them. Call your sister and tell her to keep her mouth shut especially to Henry." Megan waited only long enough to see Ida Mae nod, before she headed for to the door. Pausing there, she turned back to Ida Mae. "Nadia will need you to bring her food.

Knock twice, pause and repeat two knocks, pause again, and give one final knock. I told her to only open to that code; got it?" Megan smiled at Ida Mae's conspiring wink and nod. The old lady really loved intrigue.

At her office, she once again had to park down the street. Two black Suburbans with federal government tags had taken over the parking in front of the building. Looked like the Feds had gotten here faster than she expected. Sighing at the expected chaos, she walked into the office. Three men and one woman in suits surrounded the reception desk where Shirley looked to be almost in tears.

"Good morning, Everyone. Would you all please follow me to the conference room?" She never broke stride or looked to determine whether they were following as she walked past them and down the hall. The conference room, aka the courtroom when court was in session, or the city council room on the first Tuesday evening of the month, was deserted and quiet. Megan walked to the table at the head of the room, set down her smartphone and then turned to face the group.

Chapter Seven

Megan surveyed the disgruntled-looking group and shook her head. "Okay, let's get started. To what do I owe the pleasure of your assorted company? Let's start from left to right." Megan pointed to the suited man and woman to her left, across the table.

"We're from Homeland Security. We follow up on smuggling investigations to determine if the border that was crossed needs stronger security. I don't know who the other team is." The woman stated defensively.

The tall black man on the other side of her partner volunteered, "We're from the FBI. You called us. About the smuggling, with a possible organized-crime connection." His voice sounded bored, as though he was trying to get through to a dull child.

"Okay, let's get this party rolling." Megan faced the Homeland Security team and slowly turned to include the FBI as well. "My name is Sheriff Megan Holloway. I think the smuggling is connected to the crime-lord and possibly a murder. Why don't all of you take a seat and we can discuss the situation." She smiled and pointed to the chairs across the table before she sat down.

"Sheriff, I'm Agent Susan Strand, Homeland Security. This is my partner, Agent Arturo Escamilla. How did you discover the smuggled contraband?"

"Agent Strand, I found an injured dog and took it to the vet. Helping him to determine the extent of the animal's injuries; we found an incision into the body cavity of the poor dog. Inside her was a pouch of contraband. I've got photos of the dog, the incision, the pouch in the wound and the contents of the pouch all neatly stored with the contraband itself. Photomicrography has been used to fingerprint the contraband and the disc recording the process stored in a separate and safe location. The dog is still with the vet; I'll be taking her into protective custody." Megan noted both the Homeland Security agents busily taking notes while the FBI's lead agent had a tape recorder sitting in front of his briefcase and a nearly-empty notebook next to it.

"Possibly linked to this crime spree is an incident which occurred last night. My deputy pulled an out-of-town pickup over on the *west* side of town. Before he made it to the driver's door, someone knocked him out. Then they stripped him, and handcuffed him to a guardrail *east* of town. Using the locator in the patrol car, we found it just within town limits on the west side of town. We don't know why they put Deputy Kaleo on the east highway or why they felt it necessary to attack him in the first place, but I suspect they're trying to keep us off balance. Glancing down, she verified the information she'd given them.

"Do you have any suspects or reasons behind this attack?" Agent Arturo queried.

"A note stuck in the mouth of my deputy stated that we should 'Back off, or next time he won't be naked, he'll be dead'. From the note, I gathered the assailants were concerned about my deputy following them. He was following them, against my orders, but he actually had a valid reason for stopping them. The pickup has a broken tail light."

"Sheriff, Agent Jeremy Fowler from the FBI. What connection does this have with the smuggling and organized crime?" The black agent identified himself before asking his question.

"This is a small town in an out-of-the way county in Colorado. What are the chances that an animal from Afghanistan carrying diamonds, several out-of-town vehicles seen slowly cruising the area and a deputy attacked are not related? We don't have the population to draw more than one set of criminals, much less the places to hide them. One of our residents gave me the license plate number from a suspicious—his description—not mine, vehicle. It proved to be owned by Nicodemo Poggi, formerly of New Mexico and Chicago. He is a person of interest in the death of a deputy in New Mexico. Poggi's car was spotted driving unhurriedly around my town." Megan noted a look of boredom on the black agent's face.

"I now have a witness who overheard Poggi commanding an underling to kill one of his drivers. She saw the man follow the orders of his boss. She also heard Poggi yelling at a man, a contractor from Afghanistan to stay away from his woman. The witness is scared senseless and trying to decide if she has the courage to testify but she did see the murder. She also verified the dog carrying the contraband was in Poggi's possession. She was with the now-deceased driver when the dog was picked up at the airport." Agent Fowler suddenly looked very interested in Megan's monolog.

"I understand Poggi is also a person of interest to the Organized Crime Unit of the FBI. I feel the events of yesterday and last night are connected to him and his merry band of criminals. All we have to do is locate his new residence, referred to as a compound and/or a ranch by my witness. If we can come up with some sort of plan that will force his hand regarding his dog and then we could have him on murder and smuggling counts." Megan smiled around at the group who sat there staring with their mouths agape.

"You say you have a witness, a woman, where is she? Can we talk to her?" The second FBI Agent asked. "My name is Agent Ryan Mills. I need to question this witness."

"Agent, I'm sorry, but until I've got the witness's permission...no one is going to question her. She's been through enough and Poggi is too powerful. I swore to this woman I would make certain she's protected. You'll all need to just wait until I have confirmation from the Marshal Service and they move her to a safe house. Until then, know I've got her in a safe location. I'll get a recording of her testimony as soon as I can."

"Sheriff, while we understand your hesitation, I'm afraid we're going to pull rank and take this case away from you. We don't need a small-town sheriff interfering with our investigations." Agent Fowler stood to end the meeting.

"Agent Fowler, I can't say I will be happy to turn the case over to you, but neither will I be unhappy about it. I didn't think you would want to question the locals. They are likely to be *very* resistant. Several will meet you at the door with a shotgun, unless I miss my guess. If you feel that you can get their cooperation, then I'm happy to turn the smuggling case over to you. I'm in charge of the murder case since it happened in my jurisdiction. Now, I'm ready to be of assistance to you and your associate. If it were my case, I'd be interviewing all of the locals to see who has any information about new residents and the possibility of them having a dog." Megan paused to let the information she was providing sink in with the agents.

Megan continued, "I suggest you move very cautiously. Keeping it casual might get you some information, but once they realize you're FBI, they're likely to clam up. Past experience with the federal government has created some extreme emotions with some of the ranchers, and the businesses in town are very loyal to the ranchers," Megan offered, watching the two FBI agents confer in whispers. Smiling sweetly at them, she began again. "Tell you what. How about you and the Homeland team work the county records in Montrose and the Highway Patrol office in Gunnison? I'll question the locals and see what I can find out. Let me take the lead with them and when it's time to arrest anyone, you get the honor of the collar. You can use me as a buffer between you and the less cooperative citizens of Riverview. They never need to know that the FBI is in charge and that Homeland Security is backing up the FBI."

"Sheriff, I did some research on the way here. You've only been sheriff for less than a month by election. What makes you think the locals trust you? You've been holding the job under appointment for the past year. Also, why do you think you can handle a case this complex?" Agent Mills asked, sneering at Megan.

Taking a deep breath to control her own temper over this agent's attitude toward her, Megan responded; "Agent Mills, I appreciate your lack of confidence. However, I *have* been doing this job for well over a year. I've also attended every course in Law Enforcement and Criminal Investigations available during that time. If you want to check my records, you'll find I finished at the head of my class for each course taken. Overall, I think I can handle this investigation well enough. Letting me appear to be in charge might be a good idea if you want the locals to cooperate. I've been coming to Riverview to spend summers with my aunt since I was ten, so I'm considered a local here in Riverview."

Megan returned his look with self-confidence and defiance. "Why don't we work together? Or would you prefer to attempting to find the answers without my assistance? The decision is yours," she finished, knowing she'd made some valid points.

The two FBI agents held a quiet conversation while the pair from Homeland Security turned to Megan.

"Sheriff, how do you expect to find the people who assaulted your deputy? What leads do you have?" Agent Fowler asked, pen and notebook ready. Megan realized he was taking the lead, but not aggressively.

"Over the past week, citizens have been reporting unusual vehicles slowly moving through town. One person felt they were searching or casing the place. All the vehicles had darkened windows, which makes the locals nervous. I've even seen the fluorescent lime, lowered pickup heading west out of town. That's the truck my deputy stopped. I expect it's either a different color or out of the state by now. The people involved in this are too smart to keep something that obvious around after the occupants pulled a stunt like they did last night." Megan pulled her notes from Henry and reread them.

"Someone needs to check on the recent, at least within the past year, sales of properties between Montrose and Riverview for the purchase of a ranch or home on enclosed acreage. Something with at least three buildings, one of which is a large garage or building capable of holding four or five vehicles. Who wants to spend time at the Montrose County Clerk's office?" No one volunteered. Megan sighed.

"I think, Agent Strand, that you and your partner will get the most cooperation from that office. Homeland Security is less intimidating than the FBI and the folks around here are quick to take offense when the Federal government seems to be taking over." Megan assigned the records search. "I'm going to check with our local services and realtors to see if any vacant properties are now being leased. It's always possible they are renting a property rather than buying it." Megan looked over at the two FBI agents who nodded their agreement at Megan's suggestions

"Sheriff, I don't really trust you not to impede our investigation, but it looks like you've got some good ideas on how to handle the citizens of Riverview. Keep Agent Fowler in the loop, don't do anything to set the 'person/s of interest' off and make them run. Are we clear on that?" Agent Mills spoke for the duo.

"Agreed. My goal in this case is to protect my town. I won't stand for any intimidation of my friends, family and other citizens. The collars and the actual take down are yours once we have the necessary proof. Just be careful how you get that proof." Megan gave the men a sweet smile that ended at her mouth. "I'll look forward to hearing what you and Agent Fowler find at the Gunnison Highway Patrol office. Your FBI intimidation there should get copies of all photos and the note from my deputy's mouth. I appreciate your doing this while I speak to the locals to see if I can find out more about those vehicles seen cruising around town."

Standing up, she let Agent Fowler motion to the others to end the meeting. Walking past both teams, out the door to the reception desk, Megan approached Shirley as the teams filed out the door. "Shirley, I want you to find out who I need to speak with the Marshal Service. I want to know how to go about getting a witness into the relocation program and what they will need from said witness. I want to move this person to a safe house. Tell Cheryl when she relieves you that for the duration of this investigation, absolutely no, and I mean *NO,* discussions about it outside of the office. If any of this leaks into the gossip mill, one or all of you will be looking for new jobs. Do I make myself clear?" She stood there waiting for Shirley to nod her understanding before taking her messages and heading for her office. "Oh, I also need to have some data about funding of search-and-rescue groups in rural areas but I don't need it until Saturday afternoon so put a note up and whoever has a moment can do the research." Concluding this last instruction, she walked into her office and closed the door.

Pausing a moment to enjoy the quiet of her office, Megan frowned. She wanted control over the investigation, but the Feds weren't going to let her have it. Crap. Well, if she played her cards right, she would be the lead without them knowing it. A smile and a 'yes, sir' could go a long way in keeping them under the impression that they were leading her, rather than the other way around. The damn jerks were not rural people and because they had only city life experience they were worthless to her. Worse than worthless, they could get her people killed if they bungled any part of the investigation. *Shit.*

Heaving a deep sigh, she walked around her desk and sat. Writing herself a note to remind Shirley about the funding research, she tacked it to her computer screen. If no one gave her any data by Thursday, she would assign the chore to one or other of the girls on Friday. While she hoped one would obtain the data without her having to assign the research, she had her doubts about the self-motivation of her front desk crew. Salt of the earth, willing to do anything she asked but neither woman was a self-starter.

After spending five minutes searching, she located her local telephone directory. The book held five pages of realtors but, while there were six half-page ads for specific people, there were only five companies listed. Two each were from Gunnison and Montrose, leaving one small firm located in Riverview. Megan dialed the number, drumming her fingers on her desk while the phone rang.

"Zeke Taylor, Taylor Realty; how can I help you today?" A deep baritone voice inquired.

"Hi Zeke, Megan Holloway. I was wondering if you could help me find some people who've recently moved into the area. I don't want you to get into trouble about releasing data but I need to know if you've sold or leased any of the larger vacant homes or ranches around here, especially west of town. Within a radius of ten to fifteen miles, on this side of the Gunnison River. I won't mention where I heard of the sale." Megan played the request casually, trying not to sound demanding. "If you haven't handled any sales, do you know of any locals who might have leased their property, maybe for an extended time?"

"You know Sheriff, I missed the commission on the sale of the old man Martin's 080 Ranch at the beginning of summer. I had visited with old man Martin twice, and almost had his signature on the contract when he passed away and those greedy kids of his used an online national company to sell the place to some yahoo from New Mexico. Really pissed me off...I should have had that property in my listings! Other than that ranch, none of my larger properties are moving. Things are getting kind of lean around here. I may have to take up a different career if I want to eat this winter. Wonder if Betty needs a new cook? I'm better than the one she has now." He laughed, but his voice sounded wistful, as though cooking would be his career of choice.

"Thanks Zeke. Speaking of cooking, don't suppose you want to volunteer at the R-B to man the grill for a little event I'm putting on this Sunday, do you?"

"Grillmaster? Now, that's right up my alley. Do I get a free meal out of the job?"

"You bet. I'll even bring you a steak if you would prefer it to burgers and dogs. You'll just have to hide it from the other guests." Megan offered him the special meat she knew he loved to secure his commitment as lead grillmaster for the barbeque.

"One rib eye steak and I'm your man. What time does the party start?"

"I think the food should start about noon or so. It's a thank-you to the volunteers who searched for that boy. It's also an invitation for those who want to become part of a mounted search-and-rescue unit attached to the Riverview Volunteer Fire Department. I plan to organize a group for future emergencies like this one."

"I don't have a horse, but I can work chuck wagon for your group. Ground support is essential to search-and-rescue." Zeke offered.

"We'll put your name at the top of the volunteer list so those thinking about joining us will know the food will be the best. Thanks for the information. See you on Sunday. I'll be there about eleven to set up."

Megan broke the connection and sat staring at the phone. The 080 Ranch was about a mile short of the R-M west of town. Definitely within walking distance to town. Might take a while, especially if the person had to find the highway, but it wasn't beyond the realm of possibility. Megan had noticed a new shack next to the new iron gate since the old man passed. The current owners must have security compared to old man Martin's policy of visiting with anyone who happened to wander down his mile-long driveway.

Sitting at her desk, Megan wondered how she was going to gain entrance without arousing suspicions. An evil smile worked from her lips to her eyes as a plot entered her brain. It would mean postponing the visit to Poggi until Tuesday or even Wednesday; but it should work. City folk had no clue about the wilds of Colorado. All she needed is to scare the crap out of them. She quickly sorted through the more hazardous wildlife of Colorado. What could invade a ranch and be deadly enough to bring the Sheriff out? Bears? No, they are mostly quiet and singular animals. Cougar? No, same thing. Tarantulas...hmmm, no, too quiet. Rattlesnakes—bingo. Night time predators and no one liked them. Even most of the locals were scared of them and knew little of their habits. Nothing like the sound of a snake rattling to raise hackles and put fear into any human. All the more so if the human has never encountered them where they've lived in the past. Yeah, rattlesnakes, real or imaginary—with the help of herself and others—would do the trick.

Standing, she grabbed her hat and headed for the door. As she passed the reception desk she looked over at Shirley.

"Anyone calls for me, I'm out on patrol and out of radio range. I've got my satellite phone, but don't call me unless it's critical. I've a couple of errands to run and I don't need that damn thing going off every ten minutes." Setting her hat on her head, Megan turned back to Shirley. "Oh, get the Marshal Service's number, if they call and get me the name of the person in charge."

Shirley nodded to Megan's retreating back before going back to her crossword puzzle. With all the commotion this morning, she was only half done. Heaving a sigh, she marked her place and closed the book. First the research, then the puzzle, otherwise she would be facing the sheriff's temper. Rumor had it the sheriff could be real snarky when crossed.

Jogging down the steps, Megan pulled out her cell phone. She speed dialed Aaron. "Hi, Aaron. Hey do you still have that portable sound system? It runs on batteries, right? How long does it run before they die?" Megan listened and smiled at his responses. "That long? Great. I need to borrow it. I need your help to set up a sting. Can you think of anyone else who'd be willing to loan me a sound system like yours? I need at least two more." A smile split her face at his answer. "You're far too good to me. I appreciate your help. I'll meet you at the R-M about three-thirty. Does that give you enough time? Great. Tell everyone I said thanks and invite them to the barbeque this Sunday. With any luck, I'll hand them back their units then." Ending the connection, she jumped into her SUV and headed for the school. Between the science lab and the computer science classes, she felt certain she could get three or four cd's of rattle snake sounds and maybe even the sound of snakes slithering over the ground too.

Two hours later, Megan left the high school with four different soundtracks of snakes, more than enough to give even those who knew what was going on the heebee jeebees, much less thugs from the city who had never actually heard snakes rattling before. She chuckled all the way to the drive-in where she bought a double cheeseburger before heading out to the R-M ranch. She put the longest cd into the player in her truck and giggled. The senior computer science student had not only found great rattler noises; he also had put an underlay of slithery sounds. This hour-and-a-half-long cd was the one she planned to put closest to the 080 ranch house and turn up the loudest. The guards would be shooting at shadows by morning. Megan's eyes danced with glee. Feeling almost sorry for Poggi and company, she drove on. Thinking of the poor dog, Poggi's dead driver and the deputy in New Mexico erased any sympathy from her heart.

Waving as she pulled up, Megan watched Aaron climb out of his truck. His jeans accentuated the corded muscles of his thighs and his shirt rode up, exposing his tight abs when he pulled a sound system from his truck. *Damn* he looked sexy. Shaking her head, she tried to dispel the memory of the night before. Maybe, once a relationship shifts, the fire never dims...maybe she didn't really want to cool down. With his hands full, he smiled his welcome and continued walking to the cabin he used as his home. Originally built as a guest cabin, Roger had assigned it to Aaron after he took the foreman position. As close as she was to him, Megan had only seen the interior of the cabin once. Their relationship seemed to demand they meet in town or at her place; the town gossips would have a field day should she be found at his place in the morning. Megan seldom worried about gossips. But, Aaron seemed to be a very private person and his cabin was a stone's throw from his boss's home. Today would be her second excursion into Aaron's domain.

"Hi. Looks like I got here at just the right time. Let me get that." Megan managed to get ahead of him and open the door. "Wow, looks like you had good luck in getting portable sound systems. I managed to make four cd's. How many players do you have?" She began to help him set down his load by taking the topmost system from him.

"Well, there's mine and Jake's from the bunkhouse and I got Henry to give me the two at the library. I had to swear if any damage occurred, we'd buy him new ones. What's your plan?" With his hands empty, he snagged Megan around the waist and kissed her. "I've been wanting to do that all day."

Blushing, Megan eagerly responded his kiss. "Mmmm, I've been missing you too," she said as she broke free from his lips. Running her now-empty hands around his neck, she leaned in for another kiss. Time seemed to slow as they explored each other and desire mounted. Finally, breathing heavily, Megan stepped back. "Wow. Let's put a book mark there; to be continued. We need to get these set up and placed before it gets too dark."

"If you say so, Babe." Kissing her neck, Aaron began setting the systems up, checking batteries and figuring out how to detach the speakers on the two from the library. "I stopped and got some C cell batteries. Mine takes that size, but the ones in it were new last month. I figured the library machines would need new batteries because Henry never changes them until the units are completely dead." He tossed Megan a package of batteries. "Open this, would you?"

"You have a crow bar handy? Or a jack hammer? How about an axe?" Megan fought to open the wrapping on the package of batteries, quickly losing patience.

Laughing, Aaron took the package from her and used his pocket knife to cut around the batteries before prying the plastic open. "Since ninety percent of the retailers put batteries up by the register, you would think the makers could back off the theft-proof wrapping some. I'm surprised they haven't been sued by people who cut themselves while attempting to open the package," Aaron mused before passing the now-freed batteries to Megan.

Opening the first unit from the library, Megan laughed. "You asked my plan. Well, we're going to make those city crooks think that a mass migration of poisonous rattlesnakes is slithering across their ranch toward the house and compound. I working on a plot to draw them out, getting them to expose the fact they want that lost dog." She paused and looked inside the unit she held. "No batteries...guess that's better than old, ruptured batteries. Henry must have used a power cord." Examining the details of + and - shown in the battery compartment, she began to place the C cells to power the player. Glancing up, she smiled at Aaron who was doing the same thing to the second unit from Henry. Once finished, she reached for the player from the bunkhouse, but Aaron snagged it from her.

"Do you have the cd's? I'll finish this one and you load the discs into the players. We need to make certain they'll play continuously without noticeable breaks." Aaron pointed to his unit with his chin.

"Well, each cd is at least an hour long. One is almost two hours...that's the one I want closest to the house. It has an underlay of slithery noises as a background to the rattles. Those house guards are going to be jumping out of their skins by morning," Megan snickered.

"Well, let's hope they don't try shooting randomly at the noises...we might lose one or more of these players if they do." Aaron warned.

"We'll need to plant the players in such a way as to be hidden, but still able to project the noise toward the compound." Megan said. "I think we need to plant these close. We can ride over toward the 080 on the four-wheeler. We'll need to stop about a half-mile short and hike in the rest of the way. Sound like a good idea?"

"This is your plot, Sweetheart. We can plant these wherever you want. I think we need to plant them only one or two directions from the house; if you're planning to call it a fall migration. Snakes heading for a den on the other side of the 080." Aaron began thinking aloud and plotting.

"Yeah. We can say it's happened every year since that house was built, and once or twice, snakes have denned up in the basement. That'll get their blood running. I'll offer to check and show them how to prevent the snakes from taking up residence. You know, the friendly Sheriff just helping the public." Megan gave an evil smirk and Aaron laughed loudly.

"Oh, you're good. Those poor SOB's will be jumping at grasshoppers." Aaron picked up the library's two cd players with the speakers attached and headed for the door. "Open this, will you? I'll secure these two in the four-wheeler and come back for the others."

"No need. I'm right behind you." Megan opened the door for him, then picked up the two smaller boom-box-style cd players. Sticking one under her arm, she followed him out. With her free hand, she closed the door behind them.

Chapter Eight

Within minutes, they had the cd players secured in the back of the side-by-side four-wheeler and where headed out across the R-M to the boundary of the 080. Several times the machine went airborne over hillocks and Megan was glad for her seatbelt. The cd players were secured in carrying tubs strapped into the bed of the machine, but she still worried about the bumpy ride. She turned to Aaron when the machine stopped and he turned off the motor.

"We're still almost two miles from the house but I don't want to use the headlights and it's getting really dark. It's a forty-minute walk, or a ten-minute drive from here. I think we have to chance driving without lights. What do you think?"

"I think walking in the dark would be as hazardous as driving and I'd rather wreck the four wheeler than break my ankle. Let's chance the drive for at least another mile. By then, the moon might be up too and we'll have more light." Megan looked around in the pitch-black pre-moonrise dark. "Can you tell which direction we need to go without lights?" she asked him.

"You can see the shadow of the mountain directly ahead. If we keep it ahead or just a little to the right of center, we'll end up at the 080. There're a few arroyos between here and there and those are what worries me. I don't want to fall down into one without knowing it. I've chased cows out of this country and the first gully is almost a mile directly ahead. There's a cattle track wide enough for this machine, I think." He pointed ahead. At least Megan thought he did. She couldn't see him at all, it was so dark.

"You're the guide. Onward." Megan tried not to let her apprehension show, but driving in the dark scared the crap out of her.

Aaron turned the machine back on and moved forward at about half the speed they'd been traveling at when they had the last of the twilight. To the east, behind them, there was a brightness that could either be the town or the moon on the horizon. Megan prayed it was the moon. Once it rose above the edge of the hills, she would feel a lot better about what they were doing. Thinking about what they were planning, she couldn't help but hope they didn't manage to encounter any snakes once they were hiking instead of driving. That would be too ironic for words. Knowing snakes, they shouldn't have any problems. Most were denning up or had denned up for the winter by the first week of November, even when the weather had been unseasonably warm. Changes in daylight as well as changes in temperature sent them into the deep crevices used by rattlesnakes for winter protection. Hopefully, the criminals weren't aware of that.

While her mind played over the things she would tell Poggi, the moon popped out from behind the hills and its light created shadows behind the vegetation and the huge boulders that dotted the landscape. Aaron pulled the four-wheeler behind one of the outcroppings and turned off the motor.

"I think we'd best walk from here. We don't want to alert the guards. The path down into the arroyo is about ten yards farther and to the right. Watch your step. Once we're on the downhill, we'll be in shadow. Take your time." Hopping out of the machine, he opened the carriers. "You know; it will be easier carrying these tubs than trying to hold on to the players. Let's put them all in one and carry it between us." Putting his suggestion into words, he soon had all four loaded and moved the tub to the edge of the tailgate. "I'll grab this side; you take the other. If you feel yourself start to fall...let go of the tub. We can replace a cd player; I don't want to have to carry you out of here." Stepping to one side, he pulled the tub forward and Megan grabbed the other handle. Together they lifted it out of the four-wheeler.

"This isn't bad but I'm glad I don't have to carry it alone." Megan admitted. "Without your knowledge of this area, I'd be lost. I'd likely end up breaking my neck."

"I would never have let you come out here alone and not just because you might get lost." His expression was lost to the night, but his voice warmed Megan's heart. "Let's keep quiet the rest of the way. Sound carries in the desert. Just follow me and jerk on the tub if you need to stop." Aaron whispered.

Together they cautiously moved down into the arroyo and up the other side. It wasn't much more than thirty feet to climb but the tub and the altitude made it challenging. Hating herself for not being as strong as Aaron, Megan pulled on the tub as they got to the top. They set the tub down and Megan took a drink from the canteen she'd brought along and tapped Aaron with it. She barely saw him shake his head no. Slinging the canteen strap back over her shoulder, she bent to pick up her end of the tub. Once out of the arroyo, they moved behind a cedar and looked ahead. The mountains a blacker outline against the starry sky. A light shone lower than the mountains to the right about ten degrees from the direction they were facing.

"What's that to the right?" Megan whispered.

"The 080 bunkhouse. It's closer to us than the main house. Let's head toward it a little. I want to spook anyone sleeping there." Aaron whispered back before taking a step that direction. Megan followed.

Spending all her time looking at the ground, trying to keep from tripping over rocks and small sagebrush, Megan lost track of time. It couldn't have been more than ten to fifteen minutes later that Aaron stopped them in the shadow of a rock outcrop. "I think we're as close as we want to get. I can see figures moving in the bunk house and I thought I heard men talking. Might be guards outside the house." Aaron leaned close to whisper softly.

"If you can hear conversation, we're close enough. Now, where do we hide the one with the longer set of sound effects? Can we get it closer to the house without it being seen once the sun comes up?" Megan whispered back, breathing in his scent as she leaned into him to speak.

"You stay here. I'll take this one over to the rock ledge and hide it in the brush. Don't move." He whispered, kissing her lightly, and then was gone with the cd player. Megan pulled out another unit and looked over at the bunkhouse window. She'd love to get it right under the damn thing, but if they found it in the morning the whole plot would be exposed. Studying the land between where she sat and the bunkhouse, she spotted what looked to be an old abandoned outhouse just a little beyond the square of light shining out the window. Hmmm, with modern plumbing, no one had likely even opened the door to that thing in years. Great hiding place. Gathering up one of the units, she planned on taking it the twenty yards to the outhouse.

"Just where are you going?" An angry hissed question stopped her before she took more than her first step.

"The outhouse," Megan whispered.

"I wouldn't use it if I were you. Scorpions and real snakes have likely been making it their home for years." Aaron took the boom-box from her and pushed her back down on the boulder she'd been sitting on.

"I wasn't going to use it as a toilet. I just thought it would be a perfect hiding spot." Megan explained.

"Let me." Again a light kiss and he was gone with the boom box. Megan fumed. Damn men anyway. Even knowing she was capable, Aaron wasn't going to let her plant any of the cd players. To her left, the sound of snakes slithering and rattling was building. Megan watched as two men met at the corner of the main house and shone flashlights out toward where Aaron had planted the cd player.

"*What the fuck's that noise?* Sounds like it's coming from over that rise." A man's voice questioned and his flashlight played up the hill behind the house.

"Damned if I know and I'll be Goddamned if I'll walk out there to check. Sounds like snakes to me and I don't do no Goddamned snakes." A second voice replied, sounding both worried and pissed. "I told the boss he didn't need to be this far out in the sticks. *Shit!* Now it's coming from over there, beyond the bunkhouse. I'm going inside. I can keep watch from there." The voice faded as its owner retreated around the building. Megan heard a door slam and chuckled to herself. The remaining guard played his light over the hill then over the landscape up to the old outhouse before turning it off and disappearing around the back side of the house. Megan wanted to clap; she was so happy to hear how well the plot was working so far. A tap on her shoulder almost made her pee her pants.

"*Damn, Aaron!*" she whispered. "You scared the *crap* out of me. I hope you hid those players well. Come morning those cowardly guards will be looking for the snakes with their pistols drawn."

"Well, the batteries should run out before then. The sounds will simply die away." Aaron chuckled. "If those two are any representation of the others, you better get out here early. They might just pack up and move out."

"I don't think so. Remember, they're short a dog carrying diamonds and a witness who can put the boss at the scene of a murder. I don't think they'll be leaving until a few loose-ends are tied up. Now, I think we need to place one beyond the house to the left. In the brush and rocks, maybe?" Megan began moving that direction but Aaron's hand on her arm stopped her.

"Let's move back, away from the house. I think staying this close could get us caught." He turned and led the way until they dropped into a shallow gully. Together they followed the gully about a quarter mile before looking over the lip of it toward the main ranch house. "I'll take a unit and place it and then I think we should be done. I know we brought four, but the sounds from three are getting these guys spooked. We don't want to overplay our hand." Pulling the other library cd player from the tub, he crab walked about fifteen yards closer to the house and set it up behind a boulder and put the speakers in the sagebrush, pointing one toward the house and one to the left of the house. Turning on the unit, he cranked the speaker pointed away from the house up and softened the one pointed toward the house. Keeping down, he crab walked back to the shallow gully where Megan waited.

"This is so unfair. You've had all the fun. I hope you know the way back to the four wheeler." Megan softly whined before picking up her end of the tub to begin the long walk back.

"Yep. Point yourself toward the moon. It rose directly behind us, so it should be directly in front of us to head back. Watch your step and let's get home. You and I have some unfinished business."

Goosebumps ran up Megan's spine. She wasn't cold, Aaron's words had set off butterflies in her stomach and shivers deep into her core. Taking the lead in a low crouch, she hoped her knees wouldn't wobble. Was she really ready for this? Pausing for a second she sucked in a deep breath that had nothing to do with the exertion of carrying the almost empty tub and everything to do with her racing heart as she contemplated the night to come.

"What, is something in the way? Want me to take the lead?" Aaron whispered from behind.

"Yeah, you know the ground better than I do. I think I'd rather follow you." Megan was proud that her voice didn't falter. It would never do to let him know how much her thoughts were wreaking havoc with her emotions. Besides, even in this poor light, she loved watching his tight butt ahead of her. At the edge of the larger gulley she watched him slip over the edge and pause, waiting for her to join him.

"Keep down until you get over the edge, then we should be able to walk upright the rest of the way," Aaron instructed in a low voice, no longer whispering.

Scurrying over the lip of the gulley, Megan slid down part of the way on her seat. She managed to get her feet under her and stand, thankful that she no longer had to crouch down. Brushing off her pants, she picked up her end of the tub.

"I think I can carry this without any help now." Aaron stepped in close to take her side as well as his and Megan's pulse sped up.

Oh, uh, yeah. It's not heavy anymore. The last unit is the one with the alarm clock, isn't it?" She stammered and stepped back.

"Yep, it's a handy little thing. It's been on cattle drives and camping trips to wake us." Aaron answered as he turned to lead the way across the gulley and up the other side.

"Okay, I think we need to set this one up to come on just before sunrise. If we put it in the brush short of the guard house, it will sound like some of the snakes have moved from one side of the property to the other. Might make them buy my 'migration' spiel." Megan smiled at his retreating butt. The man filled out a pair of jeans.

The smile slid from her face as she wondered how he would feel about her body. He'd said her scar wouldn't bother him and told her he had one to match it on his thigh, but Megan couldn't help worrying. What if seeing her naked turned him off? She would die of embarrassment. Following him closely, her mind did donuts trying to find a way to keep her body from repulsing him. She finally thought of a possible way around Aaron seeing her naked. Her bedroom could be inky dark with the lights off. Especially if she turned off the hall night light. With the blinds closed, the bathroom night light off and the hall night light off, no way could he see her scar. At least, not until morning. She could slip out of bed early and put on a shirt; that would work. Breathing easier now that she'd figured a way to keep him from seeing her deformity, her step lightened and her smile returned.

Securing the tub back at the four wheeler, Aaron started and turned it without the headlights. Over the sounds emanating from the planted cd players, they could have used a siren without being heard. Headlights were a different matter. Aaron navigated the track without lights for another mile before turning them on and speeding them back to the R-M.

The closer they got to the R-M, the more Megan's nerves increased. Maybe tonight wasn't a good night to continue what had been interrupted by Dewayne. Maybe she wasn't actually ready for this. Maybe she'd never be ready. Maybe she should tell Aaron to give up on her and take up with Sheena. An almost physical pain cut across her gut with that thought. *Shit.* What was wrong with her? She'd never thought of herself as a coward before. This thing about being scared about Aaron seeing her naked was just that...cowardice. The only way to get through it was to hit him smack in the face with all her imperfections. Either he would stay or he would run, but she would finally know. Self-disgust and anger made her sit straighter as the four wheeler came to a stop by her vehicle.

"Here you are, back where we started." Aaron cut the motor, walked around behind the side by side and removed the tub.

"Can you place that unit, with the alarm set, close enough to the guard shack to make them nervous but not close enough to be found in the daylight?" Megan asked him. She smiled shyly and continued; "Once you get it set, come over to my place and we'll celebrate getting this done."

Aaron's eyes lit up with the inner fire of desire. "Sure thing, Babe. Need me to bring over anything? Beer, wine, dinner, clean clothes and a toothbrush?" He wiggled his eyebrows.

"Condoms would be a good idea." Megan was glad the darkness hid her fire red cheeks. "I'll cook dinner while you're setting the cd player. So long as you have protection, I've got a spare toothbrush. If you want clean clothes in the morning, you should bring them...I think you'd look kind of funky in one of my uniforms." Megan surprised herself by managing to keep her voice light and teasing. "See you in about an hour." She gave him a deep kiss before hopping into her vehicle. He stood there, seemingly speechless, as she started her Dodge and headed for home. Once out on the highway, Megan needed to pull over and catch her breath, her heart was racing so fast. *Holy Crap.* This was it. No more backing down, no more hiding. Aaron could make up his own mind about her scars. Taking three deep breaths, counting to ten and she was back on the highway heading for home; she had dinner to cook.

Chapter Nine

Pulling up in front of her ranch house, Megan jumped out and ran for the porch. In the freezer, she found a frozen lasagna entrée. Perfect. She turned on the oven and threw it in before the pilot kicked on the oven burner. Setting the timer for seventy minutes, she ran upstairs to grab a quick shower to freshen up. Ten minutes later, she put on her sexiest panties and matching bra. In her closet, she fanned through all her clothes, almost in tears. Damn, why didn't she have anything sexy?

Well, she could wear the same jeans as the other night, however she had no other sexy tops. Grabbing the hanger holding her favorite fluorescent blue western shirt, she smiled. Slipping into it, she snapped the second and third snaps, leaving the top one open to create a sexy amount of exposed cleavage. She smirked slyly. Grabbing the shirttails, she scrunched them up and tied them around her ribcage. Slowly she twirled in front of her mirror. Yep. Tight pants and bare midriff; enough to give any woman courage. Running her sweaty fingers through her curly hair, she raked some of the shower frizz out of it. Pulling down a curl or two, she framed her face and spread a light wisp of bangs over her forehead. Shaking her head, she let the remaining curls settle as they would and admired the results. Kind of artless, mussed, and a little like just out of bed. Unable to resist, she practiced a couple of flirtatious smiles and eyebrow wiggles, then broke out laughing at her reflection. Lord, what was she...thirteen? Picking up her favorite perfume, a musky sensual scent, she dabbed a bead on her wrist. She spread it to the other and rubbed her right against her shirt at her cleavage. Soft and sensual, not overbearing.

A knock sounded at her back door. *Damn!* She hadn't heard him arrive. She looked out the window and saw Aaron's truck. Running back into the bathroom, she checked her makeup one more time before she headed downstairs to let him in. Soon, she'd have a dog to let her know when guests arrived.

Wondering if he'd caught Megan in the bathtub, Aaron knocked a second time. He felt his body tighten at the thought of her, naked, surrounded by hot, steamy water. *Damn...*better not go there, not yet. Megan was going to need him to stay in control; she needed finesse and sweet, tender lovemaking; not hot-monkey sex. At least, not the first time. Over the past year, he'd come to know her and appreciate her strength, especially her ability to recover from her life-altering war wounds. Knowing how she still suffered from nightmares and yet was wanting to move forward with her life, he respected her as much as he loved her.

He remembered the first time he'd seen her. Dark circles on hollow cheeks, skinny, pale, hurt-dog look in those beautiful blue eyes had called up every protective instinct he had. He'd thought this was a woman he wanted to have close so he could help her recover from whatever trauma had brought her to this point. Roger had hired her and installed her in his uncle Phil's house to maintain the property while the man in prison. Bethany, Roger's wife, had befriended the wounded woman and together they had marked trails for Bethany's project, the R-B Pack Station and Equestrian Camp.

Megan gained weight, color returned to her face and her eyes lost the wounded-animal quality...until the night of the barn fire. The fire had brought back memories of her ordeal, and she had lost it in his arms. He'd given her his shoulder while she cried out her long-held storm of emotion. When she became embarrassed, he'd explained she was allowed to grieve and cry. She'd lost a part of her life that would never come back. Her plans for her future had been blasted away in that building, her military career shot to Hell by that explosion. Yeah, she had a right to cry. When she pulled back to look into his eyes, he'd lost it himself and kissed her. When she responded, he might have taken it further if Roger hadn't interrupted them. Megan seemed willing, maybe for the wrong reason, but willing.

Aaron was glad Roger had come in looking for the coffee. The timing wasn't right for their romance. They hardly knew each other and Megan was far too vulnerable for him to push the issue. Aaron had told her that night he planned to be around and when the time was right, she had only to give him a sign and he would be there. During the past year they had come to know each other, learning to be friends and enjoying each other's company. They'd shared kisses but Megan had pulled back before things got hot and heavy. Finally, the other night they would have shared her bed if her deputy hadn't shown up. While he wondered about her motivation, he couldn't help but be happy she was ready to take their relationship to the next level. A twinge of guilt fluttered in his gut, he wondered if she might be moving forward now because of his flirting with Sheena. Was it right to take advantage of Megan's jealousy? Maybe not, but he knew he loved Megan. Consequently, perhaps her jealousy wasn't a bad thing. Aaron knew Megan cared, so possibly it was time for them to give in to the passion they shared.

Hearing Megan coming down the stairs, he re-arranged himself in his suddenly too-tight jeans before she opened the door.

"Hi, Aaron. I didn't hear you drive up. I must have been in my closet." Megan looked at the handsome cowboy and felt her skin heat at the look in his eyes.

"Mmmm, something smells sexy, uh, I mean good."

Megan watched his tanned skin turn pink around his curly beard and smiled. "I don't think I've heard of food smelling sexy before, but it's lasagna so it's possible, I guess." She couldn't help but laugh. Suddenly she froze, her heart sinking... *Oh Shit!!! Aunt Marge.* Dinner at six which was several hours ago. Stepping back from Aaron she turned and headed for the phone.

"What's the matter, Babe? You're white as a ghost. Please don't say cold feet." Aaron called after her retreating back.

"I forgot I was supposed to be at Aunt Marge's place for dinner at six this evening. I'm in sooo much trouble. Will you vouch for me...tell her that I was working?" Megan asked as she dialed her aunt. "Marge, I'm sooo sorry. I got involved in this case and completely forgot about dinner. Can you forgive me? Aaron can vouch that we've been busy setting up equipment since just before dark. I'm so embarrassed. I should have and would have called you if I hadn't been so tangled in setting things up." Megan paused, holding the phone away from her ear as her Aunt's voice carried across the room.

"Megan Holloway, don't you dare make that nice cowboy lie for you. If you didn't want to come, you could have just told me. The meatloaf dried up an hour ago. I burnt it trying to keep it warm." Marge's voice cracked and Megan thought she detected sniffling.

"Marge, I owe you so much. Give me until next Monday. This mess should be cleaned up by then and Aaron and I will take you to Gunnison to your favorite restaurant. Please say you'll forgive me." Megan begged, her eyes welling up.

"You're my niece. I have no option but to forgive you. But, you better bring your best credit card because we're going to the steakhouse on Monday." A decisive click ended the call.

Stepping closer to her, Aaron pulled her into his arms. "Okay, that was embarrassing. Nice to know she thinks of me as 'that nice cowboy' but she still wasn't ready to accept my vouching for you. By the way, the food smells good and *you* smell sexy. Your scent distracted me and somehow I said what I thought instead of what I meant to say." His chuckle rumbled as he smiled down at her. Leaning closer yet, he stole a kiss. "You taste as good as you smell, too," he said when he stood back, showed her the bottle of wine in his hands and headed for the kitchen.

"Mmmm, you smell like hay, horses and romance; I like that." She followed him into the kitchen, took the bottle of wine, set it on the counter, turned back to him and ran her hands around his neck, pulling him in for another kiss. He didn't resist. Aaron's hands moved around her body, pulling her closer while his tongue teased her mouth open. Megan's pulse quickened at the feel of his arousal pushing against his jeans. A soft whimper escaped when one of his hands moved around to untie the knot in her shirt tail.

A buzzer sounded, irritatingly refusing to stop.

Breaking away, Megan laughed. "Saved by the 'bell' so to speak."

"Hmmm, that's not what I'm hungry for. Turn the damn thing off; we can eat later."

Not arguing, Megan hit one button, to turn off the buzzer and another to turn off the oven. Aaron nibbled on her neck as she cracked open the oven door before turning back to face him. "Now, where were we?" she mumbled against his beard, nibbling at it before working her way to his mouth again. Her breasts felt heavy with need and heat pooled low and wicked while his mouth devoured hers and his hands untied her top. Her hands worked his shirt loose and ripped the snaps open, exposing his lightly-furred chest. Breaking the kiss, she stood back a step. "I've got a bed upstairs." She flushed at the boldness of her offer and then winked and wiggled her eyebrows at the wicked look he gave her. "Did you bring the condoms?"

"Honey, I've been buying condoms for a year, waiting for this night. The clerk in the drug store in Montrose thinks I'm some kind of sex fiend...a safe one, but a sex fiend, nonetheless." His eyes moved from her face down to her exposed cleavage. "I've got five in my jeans pocket and an extra box in the truck." He patted his front jeans pocket as though making certain the condoms were still there.

"Do you think five is enough?" Megan laughed back at him as they hurried up the stairs to her room.

Aaron kept his hands on her hips, sliding one down to cup her ass as they made their way up the short flight. Megan jumped and squeaked when that hand slid between her legs. She felt her panties dampen and her ears burn. She dropped one hand and snaked it back to rub the front of his jeans.

Two could play this game. Aaron groaned and his lips caressed her neck as she opened the door to her bedroom.

Then clothing began flying. Megan wasn't certain later if she stripped him or herself; all that mattered was for them both to get naked as fast as possible.

Suddenly, Megan froze. She was naked, and so was Aaron. His left leg had a hole and some scar tissue, but it was nothing compared to her shoulder's massive damage. She couldn't look at his face, afraid of what she might see in his eyes.

"What, Baby? What's wrong?" Aaron's voice sounded confused.

"M-my shoulder. I wanted to have all the lights off so you couldn't be repulsed by the scarring." Unable to lift her eyes, she was immediately gratified to notice his erection hadn't changed. If anything, it had increased.

"Honey, come here. Help me find one of those condoms in my jeans, I don't give a shit about your scars. They bother you, not me." He pulled her closer as one hand fumbled in his pocket. "Ah-ha. Here. Can you get it open?" He handed her the foil-wrapped packet.

Lost in passion and the heat of loving each other, neither noticed time passing. Finally sated and snuggling for warmth in the chilling room, they slept. Aaron woke to find Megan spooned, her back to his front, and nothing had ever felt so right. His hands played over her body, again learning every crease, muscle and scar until she began to moan, wriggling her bottom against his growing erection. Nibbling her ear, he moved his lips down to kiss the side of her throat, working his way to her shoulder.

"Your beard tickles…but in an exciting way. I'll give you a week to stop that." Megan purred.

"Only a week? I'm hoping for a much longer contract than that." Aaron whispered against her throat as she rolled over to face him. He felt her tense and knew he'd said the wrong thing. Oops. Quickly he began running his hands over her body to distract her from what he'd said. It worked. Within seconds, neither of them could have made any sense, or wanted to try.

"Oh, wow. Just wow. I never knew it could feel like that." Megan felt tears leaking from the corners of her eyes. Neither of her other two lovers had made her feel like this. Neither had been as tender or as passionate as Aaron. Unconsciously, her arms tightened around him as she nestled her head against his body.

"Honey, I didn't either. I could spend the rest of my life in your arms. I'd like to, but that's not a topic for tonight." He kissed the top of her head and hugged her.

A loud growl emanated from his stomach and was answered by hers which caused both of them to laugh, ending what could have been an awkward moment.

"Guess we better go see if the lasagna is still hot." Megan moved to get up. Standing next to the bed, she looked at Aaron's scarred body and then at her shoulder. "I guess we're both marked for life. Are you certain my shoulder doesn't disgust you? The guy I'd been in a relationship with before Afghanistan couldn't even bear to come see me in the hospital. He sent flowers and a note to end our relationship. It made me feel ugly. I thought that no one would be able to look at my shoulder ever again without gagging."

"*What an asshole.* Give me his name and I'll go teach him how to treat a magnificent woman whom he obviously didn't deserve." Aaron's eyes narrowed and Megan had no doubt he would beat the crap out of William.

"He's not worth a jail sentence. Once I left the hospital, I realized I wasn't heartbroken, just pissed and depressed. Come on, I'll meet you downstairs." She grabbed her robe from its hook in her closet and headed for the kitchen.

Over lasagna and wine, they talked about unimportant things, skirting the heavier conversation they both knew was inevitable. Together, they washed dishes until Aaron began to nibble Megan's neck while running his hands under her robe.

He turned her around, took the plate she was drying from her hands, and pulled her robe off her shoulders. Feeling wanton and decadent, she stood naked before him, her skin warming as a deep rosy blush spread up her body. Watching him unzipping his jeans, she saw that his eyes never left her body. Kicking off his pants and shorts, he stepped closer and swept her up into his arms. Carrying her, he made for the closest soft surface.

"Uh, I hate to say this, but I think we should go upstairs. Remember what happened the last time we were only necking on the couch?" Megan couldn't help but giggle at the memory of Dewayne's face that night.

"Ha! I not only remember…I had to drive home with a horrible case of blue balls." Swinging her around, he headed for the stairs. At the bottom step he stopped. "Honey, I think I need to set you down here. No. You're *not* heavy, but I left the condoms in my jeans and I don't think we can pick them up if I'm carrying you." Aaron quickly explained why he needed to set her down so she wouldn't be upset. "You go on upstairs and I'll grab the condoms. Don't start without me," he teased, wiggling his brows. At her flaming face, he commented "You have an amazing ability to blush the most beautiful shade of red. I'm going to enjoy finding ways to bring out that color." He smacked her bare bottom as he turned toward the kitchen.

In her room, Megan found a candle and lit it, turning off the lights. This time, she wouldn't be worrying about her scars; she simply loved the light from candles. Candles flattered everyone and its flickering light seemed romantic to her.

Seconds later, Aaron was outlined in the door way as he applied one of the condoms from his jeans pocket. Shadows hid his expression but Megan heard him inhale when he saw her on the bed. She watched him toss his jeans on the floor at the head of the bed before he joined her.

Their lovemaking this time was warm and tender, each learning what the other liked without the wild rush of unrelenting lust. Together they kindled the flames and together they found ways to prolong each other's pleasure.

"I could have made it up the stairs. You're a light weight," Aaron valiantly lied as they lay in each other's arms enjoying the afterglow and snuggling.

"You can go to Hell for lying, you know. Let's go to sleep. Maybe later we can wake up and use another of those condoms. There are still two left." Megan couldn't help but tease him even though she felt boneless, sated, and unable to move.

"I'll be right back. I'm going to make certain the place is locked up. With the new residents in the area, locking doors seems a good idea." Aaron covered her with the blanket before going downstairs, turning off the lights and locking the door. He chuckled at her soft snore as he blew out the candle and climbed back into bed, pulling her closer and spooning her body to his. Thinking that he could easily get used to sleeping in this position, he drifted off.

Chapter Ten

Aaron woke to sunlight filtering through the blinds across his face. *Holy Shit!* Roger was going to flip out...he'd never missed their morning coffee and scheduling of the workday before. Crap. Rolling out of bed, he groped for his clothing, finding all but one sock. With everything clutched to his chest, he tiptoed from the room. In the hall, he dropped his shorts and found his missing sock about a foot from where his boxer-briefs landed. Good, he would've hated wearing only one sock back to the R-M. A smile played over his face as he pulled Megan's door closed and walked softly down the stairs to dress. He left a short note before opening the back door. Stepping out to the brightening morning he froze when he felt something poke him in the ribs.

"Who the Hell're you and where's my sister?" The voice was ice personified.

"Shhh, let's get away from the door. No sense waking her. If it's Megan you're looking for." Aaron gently closed the door and tried to walk nonchalantly down the steps away from the porch. The man holding the gun followed, twice more poking his back. "Put that damn thing away before you hurt yourself." Aaron turned to face the gunman.

"Not before you explain exactly what is going on here." Aaron eyed a tall man with sandy hair and Megan's blue eyes holding the gun now pointed at his gut.

"You're awfully brave with that pistol. Put it up and I'll answer your questions." Aaron knew he didn't want this man armed if there was a chance his explanation was going to make him angrier than he currently was. A fistfight he could win, maybe, but with fists against a gun, he'd have no chance at all. He heaved a deep sigh when the man stuck the gun in a shoulder holster.

"Well, answer me. Who are you and why are you leaving Megan's at this time of the morning?

"Your sister, Megan, and I have been seeing each other for over a year. What I'm doing here is between Megan and me... she's over eighteen." Aaron worked hard trying to keep the sneer from his voice; unfortunately, he didn't do it well enough. He watched the man's eyes go from worried to mad as Hell and knew there would be blows exchanged. Bracing his feet, he curled his fists, waiting for Megan's brother to throw the first punch.

Waking to loud voices outside, in her yard, Megan sat up and rubbed her eyes. WTF?? Rolling out of bed, she grabbed her robe, wincing as muscles complained about her swift movements. Looking out the window, her jaw dropped when she recognized who was standing toe to toe with Aaron. Both men had fists clenched and looked about to battle. Spinning, she ran down the stairs and out the back door.

"Jake Holloway! Stand. Down. NOW!" Megan screamed at her brother just as he drew back his fist to hit Aaron.

The scene froze, like a "mannequin-challenge" freeze-frame photo. Neither man looked in her direction, but neither did either move. Shaking her head, Megan walked forward until she stood between her older brother and her lover. She took Jake's fist in one hand and Aaron's in her other and addressed them both.

"Jake, I'd like you to meet Aaron Travers, my boyfriend. Aaron, I'd like you to meet Jake Holloway, my brother. Now, I want each of you to relax and keep a civil tongue in your heads. I care for each of you and I want you to get along. Understood?" She looked from one to the other and watched as fists unclenched. Neither man relaxed, but they no longer looked ready to do battle.

"Mr. Travers, I'm not going to beat the crap out of you now but, so help me God, if you hurt my sister..." Jake snarled at Aaron.

Megan stepped to Aaron's side. "What happens or doesn't between me and Aaron is none of your business. I'm a big girl and I can take care of myself. After all, what man in his right mind would hurt a woman who carries a gun and a badge in a small town? No jury in this county would convict me..." She laughed at the look on both their faces. "Anyone want coffee?" Megan kissed Aaron on the cheek before turning and walking back into her house.

With every step Megan took, her anger increased. *Damn stupid men!* Her brother had no right to question Aaron and Aaron should know better than to be caught leaving her house. No wait, that didn't make sense. Try as she might, Megan couldn't quite figure out why she should be mad at Aaron, other than maybe his gender. Jake on the other hand—this wasn't the first time he'd threatened a male in her life. In school, he'd been two grades ahead and anyone who looked at her was subject to his third degree.

She stomped across her porch, pulled open the door and slammed it behind her. *Shit!* She wasn't a kid any longer. For crying out loud, she was the damn sheriff of Riverview.

When was Jake going to let her live her own life? She'd bet about now he was calling her other brothers, damn him. Well, the others were married and she hoped their wives would be sensible enough to prevent their husbands from rushing up here to save her from someone she cared about. Her hands began spooning coffee grounds into the basket of the coffee-maker before she slammed it into the machine and snared the coffee pot to fill the maker. Not noticing the water which ran over her hands, she barely managed to pour it into the reservoir. Her hands shook badly, but she didn't notice. Water also splashed out of the top of the machine as she hit the start button with enough force to push the machine back three inches. Hearing the back door open, she turned to see which of the two men was brave enough to follow her. It was Jake.

"Aaron told me to tell you he'll call later. He's late for work. Who is he, Sis? What do you know about him? I can run a background check, have it for you in a day." Jake walked into the kitchen, acting as if he didn't see the sparks in Megan's eyes, the agitated energy of her foot tapping, or the obvious signs of anger in her crossed arms and drumming fingers. At the sight of her, his questions died and he waited for her to explode.

"Jake Holloway, I'm twenty-seven, not eighteen. I've known Aaron long enough to know he's a good guy and if you run a check on him, so help me God, I'll flatten you. I swear it. I'm tired of you being my protector and ending any possible relationships I might have before they start. I'm still mad at you because I had to go to the prom with *your* buddy instead of any of the boys in my class. I don't even remember that poor slob's name. He treated me like fragile crystal all night. You know he didn't even kiss me good night? He just thanked me for the date and wanted me to tell you he had behaved. What did you have on him, anyway? Poor guy." Megan couldn't help the smile that memory brought. At the time she'd about died of embarrassment, but now it was kind of funny.

"Mikey. Mikey owed me for getting him out of trouble with his dad. He wasn't a slob, was he?" Jake stepped over to Megan and hugged her still-rigid body to his chest. "Hi, Sis. I've missed you. Everyone says "Hi" and sends their love. Where's that coffee?"

"Sit down over there. I'll get you a mug. Want an apple fritter?" Megan pointed to a spot at the breakfast bar and moved to get him a mug and the box of fritters. She knew Jake never turned down anything sweet. From the way he ate, he should weigh three hundred pounds, but he stayed fit and trim. It made her so jealous; that was another thing about him that angered her.

Jake grinned as Megan passed the box his direction. He hadn't stopped all night and he was hungry. "Thanks. What's this about you having a witness to a murder and needing WITSEC?"

"What's it to you and who told you?" Megan glared at him. He shouldn't be privy to this information; it should be strictly on a need-to-know within the Marshal's Service.

"Oh, I'm with the U.S. Marshal's Service now, have been for about six months. They sent me up from the Texas office since the Denver office is back logged." Jake pulled out his shield and showed it to her.

"When did you switch from the Dallas police force? Mom hasn't said a word to me." Megan inspected the badge. He might be her brother, but she wouldn't just take his word before turning Nadia over to him.

"I haven't quite had the nerve to tell Mom yet. She never calls me at work, so there's been no real need to tell her." Jake had the grace to blush at his admission of lying by omission to their mother.

"Hah...you mean you've been too scared to tell her, don't you?" Megan passed him a mug of black coffee, not even trying to conceal her smirk at his cowardice. "She'd read you the riot act and you know it. But, you know once she got over the thought of you being a Marshal, she'd be proud. Dad loved his job; he'd be happy for you and Mom will be too...after a year or two." Megan chuckled at the worried look on her brother's face.

"Dad told Mom way too many stories about his close calls. The job is actually kind of boring most of the time. Mom still thinks Dad was some kind of cross between 007 and The Lone Ranger. I just don't want her to worry." Jake repeated his reasoning for his sister.

"Just keep telling yourself that. Someday she'll find out and be very hurt that you didn't trust her enough to tell her when you changed jobs. I'm surprised they didn't go to her for a character reference. You better hope she doesn't see anyone the Service did ask. I can hear the conversation in my mind now. If I were you, I'd be calling her today and letting her in on the secret," Megan advised. She knew why Jake was worried. He was the youngest of the boys and the last one not married. Mom constantly tried to find the perfect girl for him. If Mom knew he was a Marshal, she'd be pulling strings with Dad's old friends and partners, looking for a daughter of marriageable age for him. Jake had reasons for not telling her, but none would count worth a damn if he hurt her by not letting her know.

"You know; you could be right. I haven't thought that she would be hurt." Jake took a huge bite of fritter and sighed. "I'll call her tonight. Meanwhile want to tell me what's happening around here that you need WITSEC?"

Megan poured herself a mug of coffee, added sugar and creamer and moved to sit across from her brother. Over the next half hour, she told him about all that had transpired since Sunday. Including all the leads provided by locals against the unsavory new residents of the 080, the dog, the diamonds and she ended with Nadia's story which linked Nicodemo Poggi and a contractor from Afghanistan to a murder and the smuggling. Finishing her fritter and her cooling coffee, she looked at Jake. "I never thought this town could come up with so many serious crimes in two days. I'm really earning this month's salary."

Megan continued. "The Bailey sisters are hiding Nadia; she's terrified. I left her deciding whether she could find the courage to testify against her boyfriend's killer. I warned the sisters not to say a word to anyone under any circumstances. Not even to admit they have a boarder at this point. I told Nadia I would check into WITSEC and see what could be done to protect her. No one knows where she is and what code she will answer, except me. Now, I'm telling you." Megan turned on the water over the sink and the fan over the stove, then walked over and whispered the knocking instructions into her brother's ear. She'd told Jake her tale with a lowered voice and really didn't think anyone was watching or listening to her; but she wanted to make certain the final details would be heard only by Jake.

"Thanks. I'll go talk to her. Where is this place?" Jake kept his voice down.

Megan gave him driving instructions and watched him leave before turning off the water and the fan. Locking her door, she ran upstairs, showered and dressed for the day. Picking up her cell phone, she called her office. "Hi, this is Megan. Hey, are any of the 'suits' from yesterday hanging around yet?"

"Yes, Sheriff. So far, Agents Mills and Strand have shown up. I put them in the conference room," Shirley responded.

"Patch the call back there...tell them I want to be on speaker." Megan waited until she could hear the pair talking, heatedly discussing who would be lead in this conversation.

"I can hear you and honestly, I need to lead this discussion, sorry." She waited for them to quiet. "I'm heading out to the 080 Ranch. We have reason to believe Nico Poggi has bought it and is using it as his new home base. I need two things done ASAP. First, Agent Mills, I want you to meet me in thirty minutes at the diner. Borrow Dewayne's extra uniform from his locker, you can be my deputy when we go to the ranch. Second, Agent Strand, I need you to visit the local butcher at the edge of town. He handles slaughtering and packing for local ranchers and their freezers. We need any calves or goat bones he has available. Anything large, that might burn slowly. Show him your shield; he's one of the few in town who would be impressed and give you better service by seeing it. We need to create a pile of animals to burn at the dump. Once you can create the illusion of several carcasses, I want you to burn them. Use kerosene to start the fire at about nine or so." Megan had to wait a moment, while the agents whispered amongst themselves.

"You'll have to wait until eight to visit the butcher, he opens late. I'll have one of my deputies meet you at the land fill; he'll bring a package to put under some of the bones. How good is your surveillance equipment? Will it record the fire and who visits it, including voices and conversations?" Megan paused, again waiting for the attention of the agents.

"Sheriff, we've got some of the best equipment there is. However, all we brought here was basics. It can get sound and video good enough for court…but not from a huge distance. How close is there cover?" Agent Strand asked.

"The agents with the camera and sound gear will have to hide behind boulders, close enough to watch and photograph the fire. I want anyone approaching it to be photographed and recorded. I'm hoping they'll sift the ashes and pick out the smuggled goods to take back to Poggi. Just keep cameras running from at least two angles. If we're lucky, Nico will go himself, but I doubt he's that stupid or a hands-on kind of boss." Megan paused and listened while the agents spoke quietly but clearly to each other, repeating her instructions before agreeing with each other that the plan could work. "Oh, one other thing. Do not discuss this with anyone, not even my staff. Am I clear? Now, get hopping. I'll see you, Agent Mills, at the diner. Ask Shirley for the uniform." Megan hung up, smiling to herself. Giving orders to Feds was kind of fun. She could get used to it.

Outside, she headed into town. In the station, she opened the safe, took out the container of diamonds as well as the bag from the gut of the dog. Keeping her back to Dewayne, she counted out five of the lager stones and four small ones, she put them into the bag. The remainder of the diamonds she put back into the safe, knowing what she was sending to the dump should be sufficient to convict Poggi on felony smuggling.

Turning to face Dewayne, she gave the bag to him, glaring. "Okay, whatever you do, keep this bag *in your* pocket until you put it under several bones and immediately light the fire. An FBI agent should be waiting for you at the dump where you'll set up and light the fire around nine. Use gas or kerosene to start the fire, I want it to burn hot and fast. Stay with the fire until I call you." Megan waited for his nod of agreement before turning to walk out.

Leaving the station, she hiked over to the diner where she found an uncomfortable-looking Agent Mills seated at a booth while five ranchers eyed him. Walking in, three of them turned to her and voices began in a chorus:

"Sheriff, that man's stole Dewayne's uniform."

"Sheriff, you got a new deputy?"

"Sheriff, why's that dude in Dewayne's uniform? Where's Dewayne?"

She motioned for them all to be quiet and looked around the diner, seeing only residents of Riverview. "Is anyone else around here?" Everyone, including the waitress and cook shook their heads. "Okay, then. This is Agent Mills. He's working with me and I expect every single one of you to keep your mouth shut that he's not Dewayne Jacobson, you hear?" She glared at them one at a time and got a nod from each. "Good. I'll let you all in on this operation once it's complete. Until then, the less you know, the safer you and your loved ones are. I expect you to carry on your normal business and be polite to strangers, the same as you always are. Got that?" Again she watched each person nod. Turning to the booth, she let out a sigh as she slid into it. "We need to be thankful the café wasn't more crowded. I forgot that wearing Dewayne's uniform might cause an issue. This group is pretty tight lipped. Let's take our coffee and doughnuts to go. I'll explain where once we're in the Durango."

Calling the waitress over, she ordered for both of them and in silence they doctored their coffees, lidded them and headed for the door. Stopping to pay the check, Megan glared again at the ranchers and staff. "Not a word, you hear? I swear by tonight; this could be done. If it is, I'll meet ya'll here tomorrow at this time." Waving, she followed Mills out.

"I'm glad you got there. I think the guys seated at the counter were going to lynch me." Agent Mills ran a nervous finger under the too-tight collar of his borrowed uniform.

"Nah, they would have just sat on you and called Dewayne to come arrest you. My platform when I ran for Sheriff was anti-lynching." Megan chuckled as she climbed into the Dodge. "I'm going to drive out to the R-M for a few minutes. I need to speak to the foreman." She explained as they headed west out of town. "I want you to back me up. I'm going to pay an official call on Nicodemo Poggi as Sheriff of Riverview and local gossip queen. We kind of set him up and I need to bait the trap. All you need to do is be my muscle. Look mean, say nothing, and for God's sake don't look surprised at anything I tell these yoyos." Megan glanced over that the FBI agent, noting he was wearing a regulation gun belt, complete with weapon and shells. Good. Silently she prayed the gun wouldn't be necessary.

"What kind of trap? You know entrapment is against the law and can get an arrest thrown out?" Agent Mills eyed the sheriff.

"Not that kind of trap. We're simply giving the man information. What he chooses to do with it is his business.

Trust me." Megan snickered at the last phrase. Pulling up to the barn at the R-M, she got out and went inside, expecting and finding Aaron helping with the morning chores. Sneaking up behind him, she poked him in the ribs with her index fingers and jumped back before he could swat her. "Hi. Thought I'd better come by and make certain Jake gave up on beating you."

"He's a might protective of you. Is he the oldest?" Aaron turned and wrapped his arm around her waist.

"No, but he's the last unmarried brother. The other three have wives to keep them under control. Sorry about his attitude this morning."

"Can't say I blame him. Is that why you dropped by? You could have called." Aaron eyed the man who had followed Megan into the barn.

"No, I'm going to need your help. If you can take a break, I'm trying to catch Poggi's men at the dump where they will expect to find the remains of the smuggling dog. One of my deputies will be manning the bonfire with a federal agent. A couple more Feds will be out of sight, but close to the fire with video equipment. I'd feel better if one or two of the R-M best sharp shooters covered the action. Above the landfill but close enough for back-up. Never hurts to have ex-Army Rangers covering your ass." She noted Aaron's protective look and clucked. "Don't you look at me like that, I can take care of myself and don't you forget it.

"When do you need us there? I expect it will be Roger and me unless you feel an extra man is needed." Aaron eyed her, not looking happy that she might be exposing herself to danger. "Oh; John rode out this morning and collected everything except the boom box by the gate. He says the guards were all holed up by the barn, refusing to walk out away from the building."

"Thanks. I'm happy to hear the sounds had the effect we wanted. Now, I just need to give Poggi a story to go with the noises." Megan smirked, thinking of big strong and armed men hiding out from a few snakes. "I told the agent to light the fire at nine. It's eight now. Guess you should head over that direction and set up. Take something to read, you might have a kind of long wait if they don't approach the fire until it's just ashes. I'm taking a substitute Deputy Dewayne Jacobson with me to visit the 080. I expect it'll take about fifteen to thirty minutes to explain the situation and leave. After that Poggi or some of his crew should be heading to the dump. They might wait a bit longer, expecting to dig around in the ashes. Hold your fire unless you see weapons drawn." Unable to resist the urge, Megan kissed him full on the mouth. Taking note of the surprised looks on the hired hands, Megan assumed Aaron had yet to say where he spent the night. Breaking away, she laughed. "Bye, see you later." Turning, she led Agent Mills back out to the Durango.

"You better contact Strand and let her know reinforcements are heading her way. They'll be out of sight, but close enough to put bullets where needed if things go south. Just tell her if guns are drawn, these guys are good as they come."

"Is there anyone in this area who doesn't know how to handle a rifle?" Mills pulled out his cell phone.

"Nope, this is ranching country. We're weaned on rifles and how to help cows calve. Most of our men spent time in the military, and quite a few of the women too. I might run a small office, but I'm never without ready help from the citizens." Megan drove the Dodge up the highway to the next ranch gate.

This one had a shack and guard at the new metal gate attached to a mean- looking fence. She stopped and waited for the armed guard to walk up to her window. "Hi, I'm Sheriff Megan Holloway of Riverview. I need to speak with the residents about a possibly serious danger." Megan handed her shield over to the guard, watching as he walked back and called his boss. "This is where it could get tricky. Look dangerous but controlled and keep your mouth shut. No heroics."

"Yes, Ma'am." Mills muttered as the guard came back.

Chapter Eleven

"Boss says for you to come up to the house. Follow da' dirt road about a mile. House is on the right; they'll be waiting for ya'." The guard, looking dangerous himself, handed back Megan's shield before stepping away and punching buttons inside the shack to open the gate.

Glad the steering wheel of the Durango hid her trembling hands, Megan drove through the gate and headed up the road. "From here on, we have to assume there are microphones and snipers. I doubt it, but if we act like there are, we may both get back out through that gate without any gunfire." The road rounded a bend, dipped through a wash, and an adobe ranch house appeared. Behind it was an open courtyard and two other large buildings—a barn and what looked to be a metal-sided workshop/garage. The description fit what Nadia had told her. The woman had been here, of that Megan was certain. She stopped the Dodge in front of the house, turning off the engine and looking around. Two men came down the front steps, not waiting for her and the deputy to exit the vehicle. "Smile and be friendly, but also look dangerous." She laughed at the confused look on Mills face. "Just follow my lead."

Keeping her hands in view, Megan opened her door and climbed out of the vehicle. "Good morning. I'm Sheriff Megan Holloway. Which of you is the new owner of the 080?" She looked from one man to the other.

"The boss is inside, Sheriff. We would appreciate it if you would leave your weapon with us." The man closest to her reached toward her gun.

"I'm sorry. I can't do that, it's against regulations. Also, my pistol is my only protection against the snakes." Megan shook her head and stared straight into the man's eyes; daring him to try to take her gun. She heard a door open on the porch.

"It's okay, Max. The good sheriff and her deputy are officers of the law. We can trust her not to be a danger to us." Even his ultra-smooth voice gave Megan the creeps. "I am Nicodemo Poggi, the new owner of this beautiful ranch in this stunning wilderness. Come into my house and have some coffee. How may I help you?" The voice carried a mild accent that Megan couldn't place and its bluff goodwill reminded her of a used car salesman.

Smiling she turned to meet the owner of the voice. Armani suit, expensive Italian calfskin loafers, manicured hands, graying temples and thin moustache; he looked like his mug shot had been to a make-over. His black eyes pierced hers through her sunglasses and forcing a vacant smile, she stepped forward to shake his hand. "Mr. Poggi, how good to meet you. I hope the welcome committee has been out to greet you. I'm here on a more serious issue." Megan shook his soft, manicured hand and followed the slender man up the steps and into his home.

"Rika, Baby. Coffee for our guests. Get Babydoll out of here. How many times have I told you to crate that little grease ball during the day?" He kicked toward a yapping Yorkshire Terrier which had come racing toward him and the new arrivals. The dog easily dodged his foot and managed to snag Megan's pant leg. "Get. Your. Damned.

Dog." Poggi snarled, foregoing all the signs of goodwill he had been exhibiting.

"Babydoll, come here *cara*, my little *bambina*. You know you're supposed to stay in my parlor. I'm sorry, Miss, she has almost no teeth, she can't hurt you." A bombshell of a woman made her way to collect her dog from Megan's leg, keeping out of Poggi's reach. Her dress looked like a red silk body shaper, covering Rika from just above her nipples to just below the top of her thighs.

Megan had never seen anyone exposing so much skin and anatomy still be covered enough to be legal. Behind her, she heard Agent Mills swallow. Yeah, he was likely drooling. "It's okay, the dog is just being a dog." Megan smiled at the voluptuous woman when she stood up with the dog in her arms, obscuring some of her ample cleavage.

"I'll be back with the coffee. In the front parlor, Nico?" She asked.

"How many times must I tell you; I don't like being called Nico? Yes, the front parlor and make it quick, I don't expect our guests will be staying too long." Mr. Poggi turned and led his visitors into a room on the right. "We're using this as a parlor until we get the remodel done. Have a seat, please, be my guests." He pointed to the couch and the chairs. "What is this issue which brings you all the way out to my ranch?" He stepped around a writing desk and seated himself in the plush chair there.

"I'm here to warn you about the rattlesnake migration. Let me tell you a story to help you understand the situation. Legend has it that way back in the nineteenth century when this area was being settled, the spread you own now was built by a couple from New York City. The wife had a horrible fear of rats and mice because they were rampant in the city.

During her early childhood, her favorite baby brother died from an infection brought on by a rat bite. Her phobia, she felt, was justified and she considered any rodent to be suspect." Megan paused for effect before continuing.

"The high desert teems with smaller creatures. Skunks and porcupines are at the larger end of the rodent population but the marmot, the muskrat, the weasel and the beaver can also be found in the different ecosystems. If you include the several varieties of squirrels, mice, voles and rabbits, there's a lot of smaller wildlife around here." Megan had been ticking off the various creatures on her fingers. Looking up, she noticed she had Poggi's narrow-eyed attention.

"Now, this created problems as they settled here. The first time she saw a prairie dog, she was ready to head back to the city—no matter how much they lost. They had used most of their savings to purchase the land. In Nebraska, they bought a herd of prime cattle and enough supplies to last most of the first year with the remainder of the money. Together, they drove the herd out here." Megan scratched her upper thigh, next to her pistol and looked around at the rapt attention Poggi and his goons were giving her.

"Soon, Louisa realized the country was teeming with rodents. She wasn't ready to risk her children's lives by exposing them to vermin. George Olson, her husband, came up with a plan. If there were enough snakes in the area, there'd be no rodents. So, selling off a bull calf, he used the money to hire a man to find a variety of small, venomous snake to import to this area. George wanted about a dozen snakes."

"Since it was fall, all the man had to do was find a den and collect the hibernating snakes to satisfy the contract. After talking to the Native Americans east of Denver, he decided the Massasauga rattlesnakes would be the perfect variety of snake for the contract. He located a den of them well east of the ranch, just beyond Denver. The ranchers in that area told him that these small snakes could be deadly to rodents but, in most cases, humans were seldom bitten because the snakes struck low and seldom hit anything but shoe leather. However, they told him the snakes were very deadly when they manage to strike skin; their venom was potent in spite of their size. Thinking of the bounty promised by the rancher, the man managed to bag enough snakes to satisfy the contract." Megan looked over at Agent Mills who frowned, but nodded affirmation of the story.

"Once George had the snakes, he told his wife about the plan. He would find a few good spots and put the sleeping snakes into snug dens on the grounds around the main house. Not close, but within a quarter mile so the snakes could hunt out all the rodents in the spring. While she shuddered at the idea of snakes, Louisa thanked her husband for his ingenious solution. She had picked up a litter of kittens in Gunderson, and they could patrol the house and barn. Between the two predators, she felt more secure from the ravages of having rodents around her family. George had no problems finding rock outcrops, abandoned prairie dog dens and he even dug the final burrow to house the snakes. He chuckled to himself as he put the snakes into the holes. He hoped he managed to have both genders in each den, but figured the snakes would find each other come spring. So long as the dens surrounded his home, it would keep his wife happy."

Pausing Megan chuckled. "You've got to give the guy credit; it was in ingenious plan. Years went by and, between the cats and the snakes, very few rodents survived around this house and ranch. In fact, the coyotes in the area had to move farther away to find enough food to sustain their packs. Snakes were seen around the ranch, the ranch hands often shot them until trained not to by Louisa. After her passing, George found homes for the thirty-some-odd cats except one tom and told the hands shoot the snakes. However, the balance had been upset and the almost-rare Massasauga rattle snake was common on the 080 ranch by that time. In fact, they became a nuisance. Spring and fall, when they migrated or looked to mate, the snakes would often slither across the driveway or through the barns."

Shaking her head at the imbalance, Megan continued, "Dogs learned to stay clear and cats could jump beyond reach, but horses and cattle occasionally fell victim to the small snakes. Bitten on the legs, the animals would survive with only minor ill effects. However, if bitten on the nose or face while grazing, the animal could suffocate due to the immediate severe swelling. Cowboys kept pieces of hose handy and saved about an animal a season by pushing the hose up the nostrils to keep the airway from closing. Unfortunately, they often lost two or three out in the pastures because no one saw the animal get bitten." Looking around, Megan noticed even the guards were listening raptly to the tale, she coughed to hide her smile.

"It was discovered over time that any animal bitten which died needed to be burned because leaving the carcass out to feed predators only killed the buzzards, hawks, coyotes and such. The venom of the snake passed from the dead animal to the critters eating the carcass. Burning the dead animal also kept down the decaying smell and kept the lady of the house happier. Any time one of the hands found a dead cow, horse, pronghorn or other grazing animal, they automatically burned the carcass and any other carcasses in the vicinity. For some reason, a few years back there was a bumper crop of baby snakes. They were everywhere and, by fall, they were large enough to be looking for new denning spots. After the first snowfall, things quieted and no snakes were seen until spring when all Hell broke loose. Seems a good number of snakes had created a den under the house. Kept warm and cozy by the building above them, they woke hungry, earlier than any other snake den." Megan noticed the guards shifting and looking around, as if they felt the snakes might be in the room or under the house. The story was doing its job.

"The Olson family had long since died out by this time. The current owners of the 080 had heard a little about the Massasauga rattlers in the area, but in the years they'd owned the spread, there had been little sign other than a few dead animals in the spring. *This* spring was different. The teenagers got home from school and the house sounded like there were ghosts rattling chains in the basement. The girls opened the basement door, listened as the sound got louder and slammed it shut. The eldest went to put some clothes in the dryer and had a snake launch itself out, barely missing her hand. Seconds later, both girls were in the car and backing out the driveway at a rapid pace. The sheriff of the day followed them back to the ranch, but the girls refused to leave the car when they saw no fewer than five snakes in the side yard, coming out from around the basement window. Even the sheriff hesitated to leave his vehicle but, guns blazing, he did. Being a good shot, he didn't waste much ammo, but he radioed back to town for dispatch to call the fish and wildlife officers to come take care of the problem."

Poggi looked skeptical. "Fish and Wildlife? Why not an exterminator?"

Megan shook her head. "By this time the Massasauga rattler was protected because they are rare to endangered. The overabundance here is really unusual. Fish and Wildlife should always be called in place of an exterminator." Megan watched him swallow this "fact" before beginning her story again.

"That family never went back into the house. They sold the ranch, lock, stock, and barrel to a cattle company out of Denver. No one lived on the property for about thirty years. Every spring the Fish and Wildlife department would come and clear the house and basement, and every fall, the snakes would return for the winter. Finally, the authorities got smart and took the snakes to various refuges and zoos rather than turn them loose a few miles from the ranch. After five or ten years, this seemed to work and one spring, they couldn't find any snakes in the house or around it. The cattle company which owned the ranch was breaking up, so they sold the ranch 'as is' to the family who ran it until you bought it from the old man's estate. I wanted you to know about this issue, because there's always a chance the snakes will come back some year when there is an overabundance and new denning spots are needed. So, watch out and keep small animals close." Megan paused, regarding the captivated faces of her listeners, including Agent Mills.

"Have you noticed any rattlesnakes lately? We've found some dead livestock and a large dog up behind your land, on the R-M Ranch property. All of them were bitten by the Massasauga rattler. We found several snakes still moving over the ground there. I doubt if you were warned when you bought this place. The species migrates at this time of year.

The former owner had the wildlife department come out and clear his barn twice. Seems they like to nest in the hay for the winter. Have you seen any?" Megan questioned, frowning.

"My men were complaining last night and this morning about the sounds of rattlesnakes, but I thought they were full of crap and just being lazy." Poggi looked beyond Megan and Mills to the guard standing in the doorway. "Benito, tell the men to be careful. Sheriff, how deadly are these snakes?"

"Well, first off, I have to warn you they are on the 'Protected Species' list, so you can't kill one unless it's striking at you. If you spot a nest or signs of the migration, you should contact the Colorado Department of Wildlife to come and set traps to remove them humanely." Megan smiled sweetly at Poggi's scowl.

"You mean my men can't shoot'em? I thought any snake could be killed if it came onto my property." Poggi watched Rika, who had paused in the doorway listening to the story, come in and set a tray on the coffee table and begin pouring out cups of coffee.

"Who wants cream or sugar?" Rika looked up with the question, giving Agent Mills a seductive smile and a clear view down her tight dress.

"No, Sir. I'm sorry, but you can't shoot these snakes. If one should die, burn it down to ashes. The fangs might still have venom in them and be hazardous." Megan continued the story. "Their venom is deadly enough to kill children and animals up to the size of large calves. That dog carcass we found was huge, but it looked like it fell where it was bitten. We still burn the snake-bit carcasses to keep the venom from killing scavengers. All carcasses are handled with gloves to keep us safe. Oh, by the way, have you lost a large dog? Some kind of Great Pyrenees, I think."

"No, the only dog on the property is Babydoll and her meat would poison any snake." Poggi scowled at Rika who was passing out coffee, taking too much time fussing over the male deputy. "Rika, you keep that mongrel of yours in the house and have one of the men escort you when you walk her. I don't need to have to replace the dog or drive your lovely ass to the hospital."

"Well, I just wanted to warn you and your employees." Megan said. "Do you mind if I scout up the hill behind your house? If there are other victims, I need to add them to the bonfire; I don't want hawks or crows poisoned." Megan stood.

"No need to waste your time, Sheriff, I'll have one of my men check our property. Where are you holding this bonfire? I'll have my men bring any carcasses they find to you. I wouldn't want to kill any scavengers." Poggi managed to keep his question casual, as though he really didn't care where the fire would burn.

"The dump just east of town has the best ground for burning things...no vegetation to catch so it's safe to burn there any day. I expect they'll burn what's been collected so far this morning. Drive two miles east of the town limits, on the left side of the highway, turn on the dirt road. Can't miss the sign. The owner of the R-M was rather angry about losing the calves. He knows the damn snakes migrate at this time of year; I don't know why he didn't bring his stock into the barn or closer pastures." Megan snorted, shook her head and shrugged, frowning at the rancher's miscalculation. "Thanks for the coffee, Miss. It was very good. We'd best be going; we have some other ranchers to warn. You have a good day. Oh, welcome to the neighborhood. If you need anything, feel free to call my office. Shirley, on the phones, knows the answers to all sorts of local questions." She smiled at Rika and then at Nicodemo. "Nice meeting you." The hair on the back of Megan's neck stood on end when she turned her back on the couple. Even with Agent Mills following her, she still wasn't comfortable showing the man her unprotected back.

Once in the car, she forced her hands to relax on the steering wheel, smiled at the two guards standing by the sidewalk, waved at Nicodemo and Rika. Proud of herself for controlling her fears, Megan managed to drive away from the house at a controlled speed when all she wanted to do was burn rubber out of there.

"Well, that seemed to go well. Do snakes really migrate?" Mills asked with a smile.

"Not very far, but they do. They den up and hibernate in the winter, so they move between the pit to wherever they spend their summers and then back to the den in the fall. Most of the rest of that tale was pure garbage, but he seemed to buy it. We set up sounds last night after dark...that was the sound his goons complained about. I bet none of them were willing to step off the porch this morning." Megan laughed and waved at the guard on the gate as he let them off the property. "Call your partner and tell him Poggi seems to have taken the bait." Megan suggested. At the highway, she turned west, away from town. She needed to keep up the appearance that she was visiting all the spreads in the path of the snakes, just in case Poggi asked his guard.

"Agent Mills, if you're a religious man, say a prayer that Nicodemo Poggi will want his diamonds back badly enough to send his henchmen out to the dump. If not, we just rubbed elbows with slime for no good reason." Megan looked over at Mills and smiled at his expression. Yeah, Mills wanted to take this dude down. Badly.

"I hope the bastard will send his goons to the dump! I warned our people to wait until the subjects find the stones in the ashes, the cameras have directional microphones to catch conversations at a distance. Get photographs and maybe follow them back to the ranch and catch Poggi with the stones." Mills' voice revealed his concern about catching Poggi.

Megan picked up her radio transmitter to call the station. "Shirley, patch me through to Dewayne." Her Dodge cruised toward the next ranch. "Dewayne? I need you to call the judge and get a warrant to search Poggi's ranch for the smuggled diamonds. He should be agreeable when you explain the situation."

"But, Sheriff. You said we were supposed to stay and man the fire. What if they get the diamonds?" Dewayne's voice sounded confused.

"We need them to get the diamonds. We need photos of them pulling the stones from the fire. We've got the diamonds identified so if they take them to Poggi, we'll have him for smuggling and murder." Megan explained. "With the search warrant in hand, we can follow his goons onto the ranch; he won't have time to hide them. Leave the agent watching the fire and go get that warrant." Megan broke the connection and put her transmitter back on the receiving unit. "What do you think? Would we have enough to make the charges stick if we find the smuggled stones in his possession?"

"I think so. What about the witness who heard him order the killing of his driver? Has that person agreed to testify?" Mills studied Megan, waiting for her reaction to his question.

"I don't know. The marshal was going to speak with her and let me know what the decision was. WITSEC will handle that part, but I think they should inform us if we are going to charge him with accessory to murder." Megan's tone reflected her frustration at Jake's silence. She hoped it meant he was taking Nadia to a safe house.

"The only non-federal crime you can charge Poggi with is the accessory to murder charge. You don't have any jurisdiction to arrest him without that charge." Mills looked smug when Megan glanced his direction.

"I don't give a shit about arresting the man. You Feds can fight it out as to which agency gets the collar. I just want that slime ball out of my town and county." Megan pulled up at the sheriff's office. "Okay, out you go. You need to get out of Dewayne's uniform before the locals call the cops on you. I've got a couple of stops and I'll be back to do some paperwork. Feel free to wait in the conference room or wander down to Betty's Diner if you're hungry." She waved Mills impatiently out of the Durango, hardly waiting for the door to shut before she pulled out and headed for the Bailey's Boarding House.

Chapter Twelve

Driving past the boarding house, Megan waited in the shade for ten minutes before going around the block, and pulling up to the building. Well, at least no one was following her. She walked up to the door and rang the bell. "Hi, Lilabel. Has Jake been here to speak with your boarder?" she greeted the tall gray-haired woman who answered the door.

"Who? Step inside, Sheriff; let me get this door closed. Never know who's watching or listening." A strong gnarled old hand encircled Megan's wrist and pulled her into the house. Lilabel kicked the door closed behind them. "There was a handsome young man stop by earlier. He asked to see our guest and when I told him we had no paying guests at the moment, he smiled and told Ida Mae he was your brother. Then the scamp pulled a badge out and I'll be darned if his name wasn't the same as yours. Why didn't you tell us your brother was coming to town? Even Marge, that gossip, didn't mention she was expecting another relation to be visiting."

Megan followed Lilabel to the stairway and pulled her hand free, bringing the monolog to and end and them to a halt. "Marge didn't know he was coming and neither did I until he was on my doorstep. Did you let him upstairs?"

"Well, it's against our policy but since he had that badge and I knew you were keeping our guest a secret...Ida Mae and I decided to let him go up. I warned him not to close the door, at least not for longer than ten minutes. I can't believe he laughed at me. Told me 'thank-you' for the compliment. I'm not certain what he meant by that, but his eyes had that Holloway devilment in them so I think he was joking. Humph...scamp." Lilabel looked over Megan's shoulder and Megan spun to see Ida Mae Bailey coming in the door.

"Okay, did he behave? More importantly, did he take Nadia with him?" Megan tried to contain her curiosity, but couldn't.

"Do you mean, our non-existent guest? Yes, he paid Ida Mae a hundred dollars and took the poor thing with him. Her eyes were red, so she'd been crying again. I hope that he gets her some food...no woman should be that skinny. Lordy, she's as tall as he is and about half as big around." Lilabel frowned and sighed.

"Okay then, guess you don't need me. I'll call him later and find out what's happening. Thanks ladies, for helping Nadia and keeping quiet about it. I'll let you know when it's safe for her and you can tell everyone her tale. It might be a while, because the bad guys have to be arrested, and she's got to give testimony. Once it's all said and done and she's relocated to a safe area; I'll let you know."

Two hours earlier...

Walking up to the house where his sister had directed him, Jake Holloway looked around to check for anyone watching. Nothing obvious, so he knocked on the door. An elderly woman in Capri pants and a loose fitting short-sleeved shirt soon answered the door.

"Yes, can I help you?" She tilted her head back a little to make eye contact.

"Yes, Ma'am, Sheriff Holloway sent me to talk to your boarder." Jake smiled down at her.

166

"Ida Mae? Who's at the door?" A quavering voice came from further within the house.

"No one special, Sis. Just some yahoo who thinks we have a boarder." Ida Mae called over her shoulder. Turning to face the stranger, she looked more closely, noting the dark blonde hair and the blue eyes. "I don't know what you're talking about. We don't have any boarders at the moment. Sorry." She stepped back and began to close the door.

Realizing the woman didn't understand he was a marshal, Jake stopped the door with his foot and reached for his badge.

"Freeze asshole! My sister has a gun on you; move a hair and she'll blast you through the door." The petite senior citizen did a wonderful impression of Dirty Harry at his most intimidating.

Freezing with his hand half in and half out of his jacket, Jake didn't know if he wanted to laugh or shoot his sister for not warning him about these two. "Easy, Ladies. Don't do anything rash. I'm from the Marshal's Service. Sheriff Holloway is my sister; Marge is my aunt. Can I reach my shield to show you?"

"Open your jacket with your left hand, two fingers. Use two fingers to pull out your badge. Get even close to your weapon and you're dead. Got it?" Ida Mae stepped a single step farther from the man, pushing the door open to reveal her sister holding a shotgun pointed steadily at Jake's gut.

"Yes, Ma'am. Just don't get shaky on me." Jake reached for his badge with two fingers and gently pulled it from the inner pocket. Flipping it open, he turned it toward first the woman with the shotgun and then toward the other. "See? Jake Holloway, that's me. Megan didn't warn me to have my badge out when I knocked. I'm going to give her a ration about that detail. Knowing her, she's chuckling right about now." He gave both women his most charming smile.

Lilabel lowered the shotgun, but kept a good hold on it. "She told us a Marshal would be coming, she didn't tell us it would be her brother."

"Let me see that badge." Ida Mae snatched the flip holder from him and looked it over closely. "Kind of new looking. The photo could have been taken last week and the badge looks brand new too. How do we know this is real?"

"You can call Megan, or you can let me go talk to the witness. Megan told me the knocking sequence. I think that should be proof enough of who I am. No one in town knows I'm here and if you call Marge, she'll tell you I work for the Dallas Police Department. I've only been a Marshal for about six months and haven't broken the news to the family yet." Jake hoped by giving these ladies a rundown of his life and family, they would let him into the house. "Can you at least let me in the door and close it? I doubt the suspects are around, but they've been searching and could be out cruising for Nadia. Standing in an open door and arguing only gives them something to see if they happen to drive by." Jake stepped forward cautiously.

Stepping back, Ida Mae kept over an arm's length between her and the unknown man. "If you haven't told your family, you're gonna' be in so much trouble when you come clean. I think you better call your mom and your aunt Marge today and tell them. Shame on you. I don't know about young people today." Heaving a deep sigh, she nodded for her sister to close the door. The door swung closed behind Jake with a decisive clack as it latched.

"Are we good now? Will you direct me to the door I need to use the code on? Please?" Jake took his badge back from Ida Mae and smiled at both ladies.

"Up the stairs, last door on the right. Knock loudly and wait, she has to come down a short flight to unlock the door." Lilabel directed Jake, using the shotgun as a pointer, which Jake found a little unnerving.

"Thanks." Heading for the stairs, Jake still felt nervous about the senior citizen with the shotgun behind him. He kept his hands in plain sight and hoped neither would get nervous.

"Oh, we want you to leave the door open if she lets you in. If it's closed for more than ten minutes, I'm coming in. We don't normally allow our female guests to entertain gentlemen upstairs. We won't hold with any hanky-panky."

Ida Mae's clear voice followed Jake up the stairs and he found himself nodding and chuckling at her instructions. "Thanks, I think, but *my* hanky-panky takes longer than ten minutes." *Damn,* these women were tough. Remembering his Aunt Marge, he knew he should expect nothing less from the women in the town she loved so dearly. Maybe this is also why Megan felt so at home here. These people stood together and had each other's backs, literally.

At the end of the hall, he turned to the door on his right and knocked the code Megan had explained. He waited. A long minute passed without any sounds on the far side of the door. Raising his hand to repeat the knocking, he paused as he heard footsteps approaching the door.

"Who is there?" A soft, deep, feminine voice filtered through the door.

"U. S. Marshal Jake Holloway, Ma'am. I'm the brother of the sheriff you spoke with yesterday." Jake hoped his connection to Megan might ease some of this woman's fears. He smiled when he heard the key turn in the lock. Good, she might be willing to testify if she trusted him and Megan to keep her safe. The first step was for her to open the door.

It swung inward and he was looking eye to eye with a wraithlike beauty. Given some food and time, this would be one hellacious-looking woman. Huge jade-green eyes set wide on high cheekbones covered with soft-looking smooth almost olive-colored skin. Hair the color of light cherrywood curled around her face and behind her delicately long neck. Jake could look no further than her eyes and face, the misery and fear shown there brought him forward to put a comforting arm around her shoulders. "It's going to be okay. No one will hurt you. You're going to be safe, on my badge, I swear it." Jake hoped he wasn't lying but he knew Megan would keep the woman safe if the Marshal Service refused her protection. "Where can we go to sit and talk? I need to get some information from you to put the process into operation."

Nadia turned and led him up the short flight of stairs where she had a couch, a TV, small dinette set and a kitchenette. Jake followed after making certain the door was still half-open to satisfy Ida Mae.

"Would you like some coffee? Ida Mae is letting me use this coffee pot and I just made some fresh. It's Hungarian strong, so you might want to add some water." Nadia's hand waved toward an electric coffee pot and the clean mug sitting next to it. On the coffee table was a full mug sitting next to a box of tissues.

Waving her to the couch, Jake walked over and poured a cup, tasted it and added some water, cream and sugar. Yep, it was stout to say the least. As much as he wanted to join her on the couch, he wisely sat at the small dinette and pulled out his notebook and his recorder. "Thanks. Now, the first thing I need to know is if you are willing to testify against the man or men you saw commit the crime you witnessed? You need to state your name and answer this question with a simple yes or no."

Her eyes watering, Nadia nodded.

"I'm sorry, but this has to be a verbal answer and you must say your name as it will be in the records." Jake kept his voice soft and encouraging.

"Yes. I am Nadia Venczel and for the sake of the dead, I will testify to the crime I witnessed." Nadia raised her chin and her voice was adamant.

"Thank you, Ms. Venczel. Now, I need you to tell me everything you know about the crime, where it took place, who committed it—including any person who witnessed or ordered the crime to be committed and how you ended up here in Riverview. This will be transcribed and you will be required to sign it under oath. Do you understand?" Keeping eye contact and his voice firm but encouraging, Jake motioned for Nadia to begin her tale. While she spoke, he took notes of important data that might help to get a search warrant or arrest order on those in the Poggi compound. Jake was impressed that once she began speaking, the tears dried and anger seemed to be her dominant emotion. He watched the expressions flit across her mobile face. Fear, terror, revulsion and sadness, followed by anger and a new fear and then finally exhaustion as she told of arriving at the boarding house—the only house with lights still on as she entered the town. Looking down at his notes, he added that he felt she would be a very good witness. Believable, vulnerable and brave. Perfect for a jury trial.

"When I walked toward the lights of the town, I couldn't see any buildings with lights on inside. I thought I would need to sleep in a doorway, like a bum in the city, until I saw a light on the porch and upstairs in this house. Those lights drew me and gave me strength to walk the final block, knowing someone was behind the windows of this house. I felt so alone, I had been walking for hours that night and all of the night before, listening to beasts in the shadows and hiding from cars on the road. When the little old lady, Ida Mae, answered the door, I almost fell to my knees to thank God for his protection and guidance. She kindly let me in and when the door closed, I saw the other old lady, Lilabel, standing there with a shotgun. I wondered if I was going to be any safer here than with the murderer. Lilabel lowered her gun and helped me to the couch while Ida Mae got me a shot of whiskey. They made me drink it and I hate whiskey. But, how could I tell them no? They had a gun and it was their house. My momma, God rest her soul, would roll over in her grave if I was rude to these kind women." Nadia finished and looked over to Jake.

"Very good. Now, let's get you out of here and away from Riverview to the safe house. Denver office has two in this section of the state. I think the one outside of Almont is a better choice because it's further from here. We'll need to make certain we're not followed. Do you have a cell phone?"

"I left it when I ran. I didn't even stop for my purse so they have everything of mine. I haven't dared to close any accounts for fear they would be able to find me if I contact the banks." Nadia shook her head, tears in her eyes again.

"Very smart of you. We will set you up with a new identity, make certain you have a job and a home, but right now we just need to get you away from here. Since they have your license, they know what you look like. I'll run to the store and get you a few things to cover your hair and alter your age. You stay here and do as you have for the past few days. I should be back within an hour. Lock the door behind me." Jake smiled and turned to leave, pausing to wait for Nadia to follow him down to the door. "You're going to be fine. We'll see that you're safe." Jake told her before closing the door behind himself. He waited until he heard the lock slide home and then went downstairs to face the sisters. "I'm going to move her to a safe house. I'll be back in just a while with clothes and things needed for a disguise. See you then." Waving at them, he walked out the door.

An hour later, he was handing clothing, hat and dark glasses over to Nadia. "Let's see how much difference this makes. Stand the collar up on that shirt as much as you can and tuck your hair under that cowboy hat. I want you to be a middle-aged unisex rancher, neither obviously male or female. You'll have to remember to slouch and we'll put that tanning cream over all exposed skin, darken it at least two shades. I'll wait out here while you change." Jake pushed her toward the bedroom. "Once you're disguised, we'll pick up a burger at the drive-thru and get out of town, so hurry up cause I'm getting hungry." Jake walked to the couch and sat down to wait.

Ten minutes later, a long-legged, round-shouldered cowboy shuffled out of the bedroom. Exposed neck and chin looked sun weathered and her hands were darkened as he'd told her. They matched the darkened skin of her face and neck.

"Wow. I doubt if your own mother would know you. Good job. Let's get going. The longer we stay here the more chance of being seen." Jake stood and led the way out of the apartment. At the bottom of the stairs, Ida Mae glared at them.

"I told you we didn't allow gentlemen callers upstairs. When did this yahoo arrive?"

"Ida Mae, it's me, Nadia. Did I really fool you? Thank you so much for all you've done. I'm going to miss you and Lilabel. Maybe someday I'll be able to repay you." Nadia stooped and hugged the amazed old lady, careful not to rub any makeup off.

"Sweetie...you don't owe us for what we did. But, if you ever get a chance to help someone else, do it. That's the only payment we need. Stay safe and do what this marshal tells you to, he's a good man." Ida Mae stepped to the door, looked out, up and down the street, and waved the couple out of the boarding house. "Looks okay, no unknown cars or people. You two scat while you can." Sniffling, she watched the marshal and the cowboy get into his truck and drive off.

Chapter Thirteen

Megan felt a little guilty as she slipped into her office through the door farthest from the conference room. Inside, she didn't even turn on the overhead light. Her staff would know she was here, but those using the conference room wouldn't know unless Shirley told them. Choosing a mocha over a plain coffee, she put the individual serving into its holder and pushed the button for the hot water, inhaling the aroma of coffee and chocolate rising up from the brewer. Taking the cup to her desk, she sat down and contemplated the current situation.

Right about now, her brother had Nadia on the way to a safe house, Dewayne left one Fed to finish watching the bone bonfire until it burned down to ashes. Another Fed was hiding above the fire pit with a camera to record Poggi's men when they arrived to dig the smuggled diamonds out of the ashes. Dewayne was on his way to get the warrants, Poggi was likely ordering his men to the dump and impatiently waiting for them to follow orders and return with the diamonds. Finally, there were two Feds in her conference room waiting for word that the bust would be going down. Whew...all this before her second cup of coffee; no wonder her head was spinning. Looking at her watch, Megan saw it was after noon. She hoped Aaron and Roger were set up in the hills overlooking the action. Since the confrontation would be at the 080, she doubted their skills would be needed, but those criminals meant business and the last thing she wanted was a running gun battle through town.

Sipping her slowly-cooling mocha, her mind went back to last night with Aaron. She tried not to have any doubts, but couldn't keep from wondering if it had meant as much to him as it had to her. Before her injury, her love life hadn't been astronomical, but she'd enjoyed a couple of lovers over the years between graduation and her final deployment. She thought of the fiancée she knew she would love forever—until his betrayal. He couldn't even bring himself to visit her at the hospital, the coward. What would he be like if one of their future children had been severely injured or worse yet; what would he be like as they aged and began to endure the disabilities of old age? Maybe, by that time, he would have matured enough to be able to face those situations...but, she doubted it.

Even knowing she was well rid of him, it still hurt to think he cared so little that he couldn't face her injury. Well, that was his problem, not hers. She wondered if he had yet faced the knowledge that he was a coward. For a moment, she wondered what her life would be like today, if he *had* visited her. Would he have been able to look at her scars? Would they have married? Would she be as strong and confident as she felt today? Nope. If they had married, he would have kept her as his "poor little wounded veteran" to be displayed at social affairs but kept an invalid. He would never have encouraged her to become sheriff or work at any skill because if she had shown the ability to stand on her own, she would cease to be his "poor little wounded veteran" trophy wife and that wouldn't suit his plans. He wanted to go into politics, and she was certain he would be a great politician—always able to tell the public what they wanted to hear.

Chuckling, her eyes brightened as she remembered giving her engagement ring to her brother, Mike, to take back to the asshole. The man, who would forever be nameless in her memories, had told her to keep the ring but she wanted nothing to do with it or him. From the story Mike told her months later, he had confronted the future politician in a public place, giving him a loud and embarrassing dressing down in front of a restaurant full of both horrified and gleeful patrons—he wasn't as well liked as he thought he was in Dallas. Mike had railed about his cowardice and the lack of commitment he had shown Megan, the woman he vowed to marry. She could visualize the entire thing. Before this scene, the restaurant was his favorite in Dallas; now she doubted he would have the guts to face the staff there.

Mike said there were several people blatantly holding up cell phones to video the drama. When he finished, a round of applause followed him out of the establishment. At the time, Megan had been too weak to use her tablet, so she missed the viral video of Mike, in his uniform, dressing down an up-and-coming attorney in a posh Dallas eatery. She heard about it, but never saw it. Megan really didn't mind not seeing it; social media and the opinions of others never had meant much to her. Oh well, life moved on and she'd found Aaron. Strong, sexy, resilient, understanding Aaron. Life was good, but where would it go from here?

Sighing, she finished her mocha and headed out of her office to the conference room. Inside, FBI Agent Mills and Homeland Agent Strand were talking quietly. Conversation ceased when they noticed the door opening. "Good morning, uh...I mean afternoon, Agents." Megan said. "Glad to see you back in a suit, Agent Mills. I haven't heard from the Marshal yet, but I spoke with the people who had been hiding the witness and they told me he left with the witness about an hour ago, taking her to a safe house. To me, that means that WITSEC will be protecting the witness until the trial of Poggi and his cohorts and then finding her a new identity."

"I guess that means the State of Colorado will have both a murder and accessory to murder charges to be filed against Poggi and his crew. Congratulations! When do you think we should make the arrest?" Agent Mills stood, looking resigned that Megan would be able to make a collar that might precede his.

"Actually, I have my deputy getting warrants to search the 080 for contraband and arrest the perpetrators as we speak. When we have the warrants, we'll follow Poggi's men once they have the stones. I think giving them a five-minute lead up to the house will be enough for them to hand over the loot to their boss, but not enough time for Poggi to hide the contraband. What do you think?" Megan studied the agents.

"You plan to storm the compound? You want to have a gunfight?" Agent Strand stood and walked around the desk.

"No storming," Megan contradicted him. "I hope to have the gate guard in custody before he can warn his boss. I think you two agents should keep the gang under surveillance and prevent escape while Agent Fowler, my deputy and I drive up to the ranch house with the warrants. If you two go over to the R-M, I'll call ahead and a couple of the hands will set you up where you can see and cover the front and back of the compound. I think Agent Fowler will want to lead up the long drive. I'll hang back to prevent anyone getting out the gate. Will that work for you two?" Megan softly chuckled as each agent glared but reluctantly nodded acceptance of the plan. "Good. Get going. Agent Mills, the R-M is the place we went earlier, before the 080. Take along something to drink; it could be a bit of a wait out in the brush." This time she couldn't repress a chuckle at the grimace from Strand, the female Homeland agent. City folk had no appreciation of the high desert.

Both agents headed for the door, discussing which government vehicle they should take, arguing who should drive it. Megan sighed. Going back to her office she picked up the phone and called the R-M where the wrangler, John, answered.

"Hi, Sheriff. Aaron and Roger just called and said a van just pulled up to the fire pit. Two men got out and they can see a driver still behind the wheel. Does this mean everything is going as planned?" John's deep voice sounded tense.

"Good, sounds like it. How long ago did the black FBI agent leave the fire?" Keeping her voice calm, Megan worked to reassure him.

"Aaron said the second person manning the fire left about ten minutes before he called me. He should be getting back to your office any time now; if that's where he's headed." John's voice hinted that he wanted Megan to reveal her plans. Megan ignored the hint.

"Good. I've just sent two agents to the R-M. I need you and another hand to take them to good spots to cover any action at the 080. One for the front and one for the back. Take your rifles too, just in case. Stay with them until the bust goes down. It could be an hour or more since the guys at the fire will need to let it burn down enough to sift for the contraband. Thanks, and don't forget you're still deputized from the last time I needed your help." Megan laughed, she hadn't yet actually deputized any of the R-M crew, but it was a running joke that they were her deputies.

"Got it, Sheriff. I'll have the four-wheelers loaded and ready to roll when the people you sent arrive."

"Thanks again. Stay safe and keep your head down and your butt covered." Megan hung up just as the door to her office opened to reveal FBI Agent Jeremy Fowler.

"I just heard the suspects have rolled up to the fire pit. When do we arrest them?" he demanded, towering over her desk. Forcing herself to sit back and look up at him, Megan refused to cower.

"Good afternoon to you too. I thought you set it up so we'll photograph them pulling stones from the fire, and then track them to the 080. Once their van pulls through the gate and out of sight, I thought you wanted to take out the guard before he can trip any emergency button. That's what Mills told me." Megan lied with a perfectly straight face. "You'll need to be hiding out behind the gate house, waiting for your chance. I'm certain you can lure the guard out without him drawing down on you." Megan stood and walked over to her coffee maker. "Want a cup?"

"Hell no, I don't want a cup of coffee. What are *you* going to be doing while I'm busy taking out the guard?" Fowler snarled, showing his temper over 'forgetting' what he had already set up...or at least what Megan told him he had set up.

"As soon as the van enters the 080, the action is all up to you and your crew. My deputy and I will follow your instructions. Mills seemed to think you would want me to stay back, guarding the only escape route in case someone manages to get past you. Strand and Mills have gone to take up positions to cover the action at the compound. They'll provide cover and let you know if anyone tries to run. You're making the collar. My deputies and I will be there only as support for the action. I think it should work. You've got a good head for strategy." Megan stirred her coffee and smiled at the slightly confused man.

"I'm still putting your disregard of the FBI into my reports. If *any* of this fails to hold up in court, I want it obvious who's to blame. Now, when can we get out of here?" Fowler turned, grabbing Megan's office door knob.

"Soon. I'm glad I get to wait in a nice comfortable Durango while you crouch in the sagebrush. Getting there early doesn't bother me." Megan set her coffee cup down and strolled through the door Agent Fowler opened for her, almost running into Deputy Dewayne Jacobson who was just raising his hand to knock.

"Sheriff, I got the search warrants for the ranch house and outbuildings and one for Nicodemo Poggi and any other persons of interest on his property. Is that good? Judge said if you need anything else, just call and he'll have his kid run the warrant out to us." Dewayne beamed as he waved the papers at Megan.

"Thank you, Dewayne; that's perfect. I want you to go up to Highway 50, just at the edge of town, where you normally sit waiting for speeders. Face town and let me know when you see a van with blacked-out windows. Don't do anything but sit there. I do *not* want you to intercept this vehicle, even if they *are* speeding. Do you understand me? When you see them, call me on the radio and ask 'Do you want me to close the speed-trap, Boss'?" Megan waited while Dewayne wrote down what he was supposed to say. "Good.

No calling anyone on the radio until you see that van and send me that message. You can reach me on the satellite phone if you have any questions. Now go. I need you to get set up."

Turning back to face Agent Fowler, she smirked at his frustration. Megan handed him the warrants. "Now, we're ready to go," she said as she took two bottles of water from the fridge by the desk. At her Durango, she handed him one bottle. "You're going to need this. You never go anywhere in the high desert without water. Not if you want to live long, at any rate." Fowler's frown deepened.

"Just how long do you think I'll be hiding by the gate?" He paused at the passenger door.

"If you're lucky, less than an hour. Otherwise, maybe as many as three hours, depends on whether Poggi's goons take a metal rake to the fire. I'll drop you just around the bend from the gate. The hike back won't take long." Megan drove west, past the 080 gatehouse and around the bend out of sight of the guard. She stopped long enough for Fowler to exit. "I'll have Dewayne pick you up. He's going to be behind the van about a mile or so." Driving farther down the road, Megan made a U-turn to the spot she planned on parking while she waited for word the diamonds were on the way. Once parked and comfortable, she watched Agent Fowler trek back toward the gatehouse. *"Damn city folk, don't have a clue."* Shaking her head, she chuckled at his awkward movements. He stumbled into a boulder and a cactus growing next to it. She watched him shake his hand, obviously in pain. He bent over and began walking more carefully, but not very quietly. Fortunately for him, passing traffic on the highway covered the sounds of his approach.

Cracking open her bottle of water, Megan lowered her window. At least the weather wasn't as hot as last week. Fall was a wonderful time of year in Riverview, if it lasted more than a week. Often the days went from summer warm to the first snow of the season in what seemed to be only hours, but this year they were having an extended fall. The leaves had begun turning weeks ago, but only the nights were chilly so far. "Lord, please let the weather hold for this weekend. Amen." Megan had refused to watch the weather reports, fearing the forecast. The spur-of-the-moment barbeque she'd invited the volunteers to attend depended on decent weather. She wondered, did the R-B have an indoor arena or space in case of a storm? She'd have to call Bethany this evening to find out before making the final preparations for the event. Her radio crackled and Megan looked at her watch. She'd been parked just over an hour.

"Do you want me to close the speed-trap, Boss?" Dewayne's voice sounded stilted, but Megan didn't think anyone would notice. At least she now knew the thugs were on their way back to the 080, hopefully with the diamonds.

"Yes Deputy Jacobson. I need you to meet with the Highway Patrol just past 080. Pick up Agent Fowler and proceed as he directs. There's been a minor accident." Megan flicked her microphone off after telling Dewayne to come this way.

"Yes, ma'am. I'm on my way." The radio went silent.

From where Dewayne had been sitting, it should be about a ten-minute drive for the van to get to the 080; Agent Fowler should be ready to take down the guard at the gate once the van entered. Swigging another gulp of her bottled water, Megan listened for the sounds of approaching traffic. Only a distant bobwhite and the scream of a red-tailed hawk on the horizon broke the silence of the desert. Waiting made her thirsty, especially in a situation like this. In Afghanistan, she'd been on patrols that included waiting and watching for the enemy to make a move and she had never enjoyed the wait. Too many things could go wrong. She finished her water and tossed the empty behind her seat.

With time dragging, Megan finally couldn't stand it and started her Durango. Just then, she heard the sound of a slowing vehicle and the crunch of tires turning onto a gravel drive. The bust was going down. Megan rounded the curve in time to see Agent Fowler climb into Dewayne's cruiser as it turned into the 080, heading for the ranch house. An unmarked CHP vehicle followed them down the drive, Megan wondered who'd invited them to the bust. Hanging back, she let all the other vehicles get far ahead of her on the long single-lane blacktop drive. Something was niggling in the back of her mind...some little thing kept telling her to guard the gate and the exit. Letting the other vehicles pull into the compound, Megan stopped well out of sight of the ranch house, angling her Dodge to block the drive. From the direction of the compound, she heard shouts and a couple of gunshots—and then silence. The silence was broken by the roar of a powerful engine. A crash of metal on wood sounded from ahead and to her left.

A bashed-up Lamborghini swerved onto the blacktop between Megan and the compound. Tires squealing, it gained traction and speed heading directly for her Durango. Megan jumped out and away from her Dodge at the same instant a screech of brakes and the smell of burning rubber reached her. She watched the Lamborghini veer sideways sliding toward her Dodge, coming to rest with its passenger door solidly against the passenger door of the Durango.

Rika sat with Babydoll clutched to her chest, her eyes huge and terrified when she realized she couldn't open her door. Megan watched Rika's jaw drop and heard a muffled scream emanate from the woman as she gaped at Megan's drawn pistol. Poggi leapt from the driver's side, his pistol in his hand, heading to the left, into the desert, firing wildly at Megan. Ducking behind her patrol car, she watched the idiot run.

"Don't know where you think you're going." Megan called after the fleeing criminal. "Only desert, sagebrush and mountains that way."

A shrill wavering scream pierced the air and Poggi emptied his revolver at something on the ground. Chuckling, Megan trotted after the now hopping and limping man. "So, tell me, did you get snake bit or did you step on a cactus? Maybe a jack rabbit spooked you. You damned city folk are helpless out here in the wilderness." Listening to him moan as he hopped around, Megan began to feel sorry for him; until she remembered her dog. Karma is a bitch and this time it looked like Poggi got what he deserved.

Almost to the man now, she saw the dead snake. "Well, at least he managed to shoot it." She muttered to herself. Looking up at him she said, "Looks like you killed the snake, of course your blood might have poisoned it anyway. I suggest you find a rock and sit down. You're not dying but, the more you move, the faster the venom will spread and it'll hurt worse. Sit on that boulder and put your foot up." Whipping out her phone, she was relieved to see two bars and called 911.

"Sheriff Holloway here. I've got a snake-bite victim on the 080 west of Riverview. Looked like a Massasauga, but it could have been a midget faded...yeah, best to send the anti-

185

venom. SHIT!" Megan dropped her phone and emptied her pistol into the snake hanging on her pant leg. Its death those pulled it free of her pants. Cussing under her breath as she shook her leg out, she pulled her extra pistol from her boot holster. Megan was thankful for her worn tall cowboy boots which had just saved her a lot of pain. Retrieving her phone, she was pleased to see the call hadn't been cut off.

"Sorry about that. No, I'm okay. Sonofabitchin' snake struck at my ankle and hit my boot. On the patient, no tourniquets, right? Okay, I'll see if I can't keep him quiet. Thanks." Ending the connection, she looked back to Poggi. "Here's one of the many differences between us...you dress for style and I dress for the desert." Pausing she pulled the leg of her uniform pant up to show her lower leg. "Cowboy boots aren't just a fashion statement, they're a survival tool!"

The unmarked CHP cruiser pulled up behind Poggi's Lamborghini and Agent Fowler hopped out. Looking around, he stepped off the pavement in the direction of Megan and Poggi. "Agent Fowler, I wouldn't come this direction, if I were you." Megan cautioned. "Rattlesnake bites are painful." She chuckled at the speed Fowler stepped back onto the pavement. She could see him speaking into a radio, but couldn't tell what he was saying. Minutes ticked by before Dewayne pulled his patrol car up behind the cruiser, parked it and walked out to where Megan waited with a now sweating and moaning Nicodemo Poggi. In the distance, the sound of sirens relieved Megan's worry that the man might actually die before help arrived. Snake bites were seldom fatal any more, but if the anti-venom was delayed, a person with a weaker constitution could succumb to the severe shock and neurological symptoms the venom might cause.

Dewayne almost lifted Poggi completely off his feet, dragging him more than helping him to walk back to the paved drive. "There you go, Mister. Sit on the pavement and put your foot on the bumper. That's it," Dewayne instructed Poggi.

"Agent Fowler, I think if there's anything you want to know from Mr. Poggi, you can likely get a truthful answer." Megan suggested. "Pain loosens the tongue."

"Poggi, how did you know we were coming? The gate guard didn't hit any panic button. I stopped him and opened the gate myself." Fowler asked clearly frustrated that Poggi had bolted before he could be caught in possession of the smuggled diamonds.

"The gate opened without the guard calling it in. He had no reason to open the gate so I knew something was off. I keep my poor Lamborghini in the garage close to an outside wall that would be easy to crash just in case." Poggi's eyes looked watery as he surveyed his damaged sports car. "I didn't want to hurt it, but there was no other choice."

"What about your woman? Didn't you worry you might hurt her with your wild escape attempt?" Fowler pressed as the sirens got closer. Rika stepped closer to hear his response.

"She wasn't supposed to be in the car. If she hadn't been walking that damned dog as I made a run for it...she'd never have been in the car. I'm the one going to prison, not her. All she'd do is slow me down. But noooo, she managed to get herself and that damn ratty dog into the car before I could get out of the garage." Megan repressed a smile at the glare Poggi gave Rika.

"*You self-serving, egotistical bastard!* You'd leave me behind to face the Feds while you ran in your precious car?

The same way you let your contractor buddy from Afghanistan pat my ass? *You asshole!* Who's in charge of this arrest? I want to testify against this jackass. I've been with him over a year and have eyes and ears. If he doesn't want me around, I can make damn certain he spends the rest of his life behind bars. If I'm lucky, he'll be some thug's bitch." Rika looked from Megan to Agent Fowler, obviously wanting one of them to step forward and offer her a deal for her testimony.

"Well Mrs. Poggi..." Agent Fowler began.

"I'm *NOT* his wife. My name's Rika Maria Soto. There's no law against my testifying against him. I just need some sort of protection until he's permanently in jail." Rika stomped around the Lamborghini with the dog in her arms and sidled up to the FBI agent. "You'll protect me from him, won't you?" Her eyelashes fluttered and she lowered the dog, giving Agent Fowler an excellent view of her ample breasts nearly popping out of her tight top.

Shaking her head, Megan stepped away from the discussion, leaving Dewayne to guard Poggi. Walking back into the scrub, she photographed the carcass of the rattler, being careful not to get her hands within reach of the mouth since a dead rattler can still bite reflexively for several hours after death. Using her foot, she turned the snake which had bitten Poggi left and then right to get a clean photo of markings, size and head. The paramedics might need to see them.

By this time, she could see the ambulance making its way up the paved drive. Upon seeing vehicles blocking the road, they cut the sirens and stopped. "Is the snake-bite victim here? If not, I'm going to need you to clear those vehicles." Came a voice from the driver's side.

"Over here, damn it. No one else is bent over double in pain, are they? *Idiot cowboys.*" Poggi snarled, his voice showing his disgust as he waved to the ambulance crew. Dewayne helped him, not too gently, to stand.

"Mister, I don't think it's very smart for you to insult us cowboys. I could drop you and those cowboy paramedics are going to be sticking needles in you. Maybe you should be real nice to all of us." Dewayne's laconic drawl and sarcastic tone inferring that the mafioso was the idiot.

A four-wheeler side-by-side rolled over a hill, out of a gully and up to the assembled group. Megan smiled, unable to help herself, when she realized Aaron was with Agent Strand.

Climbing stiffly off the machine, Agent Strand asked Megan, "Sheriff, did you get enough on the goons who sifted the ashes of the animals at the dump? I understand there is film and sound of the discussion between them about how happy Nico was going to be with the recovered gems." Rubbing her dusty seat, the agent continued. "I know he left before they made contact, so the gems were never passed but, the association of his name with the recovery and the witness who puts the dog in his possession should make the case, shouldn't it?" Agent Strand walked up to Megan, rattling off questions one after another.

"It's your case but, in my humble opinion, you should have enough to hang his ass. The sound was a great idea. It connects the gems with Nicodemo Poggi especially when we have the witness to back up the connection. Good job." Megan grinned at her. Feeling an arm encircle her waist, Megan leaned back into Aaron's chest. "I'm glad you're okay. Who was shooting?" She dropped her voice to keep the question between themselves.

"The Fed felt the need to impress the goons with his firepower. No one had drawn a gun when Agent Fowler began to fire—which could have done some serious damage. They really shouldn't let men with inferiority complexes work with weapons. Way too fast on the draw." Aaron spit in the dirt to the left, away from the agent, the CHP officer and the paramedics. "I heard you almost got snake bit yourself. You okay?" Aaron inspected the tiny set of holes in her pant leg where the snake had struck.

"Yeah. Boots are part of the uniform and these are tall boots." Joy at his concern for her safety caused her to rub her head against his shoulder. "You know I can take care of myself, but thanks for the worry. I hope you're not going to get gray hair with me being the Sheriff of Riverview."

"We'll talk about this later. At the moment, I've got to go collect the men sitting in handcuffs in the compound. Dewayne secured them, but I think they still feel the place will be overrun with rattlesnakes any minute." Turning to her deputy, Aaron pointed to a pickup truck coming across the open ground towing a small horse trailer. "Hey Dewayne! Is that trailer going to be big enough to hold your prisoners? If they sit down, they should ride well enough to get them back to town, don't you think? Roger uses it to transport his prize stallion so the thing has great shocks and suspension."

Agent Fowler swaggered up to Megan. "I'm commandeering your deputy's cruiser and taking Ms. Soto to Montrose behind the ambulance. Poggi can have his bite treated at the hospital and if they need to keep him overnight, I'm certain I can find a deputy to guard him. The jail there is bigger and I want Poggi secured either in jail or at the hospital under guard. I'll order transport sent there from Denver, and one for the other five suspects sent here. You can secure them until the transport arrives, can't you?" Fowler's tone inferred he expected the prisoners would likely be sleeping in a barn, his opinion of the Riverview Sheriff's Department being rather low.

"Oh, yes, Sir. We can even feed them for a couple of days before we run out of food." Megan's snarky comment caused her deputy and Aaron to choke on chuckles and Agent Fowler to glare at her. "Dewayne, take Aaron and the trailer up to the compound and collect those men. Make certain they're seated and rope the cuffs together to keep them stable in the horse trailer. No pun intended." Megan laughed at the pun. "I'll see you back at the office."

"Yes, Ma'am." Dewayne and Aaron jumped into the four-wheeler and led the pickup toward the compound.

Agent Fowler aided Ms. Soto into Dewayne's cruiser and they maneuvered around the wreck. The departing ambulance and the unmarked CHP cruiser led the way down the paved drive and off the property.

"Agent Strand, would you like a ride back to my office? Looks like I've still got my vehicle." Megan pointed to her Durango sitting angled on the paved drive, barely untouched by Poggi's sports car. "I'll call a wrecker for Poggi's car and have it taken to the impound yard. He might have evidence stored in it; we'll keep it under lock and key until a crime scene team can clear it."

"Thanks, I expect Agent Mills will drive the FBI SUV to your office. Agent Escamilla still has our Homeland Security vehicle. I'll call him and tell him to meet me there. He's got all the photos and audio from the goons sifting the ashes and recovering the contraband. I was surprised to learn the contraband was diamonds. Can they be traced?" She asked, walking over to the Durango. Stopping at the front of the vehicle, Agent Strand surveyed its position and that the Lamborghini. "Hmm, I think I'll let you move before I try to get in. Did Poggi actually hit your Dodge? Can't tell from here."

Megan stood at the rear of her vehicle and scrutinized the miniscule gap between it and the sports car. "You know; I don't think they actually touched. Amazing that two vehicles could get that close and not come into contact somewhere." Taking out her cell phone, she took photos of the scene and the two vehicles. Switching back to communications, she called Shirley on the desk. "Shirley, I need Joe and a wrecker dispatched to the 080. I want the suspects' car taken to the fenced lot behind the office and left there. Have Joe follow the tow truck and lock the gate with a chain and padlock, bringing me the key. Got that?" Cutting the connection, she put the phone into her pocket.

"Should we leave it here without a guard until they arrive?" Agent Strand looked worriedly at the wreck.

A sound in the distance signaled the return of the make shift paddy-wagon horse trailer transporting the arrested suspects. Following that was John, the R-M wrangler with the four-wheeler. Megan waved the truck and trailer out the gate, but signaled John to pull over.

Grinning, John stopped the four-wheeler and cut the engine. "Hey Sheriff. Those dudes were funny. One kept whining he'd seen a snake slither under the barn while they were tied up not ten feet away. When we got there, they were trying to get to their feet to run. What a hoot!"

Megan laughed. Those men would be worried about snakes for a quite a while. "The power of suggestion is an amazing tool. So useful, sometimes. It can make people see things, especially if the suggestion is scary. I need you to sit here with this car until Joe and the wrecker arrive. I'll clear it with Roger and Aaron. Remember, you're still deputized."

"Yes, Ma'am. Won't be quite as entertaining as those greenhorns, but still beats breaking colts." John gave her a mock salute. "Can I sit in it? Always wanted a fast car and this thing looks expensive and fast."

"No. I'm sealing all the windows and the doors with evidence tape. Anything in this car could be evidence so we need you as a witness that nothing has been removed until the wrecker picks it up." Megan wanted to pat the man on the back, he looked so depressed about not being able to sit in the car. "Tell you what...once the crime scene unit from Gunnison is done with it, I'll let you sit in it and maybe drive it to the wrecking yard or wherever the Feds want it put. How's that?"

"Seriously? No one will ever believe I got to drive a car that cost more than my dad's ranch." Again the grin on John's face threatened to split the skin of his cheeks.

Megan hoped she hadn't just promised the impossible, but it would depend on the car still drivable when the federal CSI unit finished. "So long as the Feds don't have specific rules against it, it's a deal." Megan climbed into her car while John and the Homeland Agent watched. Once behind the wheel, she inched her Durango back, careful not to scrape the Lamborghini. As soon as she had her vehicle pointed down the drive, she hopped out and dug her crime-scene kit from the back. Donning gloves, she began to seal the doors and windows of the sports car. She remembered to reach in and put it into neutral before removing the keys and sealing the driver's door. Satisfied that every possible point of entry was sealed with tape or zip ties, she walked one last time around the car. "That should do it."

Chapter Fourteen

Driving back to Riverview, Megan felt Agent Strand watching her. "What? Something wrong?"

"I've been with Homeland for about three years and I've been part of quite a few cases and situations which involved small-town law enforcement...I've got to say you're different. You handle things completely unlike most small town sheriffs. I've never seen anyone handle the FBI as well as you did. Without even trying, you fooled them into thinking they had the lead in this case, while all the while you had the lead until the take-down. You're good."

"Thanks, I think. My momma taught me you catch more flies with honey than vinegar. A little reminder of what he would face trying to get information from the locals and Fowler was more than happy to let me do it my way. I will admit a couple of times I had to make Fowler think I was working on things we'd discussed. But, I no choice—these are my friends, my supporters, people I respect. I was elected to protect them and, in my book, that means from anyone and everyone, including well-meaning federal agencies and bad guys." Megan cleared her throat and shook her head. "Besides, you know I was right. Neither you nor the FBI would have been able to pull off the sting I used because you never would have thought of it. Also, we had some of the most skilled sharpshooters in the state covering our operations because I knew to call them. They were there because they trusted me enough to follow my directions."

"You're right about that. A rattlesnake migration? *Seriously?* Do they even do that? What if Poggi had called your bluff? Would you have pulled out live rattlers and pointed them toward the compound?" Strand chuckled at the thought. If Megan had been forced to do something like that, God only knew who or what would have been shot in the melee. It would have kept the goons busy, but could have put everyone in danger.

"Well, rattlesnakes move from the den to prime feeding areas in the spring and back to the den in the fall, so I guess that is a migration of sorts. Besides, Poggi didn't call my bluff and he sent his men to sift through the ashes for the diamonds. That's all that counts. You've got it on film with audio that they were working for Poggi and taking the booty back to him." Megan couldn't suppress a self-satisfied smile as she drove up to the office. Parking the Dodge, a thought came to her. "Oh, you might want to call the Montrose and Denver Airports. If Poggi has any other animals coming in, you can intercept them due to probable cause. It only took my veterinarian about ten minutes and some anesthesia to open the dog and find the goods."

"Shit, you're right." Pulling out her phone Agent Strand began the process of calling airports within two hundred miles to tell the TSA screeners to check all larger animals for body-cavity incisions. She expanded the search from just dogs to horses and cattle whether they were being flown domestically or being imported. At the Denver airport, the TSA agent in charge promised to disperse this data throughout the system in the event that other criminals had thought of using animals to carry contraband.

From the conference room, Agent Strand sent out an APB to all border crossings to be aware of this form of smuggling. All animals were to be searched for incisions and large livestock could be inspected by a veterinarian if needed and held for thirty-six hours. She even took the thought one step further and suggested if there were any suspicions, the veterinarian could check the uterus of larger animals.

Leaving Agent Strand working industriously to close this possible avenue of smuggling, Glancing at her watch as she walked toward her office, Megan began unstrapping her pistol. Her shift was over fifteen minutes ago; no wonder she was tired. It had been a busy day and Aaron hadn't let her sleep very much last night. The thought brought a smile to her lips; Aaron should likely be as tired as she was today, but she hoped not. Stepping into her darkened office, her hand reached for the light switch when it was covered by a strong work-roughened hand.

"Why don't we just leave the lights off. I've been waiting all day to catch you alone."

Instinct and fear froze Megan. "You know, all I have to do is raise my voice and this office will be crammed with armed deputies and agents."

"Yeah, but you're not going to do anything that stupid; now, are you? There's two sweet old ladies depending on you doing as you're told. Ida Mae and Lilabel said you'd cooperate. My woman's holding them while we negotiate their release." The man's voice seized her attention. She'd heard it somewhere before. Not in Riverview, not in the past year or so...but the syntax and accent as well as the timbre of that particular voice were niggling at her memory.

"What do you want to turn the Bailey's loose?" She stammered, trying to stall and buy time. "How do I know you haven't hurt them? They're old ladies, you could have given Lilabel a heart attack...she's not well." Knowing Lilabel was strong as a twenty-year-old, Megan still wanted to plant the idea that the captives he held could become a liability at any moment. Hopefully, that would make him release them. "Tell you what: I'll become your hostage—just turn those near-sighted old ladies loose. They can't hurt you, likely couldn't even identify you or your woman. You don't need to keep them. Hurt them, and there'll be no hole deep enough for you to hide. This entire county would come after you...those women have mothered every cowboy and ranch hand in the state at one time or another."

"Where are your 'cuffs?" His hands began a rough search of Megan's belt until he felt her handcuffs. "Put your hands behind your back."

Balling her hands into fists, Megan did as he instructed. Once he cinched them painfully tight, he pushed Megan farther into the room. She spun around to see what he was doing and said a prayer for the sisters' safety as she watched him text to someone. "Done. *You're* now the hostage. The old ladies are locked into a closet. Where's your brother and that slut he's taking to a safe house?"

Heaving a sigh of relief, Megan hoped the man was telling the truth. She knew the closet under the stairs was the hiding spot the women used for the shotgun; if that was where they were put; the woman might not have seen it. This could get interesting. Megan's captor stood with his back to the door and her own pistol pointed at her chest. In the dark, she couldn't see if he'd released the safety, but she hadn't heard the click so, if her luck held, the safety was still engaged.

A not-too-distant shotgun blast, followed by a second, brought scraping chairs and running footsteps in the hall outside her door. Before her captor could lock the door, it was slammed open, knocking him off balance. Scrambling, Megan called, "*He's got a gun!*"

"*Sonofabitch!*" Aaron's voice scared the crap out of Megan. *He* wouldn't be armed. *Damn.* With light coming in from the hall, Megan could see the gun swing in slow motion toward the man standing in the doorway.

Launching her body, head down, Megan managed to hit the gunman in the ribs, knocking the wind from him and forcing him to fall toward Aaron, but he still managed to hold onto the gun.

"*Bitch!* That's the last move you'll make." The man's voice wheezed, backhanding the barrel of the gun across her ear and cheek.

Pain, worse than any she'd ever felt in the Army, exploded in her head and Megan felt herself falling into blackness.

Aaron hurled himself into the Megan's attacker, grabbing his wrist and slamming it down against the edge of the desk. With an audible cracking of bones and a howl of pain, the gun clattered to the floor. More footsteps in the hall behind him and the light was thrown on. A stranger was rolling on the floor, clutching his broken wrist with his good hand. Megan lay face down, with her hands cuffed behind her back, pale and unmoving.

Agent Strand kicked the gun across the room, grabbed the disarmed gunman and pulled him to his feet. "I'm going to enjoy cuffing you, asshole." She pulled first his good hand and then the swelling right hand behind his back and used her own cuffs to secure him. "How does that feel? Don't

give me any reason to take you down—you won't like it."
She pulled him to his feet and pushed him roughly out the
door. "Deputy, where are the jail cells? This jerk can cool his
heels in one until the medics are done with your sheriff." A
disembodied voice in the hall gave her directions and she
marched the moaning man away, pushing him none to gently
as he stumbled along.

"Megan needs medical attention. Are the paramedics
on their way?" Aaron looked worriedly toward those
standing in the hall, his voice cracking and his face almost as
pale as Megan's.

One look at Aaron's face, and Shirley called the
hospital checking on the ETA for the ambulance dispatched
to Riverview. "What the *fuck* to you mean they're headed for
Bailey's Boarding House?" she screamed into the
microphone. "*Damn it, man.* Redirect them here unless you
know for a fact one of those old ladies is bleeding."

"Yes, I know shots were fired at the boarding house,
but until we know differently, we have to assume that Ida
Mae and Lilabel didn't kill anyone. Sheriff Holloway is out
cold and bleeding from the head. You need to get their asses
HERE! ASAP!" She gave Aaron a thumbs up signal and
ended the conversation.

Turning away from her com unit, she grabbed the
phone. "I'll call the Baileys. You take care of the sheriff. For
God's sake get those cuffs off of her. Sheesh, men can't do
anything without being told." Shirley muttered as she dialed
the Baileys. "Ida Mae? Calm down, Woman. Are you okay?
Is Lilabel okay? Did you hit 'em? Good job. Is it bleeding a
lot? Okay, put a pressure bandage on it. I'll send a deputy to
take over and get another ambulance for her."

Disconnecting, Shirley looked around the hallway, finally seeing Joe. "Joe, head for the Bailey's. They've got a wounded prisoner. Possible home invasion and kidnapping attempt, but I think it's connected with what just happened here. Stay with her, no matter where the ambulance takes her. Don't let that bitch get away." Shirley pointed toward the door and watched the big man move nimbly through the crowd gathering in the hall. "Okay, everyone. Let's move along. Nothing you can do here. Clear the hall so the paramedics can get in. Cheryl, go get that icepack from the freezer. It won't hurt to lay it on that wound until help arrives."

Aaron held Megan in his arms. Rocking her gently while he sat on the floor praying that she would be okay. Outside, the siren stopped as the paramedics arrived. "It's okay, Baby, the paramedics will take good care of you. I'll be right here. I won't leave you. You're going to be okay…God, please let her be okay…" Aaron wiped his cheek against his shoulder, never noticing the wetness his tears left there.

Chapter 15

Pain, voices, lights—then darkness. Megan floated between consciousness and a black well of darkness. *"Hey, Baby. Don't be a stuck-up bitch; come over here and have a drink with us. Just because we don't wear uniforms; doesn't mean we're not lonely. I know the commander told all you 'soldiers' to protect us...so, come sit on my lap. We'll talk about whatever comes up."* Rude laughter, a hand pinching her ass as she tried to get by the group of independent contractors the post used to bring in supplies. They were always trying to grope the females in her troop. The one time her friend had broken the nose of one of them for taking liberties...Mary had drawn extra duty for a week. They were the Commander's pets. He wouldn't hear anything bad against them and their often drunken rudeness to the women on post. Not only the soldiers, but some of the civilian workers had complained about this particular set of contractors. No woman was safe from their roaming hands and rude behavior.

"Shonofa... That'sh it." Her voice sounded scratchy and surreal. Pain. Megan turned her head and immediately wished she hadn't moved.

"Megan. Honey. Don't try to talk. Don't struggle; your face is bandaged. Babe, they can't give you the good stuff for the pain until they know you don't have brain trauma. Just hold still. You'll feel better soon."

A hand held hers and Megan knew it was Aaron even though her eyes wouldn't open. His gentleness soothed her confusion. The memory began fading. Wait, she needed to tell Aaron. "Know him. 'Dependent contractor. Afghanishtan. Mitsch shomething." Moving her jaw shot a

202

bolt of pain through her skull, her eyes watered and tears leaked from the corners. She felt herself fading and relaxed back into the painless dark.

Aaron felt the tension leave her and knew she'd fallen into unconsciousness again. Better that than hurting, but it worried him. Searching the drawer next to her bed, he found a pen and paper. Thank God for the candy stripers. The hospital volunteers visited rooms, stocking the drawers with incidental items like pens and note pads. Pulling out the items he needed, he wrote down what Megan had said. "Knew the guy. Independent contractor in Afghanistan. Name: Mitch ??" Tearing off the sheet, he stuck it in his pocket and left the notepad next to her bed. This could be important. Even though the guy was under arrest, this information might help find out why he attacked Megan. The woman who assaulted the Baileys had lawyered up, so without some sort of proof connecting the two incidents, the crimes couldn't be linked.

Picking up Megan's hand again, Aaron pressed it gently to his lips. "You're going to be okay. You'll be good as new. I heard them talking and you've got a crack in your right zygomatic bone and a long superficial cut across your cheek; ten stitches. Nothing too serious...as long as no damage was done to your skull or upper mandible, no brain bleeds. The jerk was off balance when he hit you, so I know you can't have any damage to your skull. Not with your hard head. A hit like you took, shouldn't do more than take ten years off my life. I think you saved my life. Using your head to throw him off balance. Damn Woman, I would rather have taken a bullet than to sit here watching you in pain. I love you and you humble me with your actions. Oh, I hear someone coming." He kissed her hand again and laid it down as the door to the room opened.

"Ah, Mr. Travers. Still here I see. You're her fiancé, right? You're the closest thing to a relative she has here in Colorado, I've been in touch with her family in Texas and they have given me permission to keep you abreast of her condition." The doctor smiled absently in Aaron's direction and looked at the chart tablet in his hand. "The tests show the fracture you know about and bruising to the mandibular condyle, just under the ear. There's no displacement on the fracture so I don't think surgery is indicated, but she might want to see a specialist if she needs reassurance."

"What about her skull; is it fractured? Why is she fading in and out of consciousness? Does she have bleeding in her skull? What did the scan show?" Aaron tossed out all the terms and comments he'd heard the medical staff use while he sat with Megan.

"No fracture in the skull, though the zygomatic fracture is close. Overall the scan is good, no depressions or bleeds except the swelling of the tissue surrounding the mandibular condyle. Nature has a way of protecting us and her losing consciousness is just her body's way of keeping her from extreme pain. Now that we have the scan to go by, we can give her stronger pain medication. It will likely keep her asleep, but when she does wake up, her pain level will be manageable. Any other questions?" The doctor asked as he tapped the screen of the tablet and turned to leave.

"Yes, how long will she be staying in the hospital? Will she be on any special diet? Any special instructions or things I should watch for since I plan on staying?" Aaron picked up Megan's hand as he spoke, his thumb stroking the back of it.

"I'll re-evaluate her tomorrow morning, but I think she should be able to return home tomorrow afternoon as long as she's not experiencing dizzy spells or nausea. Do you live with her, or would she be home alone as she recovers?" The doctor paused in the doorway, waiting for Aaron's answer.

"I can make certain she has someone to sit with her as she recovers. I work at the R-M but I'll spend my evenings and nights at her place. If you're concerned that she would be alone if symptoms suddenly occurred, don't be. No one in Riverview would allow that to happen. We take care of our own." Aaron looked the man in the eye as he replied. Riverview was a close community. One phone call to Marge or Shirley and Megan would have more house guests than she needed.

"Good, I never feel right about releasing head trauma patients unless someone can monitor them for a few days. I'm going to have her jaw immobilized as much as possible without actually wiring it closed. She'll be a lot more comfortable if she isn't talking or chewing for a week or so. Until the swelling goes down, she needs to have food put through a blender. No special diet, just make whatever she eats into something that can be sucked by a straw. Got that? The stitches on her cheek should be removed in a week, I don't think she'll have much of a scar."

"Yes, sir. I'll make a few calls and get things set up. I'll see you in the morning." Aaron finally let the man out the door, sitting back down next to Megan as the door closed. "Don't know how much of what you hear is sinking in right now; you just sleep. I'll take care of everything." He looked closely at her when he thought he felt her hand twitch in his. "Just sleep for now, Babe. I expect they'll be in soon to wrap your jaw. At least it's not broken." Releasing her hand, he pulled out his cell and called Megan's office. "Shirley, this is Aaron. Megan's going to be okay. She's got a fracture of the zygomatic bone in her cheek and a severe bruise of her mandibular condyle, that spot just under her ear. She'll be spending tonight under observation in the hospital. I'm staying here with her. She might get to go home tomorrow."

"Thank the Lord. I've been praying that she would be okay. Is there anything you need from us?" The voice on the phone sounded teary, choking Aaron up with the reaction he'd been holding back.

"Call Marge, Stephanie and Bethany. If they let her out of the hospital tomorrow, she's going to need someone to stick around her house for the next week or so. See if they can take turns or something. I'll be there every night by six, but Roger needs me at the ranch at least every other day, so I can't stay with her all the time. I'll call you in the morning and let you know when she's heading back to Riverview. At least I've got my truck here. Now I'm glad they didn't let me into the ambulance with her." He listened as Shirley repeated his suggestions and hung up before she did.

A light went off in his brain and he knew just who to call. Kam was a nurse by profession and her pregnancy had forced her to take leave from her job. Chuckling to himself, he went through his contacts list until he found David's private number. With David being FBI, this would kill two birds with one stone. "Hi, David, this is Aaron. Yeah, doing good and you?" He listened as David touched on his health and dealing with a pregnant wife.

"I'll bet it's tough. Hey, listen man. Megan is hurt. She's going to be okay, but they're keeping her in the hospital tonight because the bastard hit her with a gun barrel across her cheek and caught her under the ear. Doctor wants to make certain there's no brain trauma. Before she passed out this last time, she remembered something and told me the attacker was a sub-contractor at her last post in Afghanistan. He also may be connected to the crime boss they arrested today. I know there was smuggling and murder involved too. I don't know the name of the lead agent in the arrest, but there's an Agent Mills and an Agent Strand—I think she's Homeland—involved. Do you think you could get that information to them? The guy's name is Mitch something, he's currently under arrest in Riverview for assaulting an officer and maybe attempted kidnapping, I don't know."

"Kam's going to want to come help, is there room for her at Megan's place? I'll bring her over tomorrow, things are slow here. Agent Fowler was lead on the Riverview case. I'll let him know what Megan remembered. He's going to want to talk to her after he investigates the connection. She might lose her prisoner to him if he's part of the Federal case. Listen, I'll talk to you later. I've got to call Kam before she learns of Megan's injury from anyone else and tries to drive herself to Riverview." The line went dead in Aaron's hand and he couldn't help but laugh at David's concerns. Megan would be happy to see Kam; they could sympathize with each other as Megan healed and Kam gestated.

Chapter Sixteen

"Wat da 'ell you mean, it'sh Friday?" Managing to speak without moving her mouth was a new skill for Megan. The pain when she forgot and tried to speak normally kept her aware of the restriction.

"Babe, you slept through Thursday because of the pain meds. We could barely wake you enough to suck your food down the straw. I was beginning to worry, so we cut back on your dosage. How do you feel?" Aaron passed Megan a glass of breakfast. Today they'd made blueberry pancakes, topped with butter and syrup and blended it with orange juice. He'd tasted it and it wasn't horrible, but maybe he should tell Kam to serve each part of lunch as a separate glass, mixed with simple water.

"Feelsh like a truck hit my fashe." Slurring her words, Megan took the glass and sucked the dish up the straw, making a face at the flavors. "'sh different." Sucking harder she drew down the meal with her eyes closed and swallowed loudly. "Don't make thissh again, okay?" She handed the glass back to Aaron. "Tanksh."

"Okay, in future, we'll not mix things, just give you one flavor at a time." Aaron took the glass and leaned over to kiss the top of her head, where it wasn't bandaged. "David spent the night; he wanted to talk to you once you're awake. Do you feel up to it? I think he's got some news from Agent Fowler." He grimaced in sympathy when Megan attempted to nod then abruptly stopped moving.

"Ow. Pleashe, I need ta' know." Megan tried to smile, felt her left cheek move, but knew her right was still too swollen to lift. She'd seen her face in the mirror across the room, and it wasn't a pretty sight.

While Aaron left the room to find David, Megan took a longer look in the mirror on the dresser. Nope, she looked just as bad as she felt. A train wreck in a human body. Closing her eyes, she felt herself drifting off and forced them open to keep from falling asleep again. She had too much to do today to sleep it away. Hearing sounds in the hall, she managed to sit up straighter and pull her covers higher against her chest.

"Megan, thank heavens you're awake. I've been so worried. I even checked with Dr. Samuelson to see if you should be sleeping so much. He advised us to cut your pain meds by half and see if you would be in too much pain. How do you feel? Would you like something for pain?" Kam waddled into the room and over to the bed where she felt Megan's forehead, counted her pulse in her wrist, and closely inspected her pupils.

Unable to stop it, a chuckle escaped Megan's throat. "Kam, you look amazsing. You glow. I'm okay for now. Painsh not too bad. I jus can' talk." Frustration brought tears to her eyes. "Damn."

"You're doing great. Don't try to talk. David has all the news; he just got off the phone with Fowler." Looking around, Kam spotted her husband entering the room behind Aaron. "Come over here, honey, and tell Megan what's been happening. She's missed a whole day of developments." Her arm snagged David's and she pulled him toward Megan's bed.

"Well, where do I start? Hmmm?" David grinned down at Megan and winked. "Mitchell Banks, not the name he was born to, works for a conglomerate based in the Bahamas. We still haven't exactly figured out what his role is with the company, but it seems he roams the world 'taking care of details.' Things like witnesses, company embezzlers, whistle-blowers, a wide variety of people go missing whenever he's in the neighborhood. In talking to the murder witness, it seems he was the third person in the trio who killed Nadia's boyfriend. She described him down to a scar above his right eyebrow. She's got a fantastic memory for faces, that woman. He wasn't trying to protect Poggi; he was after her to protect his own ass."

David paused to look around and, finding the small cooler next to the bed, he opened it to discover bottled water and sodas. "You don't mind if I have one of these, do you?" He chuckled when Megan didn't attempt to answer. "No, don't try to answer, I know you like to share." He took out a bottle of water, opened it and chugged about half of it.

"So, when we investigated more into the smuggling angle of this case. We discovered the firm that sponsored the dog just *happened* to be in this same conglomerate. Now, we're looking into the possibility of more than diamonds being smuggled out of Afghanistan and other countries where this company works. They're a sub-contractor providing goods and services to our military, and the military of our allies. Poggi may have been only the money-laundering segment for the group. We've managed to take down the offices in the USA and on our military posts, but their computers are well encrypted and it could take months to discover all of their plots and crimes." Pausing to take another drink, David looked more closely at Megan. He noticed she seemed to be having trouble keeping her eyes open so he lightly raised his voice as he continued the news.

"In the meantime, we've got Poggi charged with smuggling and money laundering. For his attack on you at your office, Banks has been charged with attempted kidnapping and assault. I'm certain you'll want to change that to attempted murder and accessory to murder charges. The woman who held Ida Mae and Lilabel is holding out. No way will she cooperate at this time. All you can charge her with will be home invasion and terroristic threatening, for attacking the Baileys. Unless we find some way of connecting her to Banks, there's not much more we can pin on her. She's in it up to her eyebrows, just nothing we can pinpoint."

Drawing a deep breath, David exhaled and took a long swig of his bottle of water. "All Poggi's soldiers have been charged with resisting arrest and assault against Agent Fowler and Deputy Jacobson. Poggi's attorney has bailed them out of jail. Poggi is being held as a flight risk without bail. His old lady has turned against him and she's still singing. We'll likely have more charges against him and the others when she's done. Mitchell Banks is behind bars as a flight risk too. He's screaming about a suit against Aaron for breaking his wrist, but don't worry—it won't stick. Any questions?" David looked from Megan to Aaron, and back to Megan.

"Ish Fowler coming by to queshtion me about Banksh?" Megan felt her eyes drifting closed again and fought to keep them open.

"Not until you can talk well enough for an audio recording. You look beat. I'm out of here. You've got my wife until next Wednesday. She's got a doctor's appointment next Thursday, so I'll be back to collect her. In the meantime, sleep lots and heal. Kam will take excellent care of you and you can keep her from going stir-crazy." David patted Megan's hand, kissed his wife and left the room whistling.

"You have no idea how happy he is to be rid of me for a whole week," Kam confided as she helped Megan slide back down into the bed. "I know I've been driving him nuts, but he has no idea what it's like to be sitting around with nothing to do but knit when I'm used to being busy." Kam sighed and then chuckled knowingly when she heard the car start and spew gravel as it headed down the driveway. "Hope he doesn't get stopped for speeding on the way home."

Aaron leaned over Megan and kissed her brow. "I've got to go. Roger is waiting for me; we have some cattle to bring down from the high pastures. Snow predicted next week. We've had a long fall and I think it's about to come to a snowy halt." Reluctantly letting go of Megan's hand, he headed for the door. "See you tonight, Babe."

"Wow. You'd think we had the plague or something." Kam chuckled at the quick retreat of the men. "I think we've been deserted. Why don't you take a short nap? I'll wake you at lunch with a burger shake. It's kind of fun coming up with food we can put through the blender. I'll make you a milkshake separately. What flavor?" Kam helped Megan slide down in the bed and pulled the blanket up to her chin.

"Shockolate." Megan mumbled and her body relaxed into a healing sleep.

Kam smirked. Putting a pain pill in her breakfast had worked. Sleep was the best thing for Megan now.

From the open window, Kam could hear the coming and going of vehicles. One would be Aaron on his way to work, but who was arriving? Looking out the window, Kam watched a very pregnant Bethany roll out of her SUV. Another month or two and Kam would be moving like that. At the moment, she had only a minor waddle. Rubbing her slowly-swelling abdomen, her heart sang. A year ago she and David had married. Thanks, in part, to Megan and Bethany and this town. Too bad Riverview wasn't large enough to need an FBI office. Denver was fine, but didn't have the feeling of family she got whenever she visited here. Leaning on the sill, she waved to Bethany, motioning her to come on up. She put her finger to her lips to indicate Bethany should enter quietly, nodding when Bethany gave her a thumbs up signal. Kam walked to the bedroom door, glanced again at a sleeping Megan before exiting, closing the door softly behind her.

"Kam, my God you look amazing! I'm so jealous. I'm so huge and you're still looking wonderful. When is your baby due? Ours is due between Christmas and New Year's." Bethany expertly turned her body so she could hug Kam without each rebounding like Sumo wrestlers off the other's expanded belly.

"Our girl is due in early March. David is so excited. He says a daughter first means you have someone to care for you in your old age. Not that he's a chauvinist or anything...but isn't that sweet?" Kam stepped back to look Bethany up and down. "Are you certain it's not twins?"

"With today's imaging, there's really very little chance of that happening. Twins would be fun, but maybe next time." She laughed and Kam could see Bethany's baby moving.

Downstairs, they heard the telephone ring. "Well, let's go downstairs. I'm not running; they can leave a message." Kam led the way down the long single flight to the ground floor just as the ringing stopped and a beep invited the caller to leave a message.

"Hi Megan, this is Zeke. I heard about your injury and wondered if you're still planning that barbeque this weekend. You might want to let everyone know, one way or the other. Seems there's several debates going around town. Oh well, hope you feel better fast..."

Picking up the telephone Kam asked, "Zeke who? This is Megan's friend, Kam, from Denver. What barbeque? Where?"

"Hi. Who?"

"Kam, I'm staying with Megan. What barbeque? She hasn't exactly been coherent since the injury." Kam looked over at Bethany who was shaking her head and shrugging her ignorance of any event for the weekend.

"Oh. My name is Zeke and Megan had asked me if I would grill the hot dogs and burgers for the picnic to thank the volunteers who helped search last weekend. She wanted to use the event to set up a Search-and-Rescue unit for Riverview. I know she really was counting on this event at the R-B to get names of those interested in being part of the unit. I told her I'd volunteer to be the cook for the group. She said Shirley was researching grants and training courses. Do you think she'll be able to do it or should I pass the word the event is on hold?"

"Wait just a minute." Kam covered the mouthpiece of the phone and turned to Bethany. "Did you know anything about this? Do you think we could get it together for Megan? It's just a picnic, not big meal type of event." Her tone of voice gave Bethany the idea that Kam really wanted to get this event rolling for her friend.

"No problem. I'll bet Shirley already has things together and all we have to do is let everyone know. I wouldn't be surprised if Sheena doesn't already have the food ready to cook. We'll just need to have the sign-up sheets printed." Bethany rubbed the small of her back, thinking of what needed to be done. Sheena should be able to take care of the food, as long as Megan could stay awake for the event, they could handle it.

"Zeke. It's still on." Kam told him. "We'll have Megan there and the fixings. What time did she tell you?" Kam experienced a shiver of excitement. She hadn't had this much to do since she left her job for extended maternity leave.

"She told me to be there at eleven-thirty, but I think I'll be there at eleven, just to make certain everything is ready to go."

"Good. Spread the word, and I'll have Shirley spread it too. I look forward to meeting you. I'll be one of the two expectant mothers hovering around." She laughed when he chuckled. "See you then." Hanging up the phone, she glanced over at Bethany. "Seriously, this event is taking place at your pack station and you didn't know?"

"I expect Sheena is on top of it. She pretty much runs the place in the off season. I'll go into the other room and use my cell phone to check while you call Shirley and let her know what we're doing, and find out what she's already done. Megan will need to write a speech and then one of us or Aaron can give it. No way are we letting her stand up and try to be heard in a crowd." Bethany pulled her cell from her pocket and went into the kitchen to call Sheena.

Half an hour later, everything was set up and taken care of except the speech. Sheena had already purchased the food on the R-B account and Shirley had the sign-up sheets, grant information, and information on courses being offered within a two-hundred-mile radius. All Megan needed to do was go over the data and get the group organized. Kam and Bethany sat on the couch drinking tea and congratulating each other on how much they had accomplished.

"Megan will be happy. I heard from Marge this was a pet project that she really wanted to get started. Funds will be tough to come by, but I bet we can get a couple of donations just by calling a few favors in. I know the R-M can put up a thousand for equipment. Who else?"

"How about the Gunnison Valley Guest Ranch? They may benefit from this unit. Think they can put up some cash for training?" Kam asked. She knew Matt and Marcia would be interested in being part of the unit, but was uncertain if they would have the funds to put up to support it. I wonder if they could talk their absentee owner into making a donation?

"Let's make a list and do some calling. Invite prospective donors to the picnic and we can pass the hat during the event. What do you think?" Bethany held her breath, waiting for Kam's opinion.

"Ohhh, that sounds perfect. Have Sheena clean out a large jug from the kitchen and mark it for donations."

Two hours later, both women were exhausted and talked out. They were grinning like Cheshire cats, but that was as much as they had energy to do.

"Ugh, I need to get up and fix Megan lunch. I don't know if I've got the energy. This little girl is draining all my ambition." Kam rubbed her itching belly.

"Knock, knock...Megan? Are you up?" A deep male voice came from the back door.

"Who's there? Megan's sleeping." Kam found the energy to get up and cautiously walk toward the back of the house. She hadn't heard any vehicles arrive, but the living room was to the farthest from the drive and parking area.

"Jake, Megan's brother. Want to unlatch the screen? I can pick a door lock; but screens end up needing to be replaced when I'm done and I don't think Megan would be happy with that." A deep sigh followed his words.

"Hold on, I'm coming. Aaron told me you might show up. He didn't tell me you were so stealthy though." Entering the kitchen, Kam saw a tall, blonde, blue-eyed man standing outside the latched screen door. One look and she grinned. Yep; this was Megan's brother alright.

"No rush, you didn't tell me you're walking for two. Doesn't hurt me to stand and wait. Nice to meet you, Kam." Jake extended his hand as the Kam opened the screen.

"Nice to meet you, too. Have a seat. Have you had lunch?" Kam moved to the fridge, taking out the milk and chocolate syrup before opening the bottom freezer to grab the vanilla ice cream. Looking over her shoulder as she reached into the package of frozen burgers, she waited to find out if Jake needed a hamburger too.

"I haven't, but I can make myself something. You don't need to trouble yourself on my account."

"I'll have one of those, Kam. This boy is screaming for food about twenty hours a day." Bethany waddled slowly into the kitchen and extended her hand to Jake. "Hi, I'm Bethany Meadows. Megan once worked for my husband, and we're friends too."

"I remember when she worked at the R-M. Right before she decided to run for sheriff. Hi, I'm her brother Jake. I'm two years older, closest in age to her from the others." He took Bethany's hand and assisted her to one of the seats at the counter. "Tell you what, Kam. You make the milkshake and I'll make the burgers. I saw a gas grill on the back deck. I'll start it."

Fifteen minutes later, the three of them were eating their hamburgers when a tapping noise came from upstairs. Kam stood, but Jake waved her down. "I'll get this. *Megan Marie Holloway*, you get your ass back in bed. *Right! Now!*" He yelled up the stairs, taking them two at a time.

Opening the bedroom door, he was just in time to catch her as she fell forward. "Damn it, *Sshake*. You shcared the shcrap outta me. When did shou get here? I gotta pee, help me to the sshohn, okay?" Megan grabbed his arm in a death grip, shaking from her near fall.

"Ow! Sis, let go of my arm. Put your arm around my shoulders. That's it; now hang on." Jake swept Megan up like he used to when she was young and carried her to the en suite bathroom.

"Put me down, damn it. I can walk, jush not well."

"Yeah, I noticed when you fell into my arms a second ago. I'll let you down next to the john and leave you alone to pee. Call me when you stand again. Kam's got your lunch almost ready." Inside the bathroom, Jake let Megan's legs go and held her steady until he felt her feet touch the floor and she stopped swaying. "Just flush, I'll be outside the door." Stepping outside the bathroom door, he smiled at Kam entering the bedroom with a tray and two tall glasses with straws. "Megan's lunch?"

"Yep. I'll see she eats. Once you get her back in bed, you can go down and finish your burger." Kam set the tray on the night stand and then straightened the blankets before fluffing the pillows while Jake helped Megan walk to the bed.

Both women made shooing motions at him until he left them alone.

"Men are so damned protective. Your brother is just like all the rest. How are you? How bad is the pain?" Kam checked Megan's vitals while she spoke and noticed the lack of color in Megan's face. The trip to the bathroom likely cost her a lot of pain.

"I wish I felt better. There'sh t'ingsh I need to get done." Taking the milkshake, Megan took a long slurp. "Ahhh, that's better than breakfast. What'sh it?"

"Hamburger with lettuce, tomato, mayo and a little mustard. I had to add water to get it thin enough to go up the straw." Kam admitted.

"Shoundsh okay." Megan sucked up a gulp of it and half her face smiled. "Yummy. Need up. Pihsnish 'morrow."

"Finish your lunch, all of it. I'll be right back with Bethany and Jake and you can tell us what you need us to do." Turning, Kam left Megan working on the milkshake again.

In the hall, she almost ran into Jake and Bethany who were standing on the landing outside the bedroom door. Putting her finger to her lips, she moved the pair farther away and whispered. "I put pain meds in the burger. She needs to finish it. The medication should put her back to sleep. Sleep is the best thing for her at the moment. Follow my lead and don't let her get excited. Got it?" She looked from one to the other until they both nodded. Turning, she led them to the bedroom door, opened it and walked in. "Look who's here. Now, whatcha need?" Kam stepped aside, letting Jake hug Megan as she sucked down the last of her burger. Bethany kissed her cheek and picked up the now empty shake glass.

"Beths, pi'nish at your sshtation 'morrow. Sheena knowsh. Check ever'thin." Turning to her brother, she tried to smile until her cheek hurt. "Bro, how'sh Nadia? You talksh to ma?"

"Yep. I spoke with her and went home for dinner after dropping Nadia at the safe house. Nadia's quite a woman. She's given statements about the murder, describing Banks and Poggi as the killer and accessory. She's gutsy. Her height and looks are going to be difficult to hide, but we've got a new identity in the works for her." Jake held her hand for a moment. "Mom said to tell you to follow your doctor's orders and, if she hears you're not, she'll be up here to tie you down until you're healed. She means it too."

Megan felt her eyes closing and fought them open, glaring at her friends when she realized she'd been medicated. "You're in sho mush trouble, Kam." Her eyes closed and she felt hands helping her slide back down into the covers.

"Don't worry, Sweetie. We've got it under control. Tomorrow, we'll let you stay awake longer. The picnic is all arranged. You just sleep." Bethany's voice penetrated the fog of her drugged brain just before sleep overcame her.

Chapter Seventeen

"Megan, come on wake up. You've got a speech to write for the picnic and you have to decide who you want to read it. Look, here's a cup of coffee, warm, with a straw. I think you should be able to open your mouth some, but sucking through a straw is going to be your best option for a few more days. Ahhh, I see those eyes. Sit up and take this." Kam waited by the bed with the coffee while Aaron opened the blinds to let in the bright fall sunshine.

"Babe, you need to get it together. We're leaving for the R-B in about an hour. I'll run your bath." Brushing a light kiss on her forehead, he left the room.

Kam watched him close the bathroom door and heard the water running. "That man really fills out a pair of jeans. If I weren't married...listen to me. It's got to be the pregnancy hormones talking. David suits me just fine. Honestly though, you had better lasso him before some scheming female sinks her claws into him." Turning back to Megan, she took a quick inventory of her patient's vitals. "You'll be happy to know the swelling is going down. The bruising on your cheek has an amazing variety of hues, but we can lighten it with makeup as long as we don't get any into the stitches."

"What timezit?" Even if she worked on enunciation, Megan had to admit she still couldn't open her mouth enough to speak to those attending the picnic. *Damn it all to Hell!*

"It's nine-thirty. We let you sleep in since it's going to be a long day. Now, here's your tablet, open to a blank sheet, and two ibuprofen. Tell me who you want to read it and then get to writing what you want to say to the volunteers." Kam handed Megan the tablet. "By the way, Shirley has come up with three different classes on grid searches and basic first aid being offered in Montrose and Gunnison during the winter. There's also one on winter survival up at the ski resort and a specific CPR class at the high school next week. You might want to mention them in your speech so the volunteers can check their calendars before they sign up." Kam watched Megan tapping letters. As words began to fill the page, Kam left the room, humming softly. Downstairs, she began packing a box with items she'd collected to help Megan be more comfortable on her first day out of bed.

Sitting with her tablet open, Megan entered "Aaron" and then backed up to erase it. A woman had to give this speech, Aaron couldn't sound needy enough and she knew this speech would either encourage everyone to sign up, or the squad wouldn't happen. "Hmmm...Bethshany or Kam?" Picturing the two expectant mothers made her smile. It would have to be Bethany. Not only was she closer to term but she was married to a local rancher. Bethany's goals were closer to everyone else's in Riverview, and the townsfolk could relate better to her. Riverview residents lived by the creed of "Help your neighbors and enjoy small town living." Before she could overthink it, she entered the word "Bethany". That done, she stared at the empty screen, trying to think of an opening.

"All of you have been invited to this picnic today for two reasons. First, to tell you 'thanks for your help' last weekend in locating Jamie Stroud. We were so very fortunate he was located in the

compound, and not in the woods. This incident brought home to me how critical it is to have our own Mounted Search-and-Rescue Unit here in Riverview. We have two guest ranches within ten miles of town, and several more farther out of town which bring tourists to our area. Not only tourists could benefit from such a unit, but our own citizens. It could be one of our pre-school children wandering off after a frog, down into the canyon or into the woods. We need to be trained and ready to move into action at the first indication of a lost hiker, biker, rider, camper or simply a motorist wandering off the highway for some reason. There are classes within driving distance to teach us how to properly organize a grid search and classes to teach us how to survive the rigors of our winter cold if stranded without shelter. Next week there's a CPR class at the high school, and any of us who aren't certified already should attend that class. Anyone at any time could require CPR and knowing how to handle the situation could save a life. Shirley has the sign-up sheet. If you want to be part of this unit, put your name, telephone number and any skills you have already learned. You'll notice Megan's name is the first on the list. we hope to see all your names by the time this day is over. Once again I want to thank you all for showing up today and for volunteering last weekend to help find Jamie. Give yourselves a round of applause."

"I've been informed that there's a donation jug on the table in the pavilion for those who want to donate to this cause. Classes cost money and so does top-notch equipment. I'd like to see at least three satellite phones in this unit. Communication can be critical and there's only so much that can be signaled by shooting into the air. I've also been told that the squad already has some support from local businesses and the guest ranches. I want to thank everyone who has already donated time, or money, or both. You will be the backbone of this unit. Give yourselves another round of applause.

That's about all I can think of to say, except be sure to sign up if you think you can spare the time to help. Even if you don't ride, we *will need ground support to help in the case of an emergency. Non-riders can help with communications, supplies, or any number of needed chores that will free up riders for the search. Another thing to remember is the lost or injured party could be someone you love. Volunteer, and you'll also be in on the best gossip. Someone with a ring-side seat to the action will always have the best stories to tell. Just a few benefits to being part of the Riverview Mounted Search-and-Rescue. Food's ready and available, so help yourselves, but try not to get too much mustard on the sign-up sheet.*

Reading the speech over, Megan made a couple of minor changes before saving it and sending it to the printer attached to the laptop in her office. Heaving a huge sigh, she pushed her tablet away and leaned back into the soft pillows. Her head was pounding and her jaw was sore. Not as painful as yesterday, but she almost wished she could bypass the picnic by and go back to sleep.

"Hey, don't you go back to sleep. Your bath is ready. Do you want to wear your uniform, or those sparkly jeans? I won't let you wear that sexy top, but I can pull out a blouse from your closet, if you like." Aaron came over to the bed and reached into it, lifting Megan out of the covers. "Today, you get only ibuprofen or naproxen. No heavier drugs unless the pain becomes unbearable, okay? You don't need to get hooked over a bruised jaw when you managed to survive without a drug habit after a major wound."

Her feet dangling in space, Megan wiggled, trying to pull her night shirt lower on her exposed thighs. "No uniform. Advil, light blue sshirt, pleashe."

"Stop wiggling, or Kam will need to call Sheena and tell her we'll be late. That, or I'll just go around with blue balls." Aaron chuckled next to Megan's ear. His lips brushing it sent heat all the way to her core.

"Ummmm, I'd shay letsh be late, but I've got a headache." Megan felt his chuckle even as she laughed into his shirt.

"I hope that doesn't become a common thing once we're married."

Megan froze. Married? They hadn't discussed marriage. God, she wasn't ready for marriage. Panic rose and her breathing sped up. She was only now beginning to accept herself and the changes Afghanistan had brought to her life. Marriage with Aaron would be wonderful. But, not yet. Silently she prayed that he wasn't going to ask her anytime soon. Maybe next year, in the spring, she would be ready to think about marriage.

"What's wrong, Babe? Oh, I get it. You're not ready to hear the M word. How about the L word? I might as well toss that at you too. I love you. You gave me a Hell of a scare. Between watching you launch yourself at that bastard and then sitting with you while you were in the hospital, I think I aged at least a decade." Aaron closed the bathroom door behind them and set Megan down on the bench next to the tub. "Now don't faint on me. I didn't mean to spook you so badly. I'm in no rush. I just want you to get used to the idea of love and marriage. I don't want you to think I'm the kind of guy you can use and then walk away from." His eyes twinkled as he tried to look mortified at the idea.

"I do love you. I'm jussst not quite ready to thinksh about marrigesh. Thish iss all new. Give me a shance to ajusst, okay?" Megan watched his face. She didn't want to see hurt or pain in his eyes and when he smiled at her she caught only a hint of rejection there.

Sighing, Aaron kissed her forehead. "Don't worry. I waited a year to have you in my bed, waiting to walk down the aisle will be a snap compared to that. But, I want to have at least one kid, so we don't want to wait more than five years, okay?"

"Kids too?" Megan couldn't keep her voice level. She grew up thinking of having a large family, but somehow as an adult, she'd forgotten that dream. Now, the thought terrified her. She wasn't ready to be responsible for a child, even if Aaron was the father.

"Yeah, at least one. I'm up for adoption or fostering if we can't have any of our own. I think we should be married for at least a year before we begin our family. Come on, jump in the tub. We can talk about this when you feel better." Kissing her lightly, he left her sitting there next to the tub, in shock from all the different ideas he'd brought up.

After rubbing her temples to ease the fading pain from the headache she woke with, she stripped out of her nightgown and slid into the tubful of hot water. OMG. Love, marriage, kids...only a week ago she hadn't really thought about even being intimate with Aaron—wow had things changed. A shaky sigh escaped her as she sat contemplating her toes before she began washing her hair. So many changes on top of smugglers, lost child and the assault on her. Too much to think about now, she had a picnic and a search-and-rescue group to start. Using her right hand, she felt from her ear to the middle of her chin. It didn't seem as swollen and when she tried to open her mouth, she managed to get her teeth apart enough to touch her tongue with her index finger. She hoped wouldn't slur her words so much. Her cheek felt very tender to the lightest touch and she'd seen the colors there. She still looked like a train wreck, even if she was feeling better.

"Megan, you need any help in there? Don't try to stand without me in there. I don't want you to fall and hurt yourself. Aaron has gone out to make certain the horses have enough hay and water. He'll be bringing your Durango around shortly." Kam's voice sounded hollow through the door.

"I'm almost done. Jusst hold on a ssecond while I rinsse." Megan slid under the water to rinse her hair, thankful she'd gotten the perm so that she didn't need to do more than run a brush through it. With Kam and Aaron being in such a rush, that's about all she'd have time to do. Sitting up in the tub she reached for the chain and pulled the old plug before leaning forward to snag one of the towels on the bench. "Okay, come on in. I really don't need your help, but I'm more than glad to have you sstanding by in case I get dizzy. Thanks for everything. My brain knows you've been here two days, but my memory is really fuzzy." Megan moved to stand, clinging to the grab bar next to the tub.

"Here, let me give you a hand." Kam steadied Megan by holding her elbow and helping her to slide out of the tub and down onto the bench. "There. You dry and I'll go get the clothes Aaron laid out for you on the bed."

Megan felt a twinge of annoyance. "I can do this by myself. I've been getting dressed and walking without help for years."

"I know you can. I'm just trying to keep you from doing more damage. At this time, another fall could put you back into the hospital, or worse." Kam's voice held that firm, calm quality used by nurses everywhere.

"Damn it, Kam. Don't patronize me. Between you and Aaron, I'm going to end up in a mental ward." At the hurt look in Kam's eyes, Megan felt about an inch tall. "I'm sorry.

I didn't mean to snap. It's just that my mother is the queen of calming children and that's the tone she always uses." Megan sighed and took the clothing from Kam. "I'll get dressed and meet you down stairs, okay? If I'm not down there in ten minutes, you can come looking and I won't hold it against you if you say 'I told you so'." Megan made shooing motions with her hands to send Kam out of the bathroom, thankfully Kam took the not-too-subtle hint.

Ten minutes later, Megan managed to walk down the stairs without falling on her face, much to her own amazement. Her knees were wobbly and her hands kind of shaky, but she made it. "Hey, I don't mean to slow us down, but can I have an orange juice or toast with jam? My jaw is stiff, but I need to eat. I think some sort of sugar will stop the shakes I'm feeling."

"Kam, didn't you give her any breakfast?" Aaron glared over at Kam.

"I was kind of busy. I thought you would take up the food. Sheesh, men." Kam turned and headed for the kitchen.

Megan heard the microwave and then the blender before Kam appeared at her elbow with a glass of something unidentifiable. "Thanks, that was quick."

"The toast was still sitting on the counter already buttered and the jam was sitting there waiting for someone to spread it over the toast. I put it all in the blender with a spoon of peanut butter, added just a little water to make it blend and here I am. I'm sorry. Aaron and I missed connections on this one. Sit on the step and eat. I'll get you a glass of orange juice too. We're not really late yet." After Megan took the glass, Kam headed back to the kitchen, returning with a tall glass of juice. "Drink all of this. It's good for you."

Her eyes watering, Megan was glad Kam had thought to blend the meal. Today was not the day to start solid food again. Sniffling, she sucked down the meal and drank the juice. "I don't know why I'm sniffling. It's got to be the meds and the amount of time I've spent in bed." She glared at Kam and Aaron who stood staring innocently at her. "You have no idea how amazing that was, or how happy I will be when I can eat again. Now, let's get going or all the food will be gone by the time we get there. I'm still hungry." Her voice was low but the words carried to both of those waiting.

Pulling into the R-B, the pack station grounds seemed crowed with trucks and trailers. Megan counted twenty-seven rigs as Aaron drove around to the parking at the pavilion. "Wow. There are a lot of riders here today. Twenty-seven at least, double that if everyone brought a friend. I wonder how many are locals here for the picnic?" She'd read the logos of ranches in the area on some rigs and recognized several others. "I hope we don't run out of food."

"Sheena likely stocked up. I doubt we'll run out even if everyone in the rigs and cars want hot dogs and hamburgers." Aaron pointed at the crowded parking around the pavilion. "I'll get as close as I can, but I think you better be prepared for a walk. Unless you'll let me carry you."

"No. No way in Hell will I show up for this shindig being carried like an invalid. I got my face hurt, not my legs," Megan huffed, bringing a chuckle out of Kam.

People milled around the pavilion in small groups or wandered from group to group, socializing with their neighbors and friends. At one table, an endless line filed by a stack of paper, signing up and taking an information sheet. It didn't take long to put down your name, phone number and horse, yes or no. Everyone seemed eager to sign up for the Riverview Search-and-Rescue Squad.

One man seemed out of place. A suit and tie, loafers and a briefcase stuck out in a crowd of locals wearing jeans and cowboy hats. Once Megan managed to get to the pavilion, she made her way to the dazed and confused-looking stranger. "Hi, I'm Sheriff Megan Holloway of Riverview. Can I help you?" She extended her hand and the man shook it like a dying man grabbing a life preserver.

"Thank God, you're here. I stopped at your office and the receptionist told me where to find you, but no one here had seen you and I was beginning to think I'd been misdirected. If one more person asked me where I'm from or comments that I'm not from around here...I might have gone off the deep end." His voice had risen as he enumerated the fears he'd had of not locating Megan. Pausing, he gazed around at the sea of faces turned toward him and listening to his every word. An unnerving silence had fallen among those milling around the pavilion. He paused to draw a deep breath and continued. "I'm Jonathan Faust, of Faust and Faust in New York City. I represent George Truman Wesley of Wesley Electronics."

"Welcome, sir, but you still haven't told me what I can do to help you." Megan managed to get her hand free without having to jerk it. A ring of residents had formed around Megan and the attorney while the man was introducing himself and his employer and the hum of conversations had just about quieted.

"It's not what you can do for me, it's what Mr. Wesley can do for you and your town. You recently performed a great service to Mr. Wesley in saving his only grandchild. Jamie Stroud is the light of his life. When Mr. Wesley learned the boy went missing and was found by the Sheriff of Riverview, he decided to establish a grant in Jamie's name. This grant would be awarded every year to the person or group the town feels has shown outstanding compassion or courage in aiding others. This yearly grant will be a cash award of ten thousand dollars. An escrow account has been established at your local bank to pay for ten years of this grant. Funds will be added as needed to cover the future. I have the first check in my briefcase, I want to award it to you, Sheriff Megan Holloway, for your outstanding service and compassion in handling the child." Opening his briefcase, he pulled out a check and handed it to Megan.

Pandemonium reigned as Megan held the check and the man shook her hand a second time. Everyone clapped and began talking at once, surrounding Megan and Mr. Faust, trying to see the check.

Megan felt her eyes well up. Working hard to speak clearly, she looked down at the check in her hands. "I don't know what to say. I was simply doing my job, but you have no idea how much this money is needed. Tell Mr. Wesley that I'm putting this check toward the creation of the Riverview Search-and-Rescue Squad. With it, we'll be able to afford satellite phones and spot locators for the groups who go out searching for lost or injured citizens. On behalf of Riverview and future rescues...Thank you." The pain in her jaw was unfelt as she raised her voice to be heard over the congratulations of her friends and neighbors.

"But Sheriff, Mr. Wesley intended this check to be a reward for you. Not for your town or rescue squad. You should do something personal with the money, not give it away." Mr. Faust seemed shocked by the idea that the money would be turned over to others instead of benefiting Megan.

Sniffling through the tears now leaking from her eyes, Megan forced her bruised face into a grin. Her jaw was on fire from it and the amount of talking she was being forced into. "Mr. Faust, this rescue squad has been in the planning stages since Jamie was found. The only thing that we hadn't figured out was where we would get the money to fund it. This check takes a huge load off my shoulders. You can tell Mr. Wesley I promise that I'll spend at least a hundred dollars on something special for me...but the remainder will go into the kitty to fund the squad properly." Hands pounded Megan on the back as she escorted the attorney to his rented sedan. She stifled a snort as she opened the door...it looked like a sedan an attorney would rent—which is to say—totally out of place here at the R-B.

"Well, I'll explain your reasoning to Mr. Wesley, but I'm certain he will feel as I do that you are wasting something designed to lighten your life. I don't understand why you want to put the money into your group instead of buying clothing or putting a down payment on a home or getting an education." His muttering continued as he closed the car door and put it into reverse. He slammed on the brakes to avoid hitting the pickup parked directly behind him. One of the R-M hands ran over to move the truck. The entire time, he was frowning and shaking his head.

Laughing, Megan let the insult to her education slide and waved the man off the property. Obviously, he didn't know she spoke four languages and had been trained in cryptology and forensic computer science by top military instructors. City people often thought as low of rural Americans as rural Americans thought of city slickers. She had to admit her opinion of those choosing to live tightly-packed in a city was less than charitable.

Turning back to the pavilion, she saw that everyone was smiling at her. Sheena came forward holding a huge container that once had held mayonnaise. "Megan, we were going to wait until after lunch, but with what that dude just gave you, we thought you might want to check out the donations we've had so far today." Sheena pushed the container toward Megan.

"What have you guys been up to? A donations jar? I invited you here to eat, to thank *you* for taking part in the search last weekend—not to cough up cash for the squad. But, hey, I'm not turning money down. Zeke, how long until the food's ready?" Looking over the heads of several friends, she saw Zeke with tongs in his hand.

"Hot dogs are almost ready and the burgers are cooking. Should be about five minutes more for the first batch of 'em." He turned back to attend the grills.

"You heard him folks, Bethany is going to read the speech I put together earlier because if I keep talking...I'm going to need a doctor. Once she's done, you can start a line and fill your plates. If you'll excuse me for a few, I need an aspirin, an ice pack, and a place to sit." Holding the plastic container to her chest like a baby, Megan headed for the lodge. Sheena ran ahead and by the time Megan hit the door, the cook was reaching into the freezer for a frozen bag of peas to use as a cold pack.

Megan took the pack of frozen peas and held it to her face, sighing at the cool, numbing comfort it quickly provided. One hand to her face and one holding the jar, she sat at the counter, staring vacantly, not certain how to begin. "Wow. This is beyond belief."

"Here, Babe. Take these." Aaron passed her two ibuprofen and a glass of water he'd gotten from the sink. He stepped closer to put his arm around her shoulder, gently hugging her and kissing the top of her head. "Good things come to good people, Babe. And, you're the best. Now dump that thing so Sheena can take it back out for the latecomers to fill." His free hand helped her turn the jug upside down and then he passed it to Sheena who was heading out with more food.

Together they sorted through the checks, many of which brought more tears to Megan's eyes. They came from people who seldom had much more than they needed to get by. The one from the Bailey's caught her off balance. They must have dipped into their savings to come up with that amount. Next, they counted the cash, separating the bills by denomination and then by the number needed to create a bundle for the bank. Finally, the change, and there was a boatload of quarters. Someone had broken the piggy bank or robbed a laundromat to come up with that many. Not counting the amount Wesley had given her, the cash totaled just over seven thousand dollars.

Megan lost it. She turned her stool around to grab Aaron and wept into his shoulder. She loved this town, but it never occurred to her that they could support her so sincerely, donating this staggering amount of money. All she could do was cling to him and weep for several minutes.

As her sobs subsided, Aaron hugged her gently before pushing her away to get a good look at her face. "I'll get you a cool cloth. At least you had the cold pack, so your right eye isn't swollen...but your left is a disaster." When she raised her hand to her left cheek, he said, "you sit still. I'll be right back."

Taking the cold pack from her semi-frozen right cheek, Megan laid it against her tear-swollen left eye. A minute later, Aaron took the bag of peas from her and replaced it with a cold, wet cloth wrapped around an ice cube.

The door opened and Kam entered. "Megan, the natives are getting restless out there. Bethany gave the speech as you wrote it, but I think they want to hear from you too." She waited for Megan to climb off the stool. "Great. I'll tell everyone you're on your way. Can I ask, what's the total so far?"

"Just over seven grand." Aaron replied, grinning at the shocked look in Kam's eyes. "I think this is going to be a well-organized and well-turned-out squad. It's about time we had our own." By the time Megan got out there, everyone would know how much had been raised. Nothing was secret in this town for long. "Let's go, Babe. Your public awaits. 'Sides, I'm starved." He considered the pile of money and checks, quickly locating a large pressure cooker with a locking lid. He scraped the money and checks into it, turned the lid to locked and slid the unit onto a lower cabinet shelf. That should keep it safe until later. No one would really steal from Megan, but removing temptation from the scenario was never a bad idea.

Seeing where Aaron put the cooker, Megan chuckled and reminded him, "Don't forget where you put the money. Sheena would crap if she found it tomorrow."

Hearing the megaphone whine, arm in arm, they headed for the door. The future volunteers of the Riverview Search-and-Rescue Squad were waiting for them. Outside the light clouds parted and the sun shone down on the gathering, drawing the autumn chill from the air.

Excitement and anticipation hung over the gathering that waited for Megan. Applause deafened her as she stepped up to the pavilion. From the crowd, a massive, bushy white dog lumbered for Megan at her top speed. While Aaron held the megaphone, Megan knelt and scratched the dog's ears. "Sparkle, how'd you get here? Doc bring you? What a pretty girl you are..." She looked around in time to see the veterinarian waving to her with a huge smile.

A few people shouted, "Speech" "Speech" while rebel yells, hoots and whistles rose up from the crowd.

Stepping up to the megaphone Aaron held out to her, all Megan could do was smile and wave for a moment. When her throat cooperated, she threw them all a huge kiss and said the only thing that was left to say; "Thank you all from the bottom of my heart. *Riverview's going to have the best damned squad in the nation!*" Resounding applause, foot stomping and whistles brought pain to her ears, but the smile never left her face.

The End...for now

Author Kasey Riley

Kasey Riley (Kim) brings a wealth of knowledge to her novels. Her love of the trail, outdoors, and rural living give color and vibrancy to her books. This realism has drawn many readers to her novels. She strives to make readers see through the eyes of her characters and imagine themselves enmeshed in the plot.

She plans on each book being a stand-alone novel that can be read in any sequence without the reader missing details of the story. However, that could change in the future, if she feels the need to link novels. Do Not Assume could be the beginning of a series. It stands alone, but could have sequels which would need the reader to start with Do Not Assume. Do Not Assume came from a discussion between Kasey and her husband, Jeff, in one of the several drives between Oklahoma and their new home in Tennessee. Tossing around an idea about a young woman who keeps being involved in mysterious violence. Coming up with an idea as to why she's involved and solving the situation kept them occupied for many miles. Kasey's mind sees every news article as a possible story plot for her characters to endure. She loves alone time on the trail to work her way through the next plot and create new characters. When not writing or riding, she enjoys reading a wide variety of genre novels and sounding out new plots on her husband of 40+ years. Together, they moved two horses, four dogs, two cats and all their assorted belongings from SE Oklahoma to Central Tennessee in 2016. Starting with a fall 2015 trip to scope out the country, simply because neither had ever been to TN, the state drew them back and the small town on the Cumberland Plateau lured them into moving there. Now able to ride out the back door, Kasey finds less time to write, but has many viable ideas to work from.

Skeleton Trail is a mystery where Megan made her debut and decision to run for Sherriff of Riverview. While it essentially is Kam and Doyle's story, there is a preview of Megan and Aaron's story.

Following are the first two chapters of Skeleton Trail.

SKELETON TRAIL
By Kasey Riley

Prolog

Gunnison County, CO – October 1933

Caleb added an entry to his journal. He placed it carefully into the cracker tin with the other evidence. He put the tin with its precious evidence in the hole he was using to hide it and carefully replaced the flooring. He walked out of the one room cabin, looking back to see if the hiding spot was visible before he headed to town for supplies.

Caleb never saw the gunman or felt the rifle aiming at him as he rode home later. He never heard the shot and felt no pain from the bullet that crashed through his skull causing his body to roll down the gully into the fast rushing shallow creek below.

The killer pulled Caleb out of the creek and took his wallet. He pushed the body over his saddle, walking up the trail for about a mile before he found a large round hole left by a falling tree at the edge of a wash.

He smiled like a kid on Christmas morning. This would save a lot of work. He dumped Caleb's body off the saddle into the hole, filling it with rocks and boulders. No need to put in dirt, critters wouldn't get around those rocks.

Once done, he rode back to collect Caleb's horses. He shrugged down deeper into his coat as snow began falling, signaling the end of good weather in the Rockies and the beginning of another winter.

Chapter One

Gunnison County, CO – Present Day

Megan's blue eyes grew large as she watched in growing horror the rocky bank giving way under Bethany's horse. With the horse scrambling madly, the pair slid backward out of sight. Jumping off Radar, she threw his reins in a tree as the sounds below faded into silence. On hands and knees, she cautiously approached the unstable edge, when she heard Bethany scream. "Bethany, are you okay? Are you hurt?" She cautiously lay on her belly, extending her long frame, and pushing her head and shoulders over the edge of the embankment.

Bethany had kicked free of her stirrups to dive off her horse when she felt him begin to slip backward off the edge of the wash. Coup fought the backward slide, whipping his body around to swim with the rolling dirt and boulders, slinging Bethany's five-foot-four-inch frame from the saddle to land on her backside in the rocks. Landing, she felt a sharp pain, her hips digging into boulders lodged in the bank. She watched Coup stumble down the landslide and saw him come to a stop, on his feet, not thirty feet below where she landed. Automatically, she rolled onto her knees, smacking her helmet on the ground, coming eyeball to eye socket with a human skull. Her breath catching in her throat, her mouth went dry in the split second before her scream startled Coup into moving further away.

"Oh my God! Megan, there's a body down here! Ewww!" Bethany's voice, breathless, then wavering up to a shrill shriek, rose up from the gully to reach Megan.

"What body? To hell with the body. Are *you* okay?" Megan inspected what she could see of her friend from above, looking for blood or obvious injuries. Breathing a sigh of relief, she saw Bethany looked to be only dirty with leaf matter stuck between the bill of her helmet and her forehead. She seemed more concerned with her discovery than with herself.

"I'm okay, I think. I landed where I have the most padding." Her eyes went to Coup, who was walking over to a patch of late oats to graze. Relief flooded her. He seemed to be moving okay, but she could see some blood staining his back right stocking. Knowing he wouldn't wander farther than the closest food, she looked up at Megan. "Are you going to lie there all day, or climb down here to see this?"

"Well, I don't want to start another landslide. Does the ground look solid?"

"Yeah, I think Coup's weight was the issue that caused the ground to give way. The creek's been undermining this bank for years." She looked both directions, seeing several spots where the upper ground extended over the gully by as much as five feet. "If you work your way down from where you are, on an angle toward the bottom of the gully, you should be fine," she advised. This gully was going to be a tough one to create a decent trail across because of the constant erosion. She gingerly touched the small of her back and felt the growing welt where she'd landed against a rock. She knew it was going to hurt later. Looking again at the skull, she frowned. What had this poor person ever done to wind up buried out here with no marker? Sadness welled up in her at the thought of his or her family who had never known the reason for the disappearance of their loved one.

Megan stood up, took a deep breath, and began to work her way toward Bethany. She hated heights and steep spots, no matter if she was on foot or horseback. Bethany was standing by the time she reached her. They both leaned over the wide hole to get a better look at the skeleton.

"I wonder how it got here. That hole looks like maybe a bullet hole. What do you think?" Megan pointed to the smallish round hole on the left side of the skull, and then swallowed back nausea at the mummified tissue and cloth visible beyond the skull.

"This hollow looks like an old hole created by an uprooted tree. I've seen root holes larger than this after a strong wind." Bethany pointed to bits of what looked to be tree roots along one side of the hole. "I don't think this person died here, unless they took shelter or hid in here. No way could he or she fall so perfectly into a hole. Maybe they froze here in a storm after seeking shelter." Bethany frowned in distaste and shook her head in sorrow at the thought of a wounded person trying to hide from a killer, but knew in her heart, if it was a bullet hole, the victim likely had never known what hit him or her.

"Yeah, I don't think this boulder walked up from the creek bed by itself." Megan hefted a five-pound rock located just inside the hole. "Now what're we gonna do?" She looked at the bones with desiccated tissue surrounded by rocks nestled in the shallow hole in the bank. "I think we shouldn't move anything until a forensics expert works the scene. There might be evidence in the hole with the body."

"Let's put back the rocks we know rolled out of the hole, geocache the location, tie a ton of ribbon on the trees above the bank and across the way, and start looking for the most direct route out of here to the closest road. The authorities are going to need a trail from the road to the body, preferably a short trail. We can call them when we get back to camp," Bethany suggested. She gave her friend a kind of lopsided grin. "The only good thing I can think of about all of this is now I have a name for the trail and maybe the ride I'm planning. This will be the 'Skeleton Trail Loop' and the ride can be something to do with murder and mayhem or the skeleton. Help me think of a good name?" she asked her friend. "Maybe hold it on Halloween or as a night ride and call it the 'Ghost 50'?"

"Your mind is never far from endurance, is it?" Megan shook her head and began to brush the dirt off Bethany's back. She stopped when Bethany winced, gasped, and jumped away from her hand.

"Ouch, careful. I'm going to have a nasty bruise. Why don't you go get Radar and I'll finish brushing off my butt and head down to Coup." She turned away from Megan with her hands lightly covering the injured area. "He looks like he has a cut on his back leg," she said over her shoulder while she watched her friend climb back up to her horse. Bethany stood a moment longer, gently feeling out the size and location of the growing painful welt of bruised flesh before she cautiously climbed down to inspect her horse.

Above, Radar stood happily trimming the tree where his reins hung over a branch. He looked around as Megan approached. Damn, the day had started out so well. She frowned at the thought of the complications and the fact that Bethany seemed to be in more pain than she wanted her to know. Roger would not be happy that she failed to keep his wife from injury. Not that she could have foreseen the situation, but he had specifically told her to take care of Bethany; even though Bethany seemed completely capable of taking care of herself. Crap. She untangled the reins from the tree, unclipped them from the bit, and clipped one end on the halter part of the halter bridle.

"I'm going to ribbon the tree up here before I follow you. No sense in making two trips up and down," she called to Bethany. Taking the roll of orange surveyors' tape off her saddle, she unwound several yards. She broke it up into strips and tied them all over the tree Radar was munching, making it look more like an orange Christmas tree than an aspen. Next, she led Radar to the spot where she would begin her decent and tied several strips of tape around smaller boulders before stacking them. She led her horse past the hole with the skeleton, marking a turning spot for the zigzag path down to the bottom of the gully. Looking back up the side of the wash, the orange tape screamed out of the browns of the fall and the earth tones of the rock. Yep, no one with eyes would miss this spot along the trail she surveyed with a grim smile.

Bethany waited with Coup at the edge of the dry creek. During the wet season, it would be deep, but at the end of summer, there was only one small puddle left to be seen. "I think we can make the trail go up over there. It looks like solid footing and for some reason, the wall isn't quite so steep. I expect the Trailmaster might choose a different spot, but let's start there because it's close to the overall trail." She pointed across the gully to where the ground slanted up at a less severe angle.

"Sounds good to me. Let's go, boss lady. You lead." Megan agreed and urged Bethany onward. Megan stepped her long legs and lanky frame onto the tall Appaloosa's before Bethany mounted her more petite Arab gelding. She saw Bethany wince as she settled into her endurance saddle. "Hey, do you need a pain killer? I've got everything from Advil to Tylenol-3 in my trail kit," She offered.

"I'll take a couple of Advil. The stronger stuff just makes me dizzy and nauseous. The last thing I need on horseback is dizziness." Bethany managed to smile back at Megan, but her face was paler than normal.

Digging out the packet of pills, Megan handed them over. During the past month of living at the R-M ranch, renting the house once occupied by Roger's uncle Phil, she had come to like both her new bosses and grown protective of them. Bethany worked hard creating the new pack station and guest ranch/campground, while Roger managed the cattle and horse ranch his family had owned for generations.

The R-B, which stood for Roger-Bethany, would offer wilderness trips for eco-tourists and trails for all levels of equestrians. With electric camping spots for guests hauling rigs with living quarters or regular RV's, cabins for guests arriving without horses or RV's, and horses for those without animals, it would bring new business to Riverview. They planned guided trips up the mountains and overnight or day options, along with a beautiful lodge for dinner, dancing, and gatherings. They were sinking a big chunk of money into this venture. The purchase of an additional two thousand acres at a land auction this past spring had begun the project. Then receiving permits from the Forestry to put trails for equestrians into the woods with the assistance of a certified Trailmaster had sealed the deal for the new project.

Bethany and Megan started the day at the campground, using Megan's GPS to store the trail they marked with ribbon through the woods and over hills.

Bethany wanted this to be about a fifteen-mile loop that would have overlooks and stopping points, but work its way back to the main camp. For the eco-tourists, it would be a daylong ride with lunch at a meadow. For the more experienced riders and the endurance competitors, it would be a two- to five-hour trail ride. They hoped to have it marked out by sundown, but now with the need to locate the closest road, who knew how long it would be before they would be able to finish the loop. Her spirits drooped at the thought that the loop might not get finished before snowfall. Double crap.

At the top of the gully, Bethany pulled out a folded quadrant map from the USGS. The trail they had been following went off to the left. They were about seven miles from where they had started. "Did you geocache this spot? We'll need to be able to give the coordinates to the authorities."

"Yep. Got it safely stored. What does the map show?"

"Well, if we follow the trail to the left long enough, maybe three or four more miles, we should come to BLM 26. It's not much of a road, but it would allow vehicles to park within walking distance." Bethany pointed to the left, indicating the direction they should go. "Road access might also work in our favor, allowing crews or an event photographer access to this trail in a competition." Bethany thought aloud, imagining competitors needing water for themselves and their hot, hardworking horses.

Following Bethany's lead to the left, Megan stopped to put up ribbons of orange tape, while Bethany went ahead to mark further up the trail. Finding the closest road would give summer riders access to help if they needed it. Riders often overestimated the condition of their horses and then needed help getting back to base camp. Forest roads, even nasty ones, have saved many horses and riders.

"Boss, look up there. Is that a trail to the left? Maybe it goes to the road or a cabin on BLM 26?" She pointed at a faint Y in the trail marked by three stacked rocks followed by several rocks laid in a row.

"Hmmm, that's possible. Let's check it out for about a mile. We come up with nothing in that time, we'll come back here and continue on this track. I think this might be the old trappers' trail used between the towns along the Gunnison back before the highway was built lower in the valley." Bethany put ribbon marking the junction low in a pine tree. Three ribbons marking the turn and another past the turn, almost out of sight to show the side trail. "Why don't you put the regular trail-marking ribbon on the right, where it will draw the eyes away from this junction? I don't want to divert riders, but I want to be able to find this trail again."

Megan marked the right side of the trail they had been riding, and then rode ahead on the side trail, while Bethany was tying ribbons at the junction. She put one in the evergreen tree at the top of the rise. Bethany passed her as they had been marking trail all day, going another distance up the trail before tying ribbon on the right side of the faint trail. Megan caught her and they topped a rise together to see a cabin nestled in the broad valley below.

"Look at that! There's a cabin down there." Bethany paused to admire the serenity of the scene.

"Wow! Bet we can beat you there! Maybe the owners have a decent satellite phone for us to reach the sheriff." Megan dug her heels into Radar and the gelding surged forward, carefully finding the trail down the hill into the low, lush valley before breaking into a soft gallop toward the cabin on the far side.

They were almost there when Coup caught up, put a nose in front of Radar, pinned his ears at the gelding, and flipped his tail. Radar, having a beta-type personality, immediately pulled up and let the alpha gelding take the lead.

"Coup has the best 'sneer' in this region." Bethany laughed at Megan's surprised expression. "He can make just about any horse he gets next to pull up and let him go by, just by pinning his ears and lifting his head at them," she explained, bringing him to a slow trot and then a walk when they approached the cabin. "I once won a race to the finish by that bit of horse interaction. Oh no! We won't find any phones here, sat or otherwise. Look at the door." She pointed to the cabin door. It leaned into the frame and hung by one old leather hinge.

"You're right. This place has been vacant a while, if the debris on the porch is any indicator." Megan agreed, noticing the leaves and dirt blown against the cabin wall. She dismounted from Radar and handed his reins to Bethany before she turned to walk carefully up the rough-hewn log steps to the remains of the porch.

"Be careful. I don't want you to get hurt. If it looks like it won't open, leave it, and we'll bring the boys back to investigate," Bethany warned, gingerly dismounting from Coup. "Damn, now my pants are starting to rub where they cross that bruise."

Megan laughed over her shoulder at her friend. "Guess it's going to be some time before you ride out again. We really should head home so you can get some ice on that swelling." Nevertheless, she still lifted the door to open it and peered into the dimly-lit cabin. "Wow, it looks like someone just left it yesterday, except for the dust. Looks all ready for the owner's return." Megan's voice reflected the awe she felt looking into this snapshot back in time. She could see the cot with the rumpled bedroll along one wall, the large pot hanging over the dead fire in the fireplace, the two-plank table, and split-log bench pushed against the closest wall to her, all waiting for the homeowner's return. She sneezed three times in a row, wiped her eyes and nose on the back of her glove, and said, "Yep, lots of dust, but wow, there's even still a book lying open on the table. Wonder what was being read the last time this place was occupied?"

"I don't think you should go in there. It could be dangerous. What if the floor gives way?" Bethany warned while she stood at the bottom of the steps holding the horses.

"The floor looks strong. Those planks must be at least two inches thick. I wonder if there's a name inside the book." Picking her way softly across the plank floor, she made it to the table in three careful steps. "Wow, it's a Bible. Kind of gives me goose bumps. There's a stub of a candle and a stub of a pencil here with it. Wonder what he'd been writing?" Megan touched the candle and pencil before her hand rested on the open Bible. It was open to the book of Luke in the New Testament. No telling which verse had been the last one read. Again, she got goose bumps thinking that here was something cherished by a person who had never come back to collect his things.

"Check it to see if there's a family name or inscription. Bibles have always been used to record family events." Bethany took one step up and decided to remain where she was when the tightening of the skin across her backside made her gasp.

Lifting the dusty book without removing her riding gloves, Megan mentally noted the page number before closing the volume and opening the front page. "This Bible is the property of Caleb Preston," she read aloud to Bethany. "The first part is printed inside and the name was handwritten on a vacant line." She fanned the pages to find the original spot in Luke to set the book back down where she found it. A single folded sheet of paper slipped from the center of the Old Testament to land on the floor at her feet.

"Wow, Bethany, there was a sheet of paper folded up in the Bible." She set the book down on the table, open to the correct page before bending over to lift the sheet and shake out the folds very gently to avoid tearing the thin paper. "It looks like a letter. The handwriting is much too fine to be written by the same hand that signed the Bible." She moved a step closer to the door for better light, and then read:

October 2, 1933   Montrose, Colorado

Dear Caleb,

Thank you ever so much for the work you have been doing to find the killer of my husband. The new sheriff has been around asking questions about the "person" I've hired to investigate my husband's death. From the way he was acting, I think that not only was he unhappy with your investigation, but that he also feels threatened in some way. He told me that I needed to let go of this search and accept that the villains who shot Tuck have long since left Riverview.

Caleb, I'm worried for your safety. If Sheriff Miller is involved in Tuck's death, he can be very dangerous. Maybe you should quit searching until next spring. By then, Miller might no longer care about your investigation. I can't stand the thought of you risking your life to bring Tuck's murderer to justice.

Please be careful and let me know if there is anything I can do to help you. Tuck didn't leave much, but I know you must be getting short of funds. I can wire you money if you need help to get through the winter. Or, maybe you can get your old job back with the Cole spread.

I'm doing fine and I feel the baby move often, so I know he'll be born to carry on his father's name. I just know it's a boy; he's so feisty, kicking all the time. I'll be praying for your safety and I hope to see you soon. Maybe you can get here for either Thanksgiving or Christmas. My mother and I would love to have you as a guest to show our appreciation for all of your hard work since Tuck's death.

Respectfully,

Angelica Tucker

Walking outside while she read, Megan used the bright sunlight to see the beautiful script. "Wow, I wonder if our skeleton is Caleb Preston. Maybe he got too close to finding the killer of his friend Tuck. Since the writer's name is Angelica Tucker, we should be able to assume that her husband was called 'Tuck' because it was short for Tucker." She handed the letter to Bethany. "Wonder what Tuck's first name was. I bet we can find a history in the papers of the day, since we know the man was killed within eight months or so of October in 1933.""Yeah, even in those days, babies took nine months, so if she was feeling it kick a lot, it's likely she was in her third trimester." Bethany looked over the paper in the sunlight trying to find any further information she could about the writer or the person who received it. "No envelope? Wish we could know where he received this letter. What town, post office, or maybe even at the Cole Ranch." She turned the paper over again and searched for clues.

"I could go in and search the cabin for more," Megan offered, turning back to the cabin door.

"*No!*" Bethany ordered. "I mean, no. That's not a good idea. If anything happened, I wouldn't be able to help you. Sorry, I didn't mean to shout. It's just scary with you in there and me out here." She apologized for her outburst. "Let's keep the letter to turn over to the authorities and head out to the road."

"Yeah, you're right. We could spend hours looking around this place for clues. Let me get this door closed." Megan suited action to words, lifting the door on its single hinge back into place, leaning against the frame. She stepped lightly down to Bethany and took Radar's reins. "Do you need a leg up?"

"I think I can still mount, but, I won't get off again until I'm home." Bethany muttered, turning to lift her left leg into Coup's stirrup. She grabbed his mane to pull herself into the saddle, settling into the seat, but keeping most of her weight on her feet to avoid resting her bruised lower back against the cantle, stifling a groan, even with all the care she took.

"You sure you can ride okay?" Megan asked.

"I can make it. I once finished a twenty-five mile race with a similar injury in the first five miles. I can ride, but I won't be able to move tomorrow," she confided, trying to keep the irritation from her voice. She knew the pain was making her snappish and didn't want to hurt Megan's feelings.

"Okay, let's get back to the main trail." Megan took the lead. At the junction of the trails, she dismounted and surveyed the placement of the ribbons to make certain riders would go straight and likely never see the side trail. "The turn is almost invisible. I doubt anyone will be up this trail before we bring back the authorities," she commented, mounting up.

After marking trail for another couple of miles, they finally heard a vehicle crunching on a dirt or gravel road almost dead ahead.

"Yippee! I knew the road had to be close. I am sooo ready to reach civilization." Bethany sighed in relief.

"Why don't I ride on ahead while you mark the spot where the trail comes out to the road? I can use my phone and call the sheriff," Megan offered. She actually planned to call Roger. They needed the trailer.

"Huh? Okay, let's get down to the road first, and then you can ride up to the ridge crest to get the best reception." Bethany agreed, while Coup cautiously picked his way down the twenty-foot embankment to the gravel road. He automatically turned and angled down the slope, while she placed one hand on the cantle and the other on his neck to balance herself against the angle of decent.

Megan sat on Radar at the top of the embankment, watching until Bethany reached the bottom, and then let Radar pick his way down the same slope. Radar had watched Coup and followed the same path without hesitation. Once at the bottom, Megan turned to Bethany, who was tearing off strips of orange surveyors tape.

"Hold on to Coup and I'll let Radar canter up the hill," she warned, and then clucked to Radar, letting the gelding set off at his sweet rocking chair gait up the gravel road.

At the top of the hill, she was happy to see her phone showed reception at three bars. Relief flooded her while she speed dialed the R-M Ranch house phone.

"Hello, this is Shorty." Shorty's voice was music to Megan.

"It's Megan. Is Roger there?"

"Nope, he's out in the barn working with that new youngster."

"Okay. Here's what I need you to do. Go tell Roger we need him to bring the two-horse trailer. Take BLM 26 to the left just before the county line. Follow it south-southeast. We're coming out that way and will meet him. Bethany is in pain. She's toughing it out, but I think she needs a lift. Oh, and tell Roger we found a body. From the GPS markers, I think it's in the National Forest lands."

"WHAT?!" Shorty shouted into the phone, causing Megan to hold it out from her face. "A body? Bethany's hurt? You better give me something better than that or Roger will come unglued," he warned.

"Coup stumbled and slid down a hill. Bethany dove off and landed on her butt. She has a serious bruise, but insists on riding. She landed almost eye-to-eye with an old skeleton in a hole in the embankment," Megan patiently told the man. "Think that's enough information to calm him down?" she asked.

"Well, it sounds a dang site better than 'Come out and get us because Bethany's hurt and needs you and by the way we found us a body.' Sounds," Shorty snarled. "I'm on my way out to the barn. Don't be surprised if he calls you."

"Well, I'm headed back down the hill to help her mark the trailhead, so he might not reach me. Just get him moving with the trailer, okay?" Megan's patience slipped and her voice sounded sharp with the question. "Sorry, Shorty. I'm tired and this day has been kind of crappy. Not your fault. Just tell Roger everything is fine, but we need him…with the trailer," she told the man as she closed the call. She turned Radar back toward Coup and let him long trot back down the grade. She saw Bethany had marked the boulders with spray paint and walked up the incline to tie ribbons around the trees at the top of the embankment.

"Hey, you shouldn't have dismounted. I could have done that painting," Megan called to her.

"It's okay. I want to walk for a while anyway. It might keep me from getting so stiff." Walking back down the trail in the embankment, she was pleased that the ribbon was barely visible from the road. That would keep any nosy people from following the trail back to the body. She wanted the spot to be visible "if you looked hard on the left side."

Observing Bethany's handiwork, Megan said, "Looks good. If you know where to look, you can find it."

"That's exactly what I want. Geocache this spot for me and we can be on our way." Turning, she led Coup up the road toward the ridge. "I take it you managed to reach the ranch. How upset was Roger?"

"Well, I haven't talked to him. Shorty took the message to him out in the barn. I expect one of our phones will ring the moment we get reception." Megan no sooner finished the phrase than her phone gave a half-hearted ring and went silent. "I expect that's him. He'll try again in a minute or two. Maybe by then I'll have better reception."

Bethany laughed, but it ended in a groan. "Damn, now it even hurts to laugh. That bruise must be swelling more. It sure is rubbing on my pants." She finished just as her phone gave a demanding shrill ring. "I've got to change that ring tone. By the time I can answer the phone I'm already in a foul mood from the noise," she muttered, digging out the offending item and flipping it open. "Hi, Honey. No, I'm okay, just bruised and sore. Megan said what? Well, she's exaggerating. I can too ride if I wanted to." Bethany glared at Megan while she listened to her husband. "Okay, I know the junction you're talking about and we're about a mile from there. If you're just hitching up, we should be there within about five minutes of you. Just take something to read and wait for us." She closed the phone. "I've got a bone to pick with you. You told Shorty that I couldn't ride? What were you thinking?" her voice rising with the second question.

"Well, what I told Shorty and what he told Roger are two different things, unless Roger has a tendency to blow things he hears out of proportion." Megan looked squarely at her friend. She wasn't going to justify herself any further and if Bethany wanted to be angry, maybe it would ease the discomfort she was feeling from hiking up the road. Megan got off and took Coups' reins so Bethany could move more easily.

"Okay, I forgive you. Shorty does have a problem with retelling what he hears. You might want to keep that in mind and have him write down messages. Force him to read back what he wrote," Bethany advised.

Megan snorted. "Yeah, like he would agree to that. Some people just have no good relationship with truth and unvarnished information." She shook her head and walked on ahead of Bethany, giving the woman space enough to groan, if needed, without embarrassment.

Chapter Two

Roger's hands shook after speaking with his wife. Hitting the button to settle the gooseneck trailer onto his truck, everything seemed to be moving in slow motion except his thoughts. He shuddered at his vision of Coup rolling down an embankment over the top of Bethany.

Shorty told him she was fine, except that there was so much pain, she couldn't stand to ride. Knowing it had to be something serious to force Bethany to call for the trailer, he considered calling the EMTs to meet him out where he was going to meet the girls. No, she'd kill him for over-reacting. But, damn it, the EMTs would be better equipped to judge the severity of her injury than he was.

Fuming about the stubbornness of this woman who had captured his heart, he recalled her jumping back on a horse to finish a seventy-five mile competition after surviving a kidnap attempt before their marriage. More guts than common sense he mused, checking the connections, latching the hitch, and making certain all the doors were secure. Jumping into his running truck, he spun gravel into the air as he headed out to collect his woman and her friend.

He turned right onto the highway, trying to picture where he needed to turn off the main road. Megan told Shorty it was BLM 26, just before the county line. He knew that road. There was one junction, and that was where he could turn this rig around to wait for them. Or, at least park and leave it to walk further up the road to find them. He wasn't certain he could sit and wait patiently if the girls weren't in sight when he got there.

BLM signs never lasted out here, but he saw the road he wanted on the left. Turning onto it, he took the next turn left, making it close to a U-turn. A short distance later, he turned right and headed south-southeast into the public lands. About two miles further, he spotted the junction. Knowing this road got nasty the higher it went, he would have to park here.

Slowly pulling past the turn, he backed the trailer around it until the rig rested on the side road. Turning off the truck, he drummed his fingers on the steering wheel, watching the side mirror for any signs of riders. He gave the horn a couple of long honks to announce his arrival. His patience at an end, he locked the truck and began walking up the road, watching and listening for signs of life. From the top of the first rise, he could only see another hill in front of the higher mountains. He walked down and up to the top of that hill, only to see another. Still no riders in sight. He tapped his foot, wondering if they were just beyond the next hill. He pulled out his phone, happy to see three bars before he speed-dialed his wife.

Bethany sighed when her phone let out the shrill ring tone Roger had selected. "Damn, doesn't he know we'd make better time if I didn't need to answer the phone so often?" She muttered before opening the flip phone. "Hi, Honey. We heard your horn. You must be just over the next hill."

"I just wanted to see if you heard it. Can you tell how far you are from the junction?" He heard the exasperation in her voice and knew she must be in pain. Normally she was happy to hear from him. "Do you want me to try backing the rig up the road so you won't have so far to ride?"

"Roger, I'm perfectly able to walk. We're leading the horses because I was getting stiff riding," she soothed.

"Don't believe it, Roger! She couldn't get back up on Coup. That's why she's walking!" Megan called loud enough for Roger to pick up.

"Is that true? You couldn't get back onto Coup? That does it. I'm taking you to the clinic and you're going – no arguments." His voice sounded stern enough that Bethany knew she would have to do as he wanted.

"Yes, Dear. Just for you, I'll go to the clinic for an x-ray," she conceded quietly.

Roger hung up more worried than ever. She never allowed him to boss her. She was far too stubborn to admit to injury or illness. She must be worried. He dialed the clinic in Riverview to set up an emergency appointment for an x-ray. The receptionist agreed he could bring her in as soon as they could get there.

He sat down on a convenient boulder next to the road and again found himself drumming his fingers while he waited on the women. Staring at the top of the next hill, his eyes were watering when a couple of boulders seemed to be moving. He stood up and the higher vantage point showed the upper torsos of two women and the heads of the horses following them. Putting his fingers to his lips, he whistled and waved at them.

Megan heard the whistle and waved at Roger. She doubted he saw her because he had begun running down the hill toward them. "Damn fool man. He's going to hurt himself running on this loose gravel." No sooner was that said, than Roger's feet slid out from under him and he sat heavily in the middle of the gravel road.

"Well, at least, I won't be the only one with a sore ass," Bethany hooted, laughing at her husband.

Megan watched Roger stand up slowly before dusting himself off and continuing to walk, instead of run, down the incline. She sighed in relief. "Looks like he hurt his pride more than his butt. That's good because there's no way I could have gotten him back up the road if he broke something," she muttered.

The women met him at the bottom of the hill. Megan stood admiring the tenderness Roger showed when he gathered his wife into his arms. "Are you okay? Can you show me where it hurts? You had me worried." All the words tumbled out of his mouth while his hands roamed up and down her arms and his eyes took in the lines of stress and pain showing on her face.

Huffing in exasperation, Bethany pulled free of his arms, whipped around, and dropped her riding tights below her injury. "Both of you get a good look. It's the only chance you'll get. Now, just let me be." A black bruise ran from left to right across the top of her hipbones. It was about three inches wide from top to bottom and about six or seven inches from left to right. The entire thing was swollen above the surrounding flesh by about a half inch at the center with a defined red line across it. "Are you happy now?" Pulling her tights back over the swelling, she grimaced.

"Boy, you can really tell exactly where you hit. It must have been a flat edge piece of shale or slip rock," Megan remarked.

"Yes, you definitely need that x-rayed. You might have chipped your hipbone on either side." Roger couldn't resist pulling her back into his arms and kissing the top of her head. "Let's get you out of here. Do you want to continue walking, or would you like me to put you up on Coup? I could carry you," he offered.

"For crying out loud, both of you are treating me like I'm dying. It's only a *bruise* – get it?" Bethany pulled out of Roger's embrace. She really wanted to stay there, but knew the more she let him coddle her, the more he would worry. It wasn't like her. "Just throw me up on Coup and we'll ride back to the trailer, unsaddle, and load them while we wait for you to catch up."

Bending, Roger grabbed her calf, lifting her up so she could land gently in the saddle, smiling because her frustration and anger were more like what he expected than the quiet "yes dear" she had been offering.

"Thanks. See you at the trailer," she told him, setting off at a trot up the hill.

Scrambling onto Radar, Megan followed. She looked back only once to see Roger jogging up the road after them. Catching Bethany just as she got to the top of the hill, she said. "Okay, you can slow down now. He can't see you." She understood why Bethany had taken off, but she didn't agree with the reasoning. She knew that Bethany was proving to her husband that she was "fine."

"Was it that obvious?" Bethany slowed Coup to a walk, standing in the stirrups to relieve the pressure on her bruise.

"Only to someone who has used the same ruse," she responded. "If we keep 'em to a fast walk, we can be over the next rise before he's halfway down this hill. That way he won't see you standing in the stirrups."

They kept the horses moving so that Roger only got a glimpse of them cresting that final hill. After sitting down when he tried to run in the loose gravel, he kept his downhill pace at a brisk walk, only jogging when the angle of the grade was uphill. He knew they had slowed once he was out of sight. He trusted Megan to control the pace and she was smart enough to slow Bethany down.

Roger had a lot of faith in the common sense of his new hand. Any person, regardless of gender, who had been through what she had and kept her wits rather than give in to pain and fear, had his full respect and admiration. Uncle Sam didn't give the Silver Star for just any reason. It takes a special personality type to be able to hold terror at bay while buried in the rubble, and stay on the radio with the enemy in the same room. It was a shame her wounds had washed her out of the Army. He knew she wanted to be a career soldier and was experiencing problems returning to civilian life. Using her to help Bethany create and run the R-B was his contribution to her rehabilitation.

Topping the final rise, he saw the girls had the saddles off the horses and Bethany was leaning against the trailer while Megan put the horses into it. Her face was pale, even from a distance. One hand was against the wheel well and she wiped her mouth with the other. He guessed that she had vomited from the pain of dismounting and unsaddling, too damn stubborn to wait for assistance from either him or Megan. Frowning, he shook his head and kept walking.

Reaching her, he took her into his arms. "It's a good thing I love you, 'cause your stubbornness could test the patience of a saint." He murmured into her hair while she turned her face into his chest, resting her forehead against it.

"Yeah, I know, but you would worry more if I sat back and let you do everything." Her arms went around his waist for a quick hug before she pushed him away. "Let's get out of here. The clinic won't wait all day for us." Her smile let him know she guessed he'd called them already.

"Do you think you can sit, or would you prefer to lie across the back seat for the drive to Riverview?"

"I think I can sit." She walked to the cab of the truck.

Opening the door, he gently placed both hands around her waist, lifting her. He froze when her breath caught as she bent at the waist to put her butt into the bucket seat. "Are you certain you want to try?" He watched carefully. "There's no shame in just laying on your stomach across the back seat. I won't tell anyone and neither will Megan." He assured her, trying to get her to acknowledge that the back seat would be a better idea.

"*No. I am going to sit.*" Gritting her teeth, she would not let Roger win this battle, even if he was right. She just wasn't going to give in to his coddling. She would stay sitting, in spite of the pain.

"Okay, okay, do it your way. I suggest that you leave your seatbelt loose and sit forward, holding onto the dash so the bumps won't force you deeper into the cushion." He conceded to her pigheaded stubbornness.

Megan came around to the truck from securing the animals and tack. "You two done figuring out which is more stubborn?" She smiled at the couple. She hadn't heard much, but the sight of them made it obvious to her that there had been a mild confrontation between Mrs. "I'm all right" and Mr. "No, you're not" that she was happy to have missed.

"Yeah, I let her win. She get's really nasty if I don't." Roger grinned.

"I guess in that case, I've got the back seat all to myself?" Opening the back door on the drivers' side, she climbed into the truck.

Climbing in, Roger automatically checked the mirrors, started the truck, and gently pulled out, headed for the highway. He watched his wife from the corner of his eye, but other than her knuckles turning white on the dash a couple of times, she seemed to be handling the rough road okay. Trying to avoid any holes he could, the truck crawled along. One section was washboard for about a quarter mile and there wasn't much he could do about it. More color drained from Bethany's face until they reached the highway.

From there, they had only about a fifteen-minute drive to town, paved the entire way. Relaxing his grip on the wheel after making the right turn and slowly bringing the truck up to speed, he looked over at Bethany. Her knuckles were returning to normal color where she gripped the dash, her eyes were closed, and he could tell she was breathing against the pain. "We made it through the worst part. Stubborn as you are, I'm proud of you, but I would be happier if you had laid down on the back seat." She gave him a valiant attempt at her sassy grin, but with the paleness of her face, it fell short.

"I'm calling Shorty to tell him we're on our way to the clinic in Riverview. He can bring your car and take the truck and trailer back to the ranch," Megan suggested.

"Good idea. The car will be a smoother ride home for her. She could even lie down in the back." Roger glanced meaningfully at his pale wife. Waiting for Megan to finish talking to Shorty, he changed the subject. "So, Megan, tell me about the body Shorty said you found on the trail." He wanted to get her report while it was still clear in her mind and before the chaos of the clinic.

"Yes, Sir. Bethany found it, when she jumped off Coup. She screamed. I never realized someone her size could be that loud. I was off Radar fast. I made it to the edge, getting a good look at her before she told me why she screamed. Man, I was so relieved. I thought that moving had caused her pain and I was going to need the Spot 2 Messenger to get us out of there." She paused to find the water bottle she had stashed in her pocket, took a drink, and recapped it.

"May I ask why you two didn't use the Spot 2 to bring help in rather than try to ride out?" his disapproval obvious when he glared at his wife, then looked in the mirror to make eye contact with his employee.

"Don't give the girl a hard time, Honey. When all this happened, it didn't hurt much and I was mobile. No sense bringing in a helicopter and the Marines, if I could ride. It's only been since it started swelling that the pain got worse." Bethany chided him and protected Megan.

"Okay, but next time – if there ever is one – call for help," Roger ordered them. "Go on, Megan. Continue."

"Yes, Sir. Well, I got down to her level, and sure enough, there was a skull sticking out of the ground and rocks that had fallen away from it. We looked closer and could see what looked to be a bullet hole in one side and a good portion of the bone gone on the other." She shuddered at the memory. "The rocks were kind of piled around the skull, so we moved a few and found what looked to be the remainder of the body surrounded by rocks. We stopped there, didn't move any more, and carefully replaced what we'd moved. He wasn't laid out flat. I think I saw a kneecap up next to his scapula, if I remember my anatomy of the human skeleton correctly." She scratched her head, remembering how the form looked to be crumpled onto itself in the hole.

"Anyway, we put a mound of rocks over the skull so that it would be protected from critters and weather, like that would help him at this point." She snorted. "Then we marked the spot with ribbon to show the location of the grave. Bethany was moving okay, so we geocached the location and headed on up the faint trail we had found." She made eye contact with Roger in the mirror. He nodded at her, both to continue and approval of their actions.

"We figured we would be closer to a road by going forward than going back. The trail might be easier, so we could move more quickly. Our marking became secondary with ribbon being further apart, since the trail was obvious; faint, but obvious. It might have been the old main trail to Cimarron back in the day," she mused aloud. "Then we found a side trail. Not as obvious, but we thought that it might lead to a cabin or closer road, so we followed it about a half mile. All we found was an old, and I mean really old, cabin. It was still intact, but abandoned long ago by anything, but maybe mice." She paused. She knew that Roger was going to give her grief over the fact that she and Bethany had spent time investigating the cabin when Bethany was injured. "Bethany still was going strong, not looking that pale or giving any obvious signs of pain, so we rode over to the cabin and I went inside to check it out."

She kept her head down, refusing to meet Roger's glare in the mirror, and then quickly continued. "We found an old Bible on the table. The name in it was Caleb Preston and there was a letter from Angelica Tucker to him, thanking him for his effort to investigate her husband's death. We think the body is his and Tuck's killers found him in the woods and shut him up to protect themselves. Then Bethany began to show signs of pain when she remounted, so we made our way out to the road and called you without any more side trips." Using a positive voice, she hoped to deter the coming lecture. The label on her bottle had her full attention, while Roger experienced a mild melt down.

"Let me get this straight. First, my wife is injured in a fall, then she finds a skeleton. Next, you follow a side trail to an abandoned cabin that you take time to explore before you two decide it might be a good idea to get your asses out to a road while she can still ride. Is that a fair understanding of your actions?" Rogers's voice had not risen; in fact, it had become more controlled by the word, until the final question came through his clenched teeth. *"What were you two thinking?"* he yelled at the women. "Never mind that question. It's obvious that neither one of you *were* thinking." Slamming his hand on the wheel, he spoke through gritted teeth, gripping the steering wheel in the same manner he wanted to grab either his wife or the woman he expected to be a good influence on her. He glared in the mirror, willing Megan to raise her eyes, silently daring her to do so. Wisely, she kept her head down.

"Roger, Honey, I'm okay. When we went to the cabin, I wasn't hurting much. I think getting off Coup got the blood flowing more to the bruise and that's why it started to be more painful. You know as well as I do that swelling causes most of the pain in a bruise." Bethany's even voice did little to settle Roger's anger, other than direct it back at her.

"Damn it, Woman. I know that I can't trust you to take care of yourself, but I expected more of Megan." His voice had lost the tightness, but gained the sound of disappointment.

"Did you really expect her to control me? I'm not only older than she is, but I'm also her boss. The most she's going to be able to do is possibly make me see a different side of what I want to do. She's not going to be able to stop or even direct me. You ought to know that." She reached one hand over to rub his white knuckles where they gripped the wheel. "Don't blame her. Blame me if you feel we acted stupidly. At the time, I felt well enough to continue riding for the remainder of the day. I knew I was going to pay for the fall later, but not as much as it actually hurts now. Otherwise, I would have stayed on the main trail and come straight out to the road." She continued to rub his knuckles until he relaxed his grip. "I love you and I'm sorry that I've scared you and caused you to worry." She smiled when he took her hand in his and lifted it to his lips.

"I'm sorry I yelled. I think I'm going to get gray hair with you around, either that or keep you under lock and key." He smiled over at her. Glancing in the mirror, he caught a smirk on Megan's face and glared back at her, forcing her to study her water bottle again. "You, I'll talk to later," he darkly promised.

Pulling up next to the clinic door, he set the truck in park before hopping out and running around to assist his wife. By the time he opened the door, Bethany had undone her seat belt. Grasping her around her waist, he lifted her carefully from the truck, taking care not to let any part of her back touch the frame as he set her on her feet. "Megan, haul the horses over to the far side of the lot, lock the truck, and meet us inside," he ordered, taking his wife's arm to assist her up the small step and in through the sliding doors.

The new office nurse met them with a wheelchair. Bethany eyed the chair and made a face that caused Roger to snort. "I'm not certain I can sit. Is it okay if I walk to the exam room?" Bethany asked.

The nurse made eye contact with Roger over Bethany's head, asking his opinion with her bright green, expressive eyes. He shrugged and nodded, knowing his wife would be uncomfortable in a wheelchair.

"Okay, Ma'am. You'll be in the first exam room. Right through this door and to the left." The petite curly-headed nurse pushed the chair ahead of her while she led the slowly-moving couple into the examination room. "Can you get up on the table?"

"I'll lift her for you." Roger picked up his wife and set her in the middle of the exam table with great care.

"Okay. Let's get your vitals while you tell me what happened and where it hurts." The nurse tightened the cuff while Bethany held the electronic thermometer in her mouth. Making notations in Bethany's chart after taking her pulse and reading the thermometer, she listened to the tale.

"I jumped from my horse as he was falling down an embankment and landed on my butt. I have a horrible bruise at the top of my hipbones. Not my seat, my hipbone." Her voice faded toward the end of the statement because the nurse had moved around and pulled her riding tights away from her body to see the bruise.

"Well, your pulse is elevated, along with your blood pressure, but your temperature is normal." Sympathy shown in her bright green eyes.

Noting the oddity of the green eye color against the warm brown hues of her skin and the extreme curl to her blue black hair, Roger wondered about her heritage.

"Hmmm, I think the doctor will want an x-ray. You're not pregnant are you?" The nurse eyed both of them, noting Roger's possessive and protective stance over his wife.

"I don't think I am, but we don't practice any birth control. I'm not due for my period for another week. Your guess is as good as mine." Bethany's chin had gone up in a challenging manner.

"Hmmm, I'll give this information to the doctor and let him make the call. You two just wait here and he'll be right in." Pushing the unneeded wheelchair out, she closed the door.

"I wonder when Doc hired her," Bethany snorted. "Kind of stern and sad, if you ask me." She leaned her head against Roger's shoulder. He had kept his arm behind her and refused to move when the nurse gave him the evil eye for getting in her way. "I'm so tired right now, I could just cry. I know it's shock from the injury, but I just want to either cry or sleep."

Hearing the strain in her voice, Roger felt his heart tighten. "It's okay, Honey. Whatever you want to do is just fine. You're injured. It's okay for you to cry." He murmured into her hair, rubbing the top of her head with his chin.

The door opened and Dr. Samuelson entered. "Well, if it isn't my favorite kidnap victim." He smiled, remembering the first time he met Bethany after she had foiled an attempt to kidnap her. "What happened this time?" he asked, looking at the notes his nurse had made. He frowned, shaking his head at their brevity, and the lack of information they provided. He looked up, noting the

271

closeness of the couple, and smiled more broadly. They made a good-looking couple, even with her face so pale.

"I came off Coup when he fell and managed to hit myself on a boulder or something. I have a nasty bruise across the top of my hips. I guess that means I didn't exactly land on the rocks, but rather hit them when I landed," Bethany explained. She was beginning to feel that she should have the story printed to hand out.

"I'm sorry. I know you're in pain. I'll get you something for it in just a minute. Nurse Marjani noted that you could be pregnant. That's going to affect both medication and possible x-rays." He raised his eyebrows at them.

"What my wife told your nurse was that she is just past mid-cycle for her period, so we have no way of knowing if she could be pregnant of not." Roger took over for Bethany, feeling her lose strength as she leaned more heavily against him.

"Oh, I see. Well, I'd like to run a blood test. It might not be accurate at this point, but if it comes back positive, then we'll move as though you are pregnant and avoid heavy meds and x-rays." He found a tube and a syringe before gently drawing blood from Bethany. "Are you two working at starting a family?" he inquired with his back to them while he put the blood into a test tube.

Roger and Bethany exchanged looks over his bent head. "Well, we've discussed it and decided to let nature be our birth control. We want a family, but maybe not for another year, but if we conceive, then we'll have a family earlier," Roger explained, smiling when the doctor looked over at him.

"Sounds reasonable to me. I've always felt those who work too hard to have a family don't do themselves any service and create more stress than needed in a marriage. Best to let the future decide itself at this point," he agreed. "I'm going to run this over to the lab. I'll be right back." He waved at them with the test tube, as the door closed behind him.

Bethany sighed. She just wanted to lie down and sleep. She eyed the exam table, running her hand over the paper cover sheet to smooth it. She saw Roger reading her mind and smiled at him. "Think the doctor would mind if I just stretched out here for a rest? I can barely hold my eyes open."

"Here, let me help you. I'll lift your legs as you move your upper body over the table." He put actions to words and she managed to stretch out on her stomach as the door opened.

"There you are." Megan entered the exam room with Shorty hot on her heels. "What's the doctor say?"

"He wants to run some tests before they can do any x-rays, so we may be here a while," Roger told the pair. "Shorty, I know you want to stay, but it's not good to leave the horses standing in the trailer. I want you to take Megan and head home." He gave a stern look to the man who was as much a friend as he was a cook and housekeeper. "I'll call as soon as we know anything. I seriously doubt that Doc will send her to Montrose for anything, so we'll be home before the evening's done."

Shorty's face fell, but he took Megan's elbow and directed her toward the door. "Okay, Boss. I'll make something easy on the tummy for dinner and see you when you get home."

Megan paused at the door and glanced over at the couple. "I'll wait until tomorrow morning to call about the skeleton. No sense getting the town gossiping and some yahoos trying to beat the forensics people out there."

"Good idea. Nothing can be done tonight and it's not as if it's going to disappear before anyone can get back out there. Shorty, keep it quiet so no fools go out there searching at dawn, okay?" Roger's stern expression as he looked at Shorty quelled the excitement in the older man's eyes.

The door closing behind them, Roger pulled a chair closer to the exam table and sat down before picking up Bethany's delicate hand in his rough one and kissing her fingers. "I guess now we wait."

Other Books by Kasey Riley

August Fire

Desperate Endurance

Do Not Assume

Skeleton Trail